SUNRISE
CROSSING

Center Point
Large Print

Also by Jodi Thomas and available from Center Point Large Print:

Promise Me Texas
Betting the Rainbow
A Place Called Harmony
One True Heart
Ransom Canyon
Rustler's Moon
Lone Heart Pass

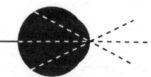

**This Large Print Book carries the
Seal of Approval of N.A.V.H.**

SUNRISE CROSSING

JODI THOMAS

CENTER POINT LARGE PRINT
THORNDIKE, MAINE

This Center Point Large Print edition is published
in the year 2017 by arrangement with
Harlequin Books S.A.

The text of this Large Print edition is unabridged.
In other aspects, this book may vary
from the original edition.
Printed in the United States of America
on permanent paper.
Set in 16-point Times New Roman type.

ISBN: 978-1-68324-228-4

Library of Congress Cataloging-in-Publication Data

Names: Thomas, Jodi, author.
Title: Sunrise crossing / Jodi Thomas.
Description: Center Point Large Print edition. | Thorndike, Maine :
Center Point Large Print, 2017.
Identifiers: LCCN 2016044596 | ISBN 9781683242284
    (hardcover : alk. paper)
Subjects: LCSH: Large type books. | GSAFD: Love stories.
Classification: LCC PS3570.H5643 S86 2017 | DDC 813/.54—dc23
LC record available at https://lccn.loc.gov/2016044596

SUNRISE
CROSSING

Chapter ONE

Flight

January 2012
LAX

Victoria Vilanie curled into a ball, trying to make herself small, trying to disappear. Her black hair spread around her like a cape but couldn't protect her.

All the sounds in the airport were like drums playing in a jungle full of predators. Carts with clicking wheels rolling on pitted tiles. People shuffling and shouting and complaining. Electronic voices rattling off numbers and destinations. Babies crying. Phones ringing. Winter's late storm pounding on walls of glass.

Victoria, Tori to her few friends, might not be making a sound, but she was screaming inside.

Tears dripped off her face, and she didn't bother to wipe them away. The noise closed in around her, making her feel so lonely in the crowd of strangers.

She was twenty-four, and everyone said she was a gifted artist. Money poured in so fast it had become almost meaningless, only a number that brought no joy. But tonight all she wanted was silence, peace, a world where she could hide out.

She scrubbed her eyes on her sleeve and felt a hand touch her shoulder like it were a bird, featherlight, landing there.

Tori turned and recognized a woman she'd seen once before. The tall blonde in her midthirties owned one of the best galleries in Dallas. Who could forget Parker Lacey's green eyes? She was a woman who had it all and knew how to handle her life. A born general who must manage her life as easily as she managed her business.

"Are you all right, Tori?" Parker asked.

Tori could say nothing but the truth. "I'm living the wrong life."

Then the strangest thing happened. The lady with green eyes hugged her and Tori knew, for the first time in years, that someone had heard her, really heard her.

Chapter TWO

The stone-blue days of winter

February
Dallas, Texas

Parker Lacey sat perfectly straight on the side of her hospital bed. Her short, sunny blond hair combed, her makeup in place and her logical mind in control of all emotions, as always.

She'd ignored the pain in her knee, the throbbing in her leg, for months. She ignored it now.

She'd been poked and examined all day, and now all that remained before the curtain fell on her life was for some doctor she barely knew to tell her just how long she had left to live. A month. Six months. If she was lucky, a year?

Her mother had died when Parker was ten. Breast cancer at thirty-one. Her father died eight years later. Lung cancer at thirty-nine. Neither parent had made it to their fortieth birthday.

Longevity simply didn't run in Parker's family. She'd known it and worried about dying all her adult life, and at thirty-seven, she realized her number would come up soon. Only she'd been smarter than all her ancestors. She would leave no offspring. There would be no next generation of Laceys. She was the last in her family.

There were also no lovers, or close friends, she thought. Her funeral would be small.

The beep of her cell phone interrupted her morbid thoughts.

"Hello, Parker speaking," she said.

"I'm in!" came a soft voice. "I followed the map. It was just a few miles from where the bus stopped. The house is perfect, and your housekeeper delivered more groceries than I'll be able to eat in a year. And, Parker, you were right. This isolated place will be heaven."

Parker forgot her problems. She could worry

about dying later. Right now, she had to help one of her artists. "Tori, are you sure you weren't followed?"

"Yes. I did it just the way you suggested. Kept my head down. Dressed like a boy. Switched buses twice. One bus driver even told me to 'Hurry along, kid.' "

"Good. No one will probably connect me with you and no one knows I own a place in Crossroads. Stay there. You'll be safe. You'll have time to relax and think."

"They'll question you when they realize I've vanished," Tori said. "My stepfather won't just let me disappear. I'm worth too much money to him."

Parker laughed, trying to sound reassuring. "Of course, people will ask how well we know one another. I'll say I'm proud to show your work in my gallery and that we've only met a few times at gallery openings." Both facts were true. "Besides, it's no crime to vanish, Tori. You are an adult."

Victoria Vilanie was silent on the other end. She'd told Parker that she'd been on a manic roller coaster for months. The ride had left her fragile, almost shattered. Since she'd been thirteen and been "discovered" by the art community, her stepfather had quit his job and become her handler.

"Tori," Parker whispered into the phone, "you're not the tiger in a circus. You'll be fine.

You can stand on your own. There are professionals who will help you handle your career without trying to run your life."

"I know. It's just a little frightening."

"It's all right, Tori. You're safe. You don't have to face the reporters. You don't have to answer any questions." Parker hesitated. "I'll come if you need me."

"I'd like that."

No one would ever believe that Parker would stick her neck out so far to help a woman she barely knew. Maybe she and Tori had each recognized a fellow loner, or maybe it was just time in her life that she did something different, something kind.

"No matter what happens," Tori whispered, "I want to thank you. You've saved my life. I think if I'd had to go another week, I might have shattered into a million pieces."

Parker wanted to say that she doubted it was that serious, but she wasn't sure the little artist wasn't right. "Stay safe. Don't tell the couple who take care of the house anything. You're just visiting, remember? Have them pick up anything you need from town. You'll find art supplies in the attic room if you want to paint."

"Found the supplies already, but I think I just want to walk around your land and think about my life. You're right. It's time I started taking my life back."

"I'll be there as soon as I can." Parker had read every mystery she could find since she was eight. If Tori wanted to disappear, Parker should be able to figure out how to make it happen. After all, how hard could it be?

The hospital door opened.

Parker clicked off the disposable phone she'd bought at the airport a few weeks ago when she and Tori talked about how to make Tori vanish.

"Miss Parker?" A young doctor poked his head into her room. He didn't look old enough to be out of college, much less med school, but this was a teaching hospital, one of the best in the country. "I'm Dr. Brown."

"It's Miss Lacey. My first name is Parker," she said as she pushed the phone beneath her covers. Hiding it as she was hiding the gifted artist.

The kid of a doctor moved into the room. "You any kin to Quanah Parker? We get a few people in here every year descended from the great Comanche chief."

She knew what the doctor was trying to do. Establish rapport before he gave her the bad news, so she played along. "That depends. How old was he when he died?"

The doctor shrugged. "I'm not much of a history buff, but my folks stopped at every historical roadside marker in Texas and Oklahoma when I was growing up. I think the great warrior was old when he died, real old. Had six wives, I

12

heard, when he passed peacefully in his sleep on his ranch near a town that bears his name."

"If he lived a long life, I'm probably not kin to him. And to my knowledge, I have no Native American blood and no living relatives." By the time she'd been old enough to ask, no one around remembered why she was named Parker and she had little interest in exploring a family tree with such short branches.

"I'm so sorry." Then he grinned. "I could give you a couple of my sisters. Ever since I got out of med school they think I'm their private *dial a doc.* They even call me to ask if TV shows get it right."

"No, thanks. Keep your sisters." She tried to smile.

"There are times when it's good to have family around." He said, "Would you like me to call someone for you? A close friend, maybe?"

She glanced up and read all she needed to know in the young man's eyes. She was dying. He looked terrible just giving her the news. Maybe this was the first time he'd ever had to tell anyone that their days were numbered.

"How long do I have to hang around here?"

The doc checked her chart and didn't meet her gaze as he said, "An hour, maybe two. When you come back, we'll make you as comfortable here as we can but you'll need—"

She didn't give him time to list what she knew came next. She'd watched her only cousin go

13

through bone cancer when they were in high school. First, there would be surgery on her leg. Then they wouldn't get it all and she'd have chemo. Round after round until her hair and spirit disappeared. No, she wouldn't do that. She'd take the end head-on.

The doctor broke into her thoughts. "We can give you shots in that left knee. It'll make the pain less until—"

"Okay, I'll come back when I need it," she said, not wanting to give him time to talk about how she might lose her leg or her life. If she let him say the word *cancer,* she feared she might start screaming and never stop.

She knew she limped when she was tired and her knee sometimes buckled on her. Her back already hurt, and her whole left leg felt weak sometimes. The cancer must be spreading; she'd known it was there for months, but she'd kept putting off getting a checkup. Now she knew it would only get worse. More pain. More drugs, until it finally traveled to her brain. Maybe the doctor didn't want her to hang around and suffer? Maybe the shots would knock her out. She'd feel nothing until the very end. She'd just wait for death as her cousin had. She'd visited him every day. Watching him grow weaker, watching the staff grow sadder.

Hanging around had never been her way, and it wouldn't be now.

A nurse in scrubs that were two sizes too small rushed into the room and whispered, loud enough for Parker to hear, "We've got an emergency, Doctor. Three ambulances are bringing injured in from a bad wreck. Pileup on I-35. Can you break away to help?"

The doctor flipped the chart closed. "No problem. We're finished here." He nodded to Parker. "We'll have time to talk later, Miss Parker. You've got a few options."

She nodded back, not wanting to hear the details anyway. What did it matter? He didn't have to say the word *cancer* for her to know what was wrong.

He was gone in a blink.

The nurse's face molded into a caring mask. "What can I do to make you more comfortable? You don't need to worry, dear. I've helped a great many people go through this."

"You can hand me my clothes," Parker said as she slid off the bed. "Then you can help me leave." She was used to giving orders. She'd been doing it since she'd opened her art gallery fifteen years ago. She'd been twenty-two and thought she had forever to live.

"Oh, but . . ." The nurse's eyes widened as if she were a hen and one of her chickens was escaping the coop.

"No *buts*. I have to leave now." Parker raised her eyebrow silently, daring the nurse to question her.

15

Parker stripped off the hospital gown and climbed into the tailored suit she'd arrived in before dawn. The teal silk blouse and cream-colored jacket of polished wool felt wonderful against her skin compared with the rough cotton gown. Like a chameleon changing color, she shifted from patient to tall, in-control business-woman.

The nurse began to panic again. "Is someone picking you up? Were you discharged? Has the paperwork already been completed?"

"No to the first question. I drove myself here and I'll drive myself away. And yes, I was discharged." Parker tossed her things into the huge Coach bag she'd brought in. If her days were now limited, she wanted to make every one count. "I have to do something very important. I've no time to mess with paperwork. Mail the forms to me."

Parker walked out while the nurse went for a wheelchair. Her mind checked off the things she had to do as her high heels clicked against the hallway tiles. It would take a week to get her office in order. She wanted the gallery to run smoothly while she was gone.

She planned to help a friend, see the colors of life and have an adventure. Then, when she passed, she would have lived, if only for a few months.

After climbing into her special-edition Jaguar,

she gunned the engine. She didn't plan to heed any speed-limit signs. *Caution* was no longer in her vocabulary.

The ache in her leg whispered through her body when she bent her knee, but Parker ignored it. No one had told her what to do since she entered college and no one, not even Dr. Brown, would set rules now.

Chapter THREE

Crossroads, Texas

Yancy Grey walked the midnight streets, barely noticing where he was going or caring that winter's breath still circled in the breeze.

Today was his birthday. Or at least he thought it was. His mother's memory had been smothered with pills most of his childhood. She'd told him she'd filled out the birth certificate a week or so after he'd been born when she'd finally healed and sobered up enough to walk to the clinic in Crossroads, Texas.

When Yancy had run away at fourteen, he doubted she'd noticed. She'd never celebrated his birth, and after he left, he continued the nontradition through his wandering teen years and his early twenties, which he'd spent in prison. And now, he thought, during his calm years in Texas.

He was alone at thirty-two and wise enough to realize that it wasn't a bad place to be. The old folks at the Evening Shadows Retirement Community, where he worked, would have thrown him a birthday party if they'd known, but they were all tucked in their beds by dark. They counted away what was left of their lives, but Yancy wanted to count forward.

He'd been with the retired teachers for seven years now, repairing their homes, managing the twenty-cottage complex that had started as an eight-bungalow motel set in a town where two highways crossed. The school system had originally bought the old motel, hoping to offer small homes to new teachers, but those retiring from teaching had wanted to stay in town and together.

Yancy drove the old residents to the doctor and picked up their prescriptions. He cared about and for them. He repaired everything around the place and built a new cottage now and then when a single teacher needed a place to live out his or her days in peace.

In return, they all loved him and tried to pass down their wisdom. Cap taught him carpentry and plumbing, and Miss Bees had taught him to cook. Leo was a wizard with money and had him investing, and Mrs. Abernathy had even tried to teach him to play the piano. No matter what project he took on, Yancy knew there would be someone waiting to advise him on every detail.

Yancy sometimes thought he'd gone from high school to grad school in the years he'd been employed by the teachers. They were a wealth of knowledge, and he was a ready pupil.

But when it came to women, nothing they said worked. He hadn't had a date in months, and the two he'd had last year had convinced him that being single wasn't so bad. There seemed to be no family for him, past or future. No girl wanted to be seen with an ex-con, handyman, drifter, no matter how nice he was or how much her grandmother bragged about him.

Looking up, he saw the old gypsy house a quarter mile away, far enough from the lights to not be in town and close enough to not be completely outside it. His place. Nestled among the barren elm trees, the house still looked haunted, even if he had framed up the second floor and repaired the roof. The trash and tumbleweeds were gone, but no grass or flowers grew near the porches. Like him, the place didn't quite fit in among the others in town.

Yancy had built a workshop behind the hundred-year-old crumbling remains so that he could rebuild the old house better than it had been built a century ago. The workshop looked more like a small barn, with a high roof and a loft for storing supplies. Inside, the bay was big enough to hold six cars, but he'd set up long worktables and saws he'd bought at flea markets and yard sales.

This crumbling home and five acres of dirt surrounding it might not look like much, but it was his, all his. A grandmother he'd never met had left it to him, along with enough money to pay the taxes for years. He didn't care that he had no relative to ever send a birthday or Christmas present for the rest of his life. This was enough.

Last Christmas, the ladies at the Evening Shadows had held a fund-raiser in his barn. They'd hung quilts to cover the walls of tools and shelves, then loaded the tables with homemade sweets and crafts. He swore everyone in town had come and bought an armful, whether they needed a new tissue-box cover or reindeer coaster set or not.

He'd loved helping the ladies out, but was glad when his shop was back in order. Old Cap had taught him that there needed to be a place for everything, and Yancy believed he could have located, with his eyes closed, any tool on his walls.

From the first day he found out the place had been willed to him, Yancy had decided to start remodeling from the inside out. When he finished, the place would shine. He'd move into a real home for the first time in his life. The house might have held only sadness and hate thirty-one years ago when his mother lived here during her pregnancy, but he'd rebuild it with the love of a craftsman who'd learned his skills in prison and had dreamed of a project like this one.

The workshop door creaked a little when he opened it.

Yancy smiled. He liked the sound; it was like the place was welcoming him.

As he did every other night, he tugged off his coat, hung it on the latch and began to work. Tonight he'd sand down aged boards that would eventually be polished and grooved to fit perfectly in the upstairs rooms of the house. He'd turned the four little rooms downstairs into one open space, with a kitchen on the back wall and a long bar separating it from the living space. The bar had taken him three months and was made out of one piece of oak.

He'd bought a radio months ago, thinking that music might be nice while he worked, but most nights he forgot to turn it on. He liked the silence and the rhythm of the midnight shadows, and he liked being alone with his thoughts and dreams. Seven years ago, when he'd arrived, he'd had nothing but a few clothes that were left over from before he'd gone to prison. Now he was a rich man. He had a job he loved and he had the silence of the night in which to think.

As he began to sand the wood and carve away the stress of the day, the loneliness of his nights and the worries he always had about the tenants

21

he cared for all slipped away as his muscles welcomed the work.

This was what he needed. A passion. A job. A goal to move toward. When he finished, he'd have pride in what he'd done, and no one could take that from him.

After a while, he heard a sound above his head. A slight movement, as if someone had shifted atop the loose boards stacked along one side of the loft.

Another sound. The creaking of the flooring.

As he had each time for a week when this had happened, he didn't react. He simply kept working. If the invisible visitor had meant him any harm, he would have known it long before now. Maybe some frightened animal had taken shelter from the last month of winter, or maybe a drifter just wanted a warm place to rest before moving on. He'd been there in his teens. He knew how much a quiet, safe place could mean.

Yancy was lost in his work an hour later when a loose board shifted above and tumbled down.

A little squeak followed.

Yancy waited, then said calmly, "If you're trying to kill me, you'll need to toss down something bigger than a two-by-four."

"Sorry," came a whisper.

"No harm. I've known you were up there for a while. Want to come down and say hello?"

No answer.

"I got a thermos of hot coffee I haven't had time to drink. You're welcome to it."

"You're not calling the police?"

"Nope. Sheriff probably has his own coffee."

Yancy thought he heard a hiccup of a laugh.

A slight woman dressed in jeans and a blue-checked flannel shirt moved down the ladder. Her long, dark braid brushed her backside as she lowered from step to step.

"I didn't mean to spy on you," she said, without looking at him. "The barn wasn't locked, and I just wanted to be out of the cold a few nights ago. It smells so good in here I've found myself coming back."

"It's the fresh-cut wood. I love the smell, too." He went back to work. "So, you walk at night also? It's a habit of mine."

She nodded. "I don't usually come this close to town, but walking seems better than trying to sleep."

"I know what you mean." He handed her the thermos. "Coffee's strong. It was left over from where I work, but it's hot. Should take off the chill."

She untwisted the lid and poured herself half a cup. "I like the sounds of the night and the way I can walk without having to speak to anyone. I can just walk and be a part of the land, the trees, the air."

"You don't like talking to folks?"

"Not much. I've just said more to you right now than I've said to anyone in days."

He grinned, thinking no one at the retirement home would believe this story when he told it tomorrow. A pretty woman, about his age, with hair as black as midnight, hiding in his loft. And even stranger, she said she didn't like to talk but yet she still talked to him.

He liked the idea that they shared a love for walking the shadowy roads and also for not having much to say. He was usually the one folks skipped talking to. "You're welcome here any-time. I'm Yancy Grey and I'm remodeling—or probably more accurately, rebuilding—the old Stanley house."

"I know. I can see that."

She had a soft, easy smile, but sad eyes. Old-soul eyes, he thought, like she'd seen far more sadness than most. He remembered a few people in prison like that and had watched sad eyes go dead, even though the person looking out of them was still breathing.

"You live around here?" Yancy knew he would have remembered if he'd seen her before. At first glance she looked more like a sixteen-year-old kid, but in the light, she seemed closer to her late twenties.

"I have to go." She backed toward the door. "I shouldn't have bothered you."

He saw panic in those beautiful winter-blue

eyes. He forced himself not to react. One more question and he knew she'd bolt.

"No bother." He turned back to his work. "It was nice to have the company, even if I did think you were a rabbit."

She whispered, more to herself than to him, "How would a rabbit get up there?"

He shrugged. "How would a pretty lady? Come back anytime, Rabbit. No questions, I promise."

She took one more glance around the shop. "I like this place. It makes me feel safe. My father had a shop like this one."

"You are safe," he added, knowing without asking that her father must be dead. If he'd been alive, she wouldn't be searching for a safe place. "Drop by anytime. Only, beware—I might put you to work."

She ran her small hand over the wood he'd just sanded. "I'd like that. I grew up helping build things. Some folks said my daddy was an artist, but he always said he was just a carpenter."

Without a word, he handed her the sander and went back to work. She stood on the other side of the workbench for a few minutes, then began to polish. For an hour, they simply worked across from each other. Her skill was evident, and he found himself wishing that a woman would touch him as lovingly as she touched the wood.

When he lifted the final board, she set her tools

down and whispered, "I have to go. Thank you for this calm evening, Yancy."

"You're welcome, Rabbit. Come back any night." He sensed what she might need to hear. "I could use the help, and I promise, no questions."

She slipped through the doorway so silently he almost thought he'd imagined her.

Folding up his toolbox, Yancy turned out the light. He'd enjoyed her company, even though he knew nothing about the woman, not even her name. For all he knew, she could be crazy. Maybe she'd run away from prison or a husband who beat her. Or maybe she was a drifter, just waiting to steal everything she could get her hands on. If so, it wouldn't be too hard; he'd never bought a lock for the barn.

But she had no car. She couldn't have come far walking and she wouldn't be able to carry off too much. She also had no wedding band, so no one was probably waiting up for her. He sensed that she was as alone as he was.

He reached for his coat and wasn't surprised to find it missing from the latch.

As he started back toward his little room behind the activity hall of the Evening Shadows Retirement Community, he smiled, glad that Rabbit was warm at least. At her size, his coat would be huge, for he had to be over a foot taller than her and probably weighed double.

Maybe he should have more questions running through his head, but the only one he could think of right now was, could he call what they shared tonight a date?

Yancy swore to himself, thinking how pitiful he was to even consider the question. She was probably just lost, or maybe hiding from something, and definitely a thief—she'd stolen his coat. Not dating material even for someone as desperate as he was to just do something as ordinary as holding a woman's hand.

But, considering all her possible shortcomings, she was still the best time he'd had with a woman in months.

Chapter FOUR

Deputy Fifth Weathers rushed into the county offices on Main Street in Crossroads, Texas, as if he were still running offensive tackle for the Texas Longhorns.

Grinning, he realized it had been four years since he'd graduated. He was forty pounds leaner and long past talking about his football days, but now and then he yearned to run with the crowds roaring once more.

He headed straight for the sheriff's office. All hell was about to hit and he hadn't even had breakfast.

He'd overslept, *again,* and that was something Sheriff Brigman thought should be a hanging offense. Plus, even though he'd worked until long after midnight, the report due today still wasn't done.

Pearly, the county's receptionist and secretary, who sat just right of the main entrance, always jumped when Fifth walked past. She was a thin, little woman who'd probably blow away if he sneezed, and in the two years he'd been working with the sheriff, she'd never smiled at him.

The first six months he'd been in town she'd asked weekly when he planned to leave. Lately, the question hung silently between them like last year's Christmas tinsel caught on a slow-moving fan, fluttering silently as it circled.

He nodded at her.

At six feet seven inches, Deputy Weathers wasn't likely to sneak up on Pearly, but she frowned like she could see doomsday coming when his shadow blocked the sun.

"There you are," she snapped. "The sheriff's looking for you."

Fifth moved closer to her massive desk. If he got any nearer than five feet, it always made Pearly start to fiddle with her shawl fringe like she planned to unknit the entire thing if he came within touching distance.

"You all right, Miss Pearly?" he said in a tone he hoped sounded more kind than threatening.

"I'm fine," she snapped. "You just startled me. Someone should have put a brick on your head ten years ago, Deputy Weathers."

Fifth gave up any attempt at conversation and headed toward the sheriff's office. He couldn't help it if his father had cursed him with height and his mother hadn't been able to think of a name for her fifth son, so she'd just called him a number. Everyone had crazy families. His was simply supersized.

"Sheriff Brigman is *not* in there," Pearly announced, about the time he reached the door. "He's out on the Kirkland Ranch. Said to bring the missing-persons flyers for the past month and maps of the county. Wants your help as soon as possible, so I'd suggest you start backtracking all the way to your car."

Fifth thought of asking her why she hadn't let him know right away. She could have radioed the cruiser he drove, called his cell or dialed the bed-and-breakfast where he'd overslept this morning. But he knew what Pearly's answer would be if he asked: she always said that she'd been about to. The woman's *about to* list would last her into the hereafter.

He turned and walked back past her desk, trying not to notice how she leaned away like he'd accidentally knock her down on his way out.

A few minutes later he climbed into his cruiser, wondering why some people treated men over six-six like they were alien invaders. Men who were six-four were apparently fine, but grow a few more inches and you're out of the normal zone. It also didn't help that deputies in Texas wore boots and Stetsons. That added another three or four inches.

When he'd played football in college, his height hadn't been a problem. But now anyone lower by a foot seemed to think he might just accidentally bop them on the head. He'd made it through the academy and had served two years as a deputy without accidentally killing anyone.

As he drove toward the Double K Ranch that had been in the Kirkland family over a hundred years, Fifth Weathers tried to relax. He'd been in Crossroads since Sheriff Brigman was shot and almost killed two years ago.

At first it had been just a job, a chance to step out of a big office and work with a sheriff everyone in Texas respected. But lately, it was more than that. He was starting to care about the people. He'd matured from a green rookie looking for excitement to a seasoned officer who hoped never to have to pull his weapon again.

That is, if shooting a snake counted as a first time.

For the most part, the folks in the county were good, honest citizens who loved to tease him once ᵗʰey figured out he was on the shy side. The ᵉr offered to stack his daughters if Fifth would take both of them out. The Franklin sisters, who ran the bed-and-breakfast, were always trying to match him up with one of their relatives because they claimed the family tree could use the height. And from what he'd seen, Franklins tended to grow out instead of up.

Fifth wouldn't have minded having a date. It had been a while. But even in college, when girls flocked around athletes, he hadn't gone out much. He'd always felt awkward and never knew the right thing to say.

He blamed his mother for his awkwardness around women. You'd think with a dozen pregnancies she could have popped out one girl so her sons could learn to relate.

When he turned onto Kirkland land, Fifth put his problems aside and was all business. If the sheriff was here, there must be something wrong. Staten Kirkland was a good man who ran his ranch like a small kingdom. He wouldn't be calling the law in on something minor.

Dan Brigman was on the porch talking to the rancher. All signs that Brigman had taken four bullets in an ambush were gone: the sheriff looked fit and strong; his hair had grayed to the color of steel, and his eyes always seemed to look right into the heart of folks. Fifth could think of no better goal than to model his career after this legend of a man.

"About time you arrived," Dan said with a hint

of a smile that told Fifth he wasn't in any serious trouble this time.

"Sorry, sir. I overslept." Fifth climbed the steps and offered his hand to Kirkland.

Dan nodded once. "I thought you might when I passed the office around midnight and saw the lights still on."

"You're working the kid too hard," Kirkland said as he shook Fifth's hand. "Come on inside, Deputy. We've got coffee and cinnamon rolls waiting. I need to show Dan the map in my office before we start planning."

"Thanks," Fifth answered politely, grateful that he didn't have to admit that right now he was far more interested in the rolls and coffee than looking at any map. Caffeine and sugar should wake him up.

Fifth followed the two men through the massive double doors of the Kirkland headquarters as they talked about the weather. The sound of their boots thumping across the hardwood floor blended with the jingle of spurs Kirkland wore.

Fifth had been at the headquarters a few times before. A New Year's party. A meeting of the new city planning committee. He liked the big old home, and it was one of the few places he didn't have to watch his head. The Kirklands were tall and built their house to accommodate.

The main room was a forty-foot-long living area built with mahogany and leather. A dining area to the left had a table that would seat thirty. Kirkland's huge office opened through double doors on the right, and a modern country kitchen was in the back.

The house reminded him of a remade set from the movie *Giant*. Pure Texas. Western, all the way.

Only it didn't seem like a house that people lived in. It was the headquarters, set up for work and meetings. Fifth had heard that the family lived in a smaller place a few hundred yards away, which made sense. Kirkland had two toddlers, and no one would want to have to chase them all over this amount of square footage.

Fifth had just begun to feel his muscles relaxing when he turned the corner off the main room and saw Kirkland's wife, Quinn, sitting at the kitchen table, talking to a woman about his age.

The stranger had short, reddish-brown hair, naturally curly, and blue eyes; she was dressed in a leather jacket and tan pants with boots laced almost to her knees. For a second he thought she looked like Amelia Earhart. Then he added one more fact as she turned directly to him and glared.

One look at him and, for some reason, the woman seemed to become angry as hell.

For a second, Fifth fought the urge to step back, maybe all the way to the door. Maybe farther. He might not have a lot of experience with women, but he could see rage flashing in her icy-blues like white-hot lightning. Take cover or run seemed to be the safest options.

The anger didn't fit until he watched her slowly stand. He added one last statistic. Over six feet tall. The possibility they'd both stepped into a match-up trap occurred to him, just as it probably had to her.

Quinn just grinned, but Kirkland made the introductions. "Fifth, I'd like you to meet my wife's niece, Madison O'Grady." Now Kirkland was grinning, obviously unaware that his kin was firing a look that might kill the only deputy for miles around. "We asked her to come in this morning. Thought you two might like to get acquainted."

"Welcome, Miss O'Grady." Fifth removed his hat and offered his hand, hoping she didn't bite it off.

The sheriff slapped his deputy on the shoulder. "So . . . ah . . . enjoy your coffee and rolls, Deputy. We'll be back before you finish." At least Brigman had the sense not to grin.

Quinn, Staten and the sheriff vanished, leaving him alone with the angry woman. The instinct to run was so strong he couldn't get his tongue untied enough to speak.

Without asking if he wanted one, she poured him a cup of coffee and slid it across the table, not seeming to notice, or care, that boiling liquid spilled out.

He sat down. He'd had women look at him with total disinterest, or sometimes even with fear because of his size, but he'd never been the kind of guy to bring out hate—or passion, for that matter—in anyone. In fact, he'd always kind of thought that women his age viewed him as a friend more than anything else. He guessed he'd be like his two older brothers where women were concerned. He'd marry a woman who was a friend and settle into an easy kind of partnership.

Fifth drew the plate of rolls close before she decided to shove them over. Maybe if he ignored her she'd calm down. He downed the first roll in two bites. It smelled good, but he swallowed so fast he didn't bother to taste it.

The second of Quinn's famous cinnamon rolls was almost to his mouth when Madison O'Grady spoke.

"Well," she snapped as she paced, "where do you want to do it? Here on the table? The couch is long enough but it might not be wide enough for us, or there are several bedrooms upstairs. Pick one."

Fifth stared at the roll, figuring she probably wasn't talking about eating. "Do what?" he said quietly.

"Have sex, of course. We were obviously brought here to meet. My whole family has been trying to match me up like the expiration date on me is about to run out. Last month it was a six-five trucker who stopped at the café. They thought I should drop everything and come meet him. Thank goodness he turned out to be married or I'd be on an eighteen-wheeler to Des Moines, Iowa, right now."

Fifth must have still looked confused because she added, "Why waste time talking or dating or getting married? Let's just do it right here, right now. We're obviously meant for one another. We're both over six feet."

Fifth didn't know what to do. She may have been angry, but damned if she wasn't the sexiest woman he'd ever encountered. He must be a masochist.

He'd always been hesitant to have any one-night stands because he feared he might hurt a small woman. Now he wasn't sure Madison wouldn't hurt him.

"Madison!" Kirkland yelled from his office. "You fully gassed and ready?"

She didn't take her eyes off Fifth. "I can be in the air in five."

"Good." The sheriff appeared in the office doorway. "Fifth, inhale another bite and follow Madison. I want you two gone as fast as possible."

Fifth caught the surprise in her eyes a moment before she grabbed a satchel and ran for the back door.

He was right behind her. He had no trouble matching her long strides as she stormed toward a

36

helicopter parked on the other side of Kirkland's barn. "You're the pilot." It wasn't a question.

"Yes, and you must be the passenger I came all the way from Wichita Falls to pick up." She glanced over at him. "You're the expert on rough terrain they were talking about. I thought—I thought . . ."

"I think I know what you thought." He grinned. "You're not the only one who gets set up with strangers because of their height."

"I'm sorry," she said as she opened the passenger door.

"Forget it. How about we start over?" Fifth dropped his hat in the cargo bag and put on headphones. "You're the pilot and I'm the expert." He watched her circle the chopper and climb into the pilot's seat before adding, "Only, I hope you're a better pilot than I am an expert. I've been studying up for months, but I've had no field experience."

"Climb in," she shouted as she started the helicopter. "You're about to have the ride of your life."

Fifth folded into the passenger seat, bumping her shoulder as he buckled himself in. "So, I guess sex on the kitchen table is off the agenda?"

She laughed, then winked at him. "Not necessarily."

Fifth froze. Now he was shocked, but by the time his brain cells fired, it was too late to run. They were already in the air.

Chapter FIVE
Peace

Tori walked the rocky ground behind Parker's house near Crossroads. The land didn't look good for much as far as farming. One field near the road was plowed, but the rest seemed like it had always grown wild. Whoever built this house had wanted peace, she decided. The front porch faced the morning sun. Trees had been planted in a circle out back years ago and now offered a small meadow of shade.

She already loved it here. Her mind had settled, and she could feel herself growing stronger. When—or if—her stepfather found her, she wouldn't be the same person as she had been two weeks ago when she vanished.

She was twenty-four, and it was time she took control of her own life. She should have done it years ago, but her mother kept saying that her new husband, Tori's stepfather, knew best. He was a businessman, and he would run everything so that all Tori would have to do was paint. When Tori had protested again, at nineteen, her mother had reminded her of how the mixing of business and art had driven Tori's father mad. He'd loved being the carpenter, working with his hands, but when his carvings began to sell for thousands, he lost the simple joy in creating.

Tori had backed off, letting her mother win, again. And again. And again. Letting her mother and stepfather handle the business side of her career so she could paint. Only lately she'd felt like a factory, always pushed to produce.

She twirled in the meadow. "Freedom," she yelled, then laughed.

Maybe she'd paint today. Maybe she'd sleep in the sun. Maybe she'd go visit the man at the edge of town who called her Rabbit.

But, no matter what, she'd do what she wanted to do. She'd live her own life.

Chapter SIX

Dallas in cadet-gray rain

Parker loved the gallery after dark. The lights of a rainy Dallas surrounded her as they glowed through the forty-foot wall of glass that framed the building. Paintings seemed to float between the city and the rich, earthy reds of Saltillo tiles.

Somehow the art seemed to come alive as shadows bordered each creation's elegant grace. Her gallery was a still, unpolluted kind of paradise that always made Parker feel safe and comfortable.

The possibility of dying couldn't reach her here. She could push the prospect from her mind and just breathe.

She took one last walk through her world. She almost had everything ready. Her staff believed she had a scouting trip in the planning stages but she was, for the first time in her life, running away to have an adventure. To paint. To live. To help a friend.

For years, she'd been saying she'd take off when everything slowed down. She'd go to Crossroads, Texas, where she'd bought a farmhouse almost ten years ago. Her someday dream had always been to paint. She'd been driving from Dallas to Albuquerque one summer on the back roads and seen a For Sale sign hooked to a barbed-wire fence in the middle of nowhere.

On a whim she'd turned off a road that was posted as private. The land, if it had ever been tamed, had gone back to nature. One edge dipped down into a canyon with rich earth shades that took her breath away. The other direction spread over rolling prairie spotted with wildflowers and clusters of trees surrounding small ponds. She remembered seeing the little two-story farm-house peeking out from behind a huge oak planted at the bend in the lane leading up to the place.

The old house was perfect. Small, with an unfinished attic that could serve as a studio. High ceilings with good light streaming in. Tall windows in the back with a canyon view. Heaven at the end of a private road. A painter's hideaway. The rancher next door owned the small chunk of land and had said he needed money to pay taxes. She'd made an offer and he didn't even bother to counter. Within hours she'd bought the place, hired a couple to clean once a month and headed back to the city.

Her someday place would be waiting for her.

A few years later, the rancher offered to lease the small field that bordered his place for a percentage of the profits. She said she would if he'd use the money to keep up her house and the road they shared. "Whatever you pay out, spend it on repairs and paint," she'd said, knowing she had little time to even think about the farm. She was almost thirty and had had a business to build.

"Will do, lady," he'd said.

A month later he'd called and asked what color she wanted the outside painted.

"The color of the Texas sky in summer. And, cowboy—" she'd forgotten his name by then "—when you have enough in my balance to paint the inside, don't bother to call me—just paint each room the color of a different flower that grows on my land."

"Will do," he'd said again and had hung up without saying goodbye.

But Parker knew the colors didn't really matter. She'd probably go the rest of her life seeing the place only in her mind. It'd be blue, like the sky. One room would be the yellow of sunflowers, another the violet of morning glories or the scarlet in Indian paintbrush.

The cowboy never called again, and the house slowly became more of an imaginary place in Parker's thoughts than a reality.

Until now. Maybe, with Tori visiting, Parker might actually start creating her own work. She smiled. With her luck, the cranky cowboy would be color-blind and she'd have to repaint the whole house before she even set up a canvas.

The buzzer on the gallery's main door pulled her from her thoughts. Parker moved close enough to hear the security guard, but stayed in the shadows.

"I'll need IDs," she heard the guard yell through the glass. "Then I'll see if Miss Lacey is available."

Two men in suits stepped forward and slapped what looked like very official badges on the glass.

After talking to someone on the phone for a minute, the guard nodded at the suits, but didn't open the door.

Parker moved farther into the shadows as he hurried toward her.

"Miss Lacey, two FBI agents want to talk to you. I can tell them you've already gone if you like."

"No. I'll talk to them. Bring them to my office." Parker smiled; she'd been expecting this. Tori had been gone for over a week, so it was about time they got around to asking questions. And if she wasn't willing to answer them, she might raise their suspicion. Parker worked with easily a hundred artists, and Victoria Vilanie was only one. There was no reason to believe Parker had anything to do with or knew anything about her disappearance. But she had a feeling it was the press that really wanted answers.

The guard nodded and turned to the door.

She watched the two men moving toward her. One was taller, older. The other was beefy, like he'd overdone the workouts. Neither man even glanced at the art on either side of them.

Ten minutes later, she'd answered all their standard questions. Yes, she'd met Victoria Vilanie in person once at a conference in LA, and she believed they might have been on the same plane back to Dallas. She got off then, but seemed to remember Victoria staying on the flight heading to Detroit. Yes, she knew how talented the woman was. No, she didn't know if Tori was unstable. No, they were not friends. No, she didn't know if the artist took drugs. Yes, she did keep Victoria's number on file.

She passed them the form that she asked all her artists to fill out. The younger man looked over it and handed the paper back. Obviously, she had nothing that they didn't already have in their records.

"Why'd you write 'Tori' on the top corner?" the older one asked.

"She asked me to call her that," Parker answered.

"Are you aware that she had death threats before the LA showing? Her parents are very worried that some harm may have come to her."

"Yes. I read about it in the paper. If I remember the story, a man had seen her picture and started writing her through the galleries."

"Right." The agent looked bored. "You ever get any of those letters, Miss Lacey?"

"No." Parker thought of adding that no gallery that she knew of had got a letter. She suspected the story might have been a lie Tori's stepfather told or a publicity stunt.

As she walked them to the door, she asked, "What's the big deal? Doesn't a woman have the right to take a vacation? Maybe she's lost in her work. Artists tend to do that." She knew it was more than that, but Tori hadn't gone into much detail that night at the airport when they'd huddled together in a corner of the crowded terminal and planned her disappearance. She'd just said she wanted to run away from a life she hated, and that she had no one to turn to but Parker.

At first it had seemed like a game. Planning each step. Even seeing if they could buy untraceable phones. But as they'd boarded their flight, Tori had smiled, as though part of her panic had vanished. Her life was like a rocket speeding out of control, and Parker had offered her an escape hatch.

Now the game felt real, and Parker had never felt so alive.

The taller agent looked at her with cold, black eyes. "The press believes Victoria Vilanie to be one of the finest artists in the world. She may have been kidnapped. In fact, according to the press, the stepfather is sure of it."

"Or," Parker tried again, "still, she might just be on vacation. Maybe she doesn't like all the attention. Maybe she's shy." The minute the words were out, Parker knew she'd said too much.

The older agent suddenly seemed to wake up. He stared at her as if he'd just heard something that would put her on the watch list.

The beefy guy shook his head. He seemed more interested in arguing than picking up clues. "The press says the public has a right to know, and besides, where would she go? She's been a recluse for years."

"I can't think of anywhere, but after all, I don't really know Tori."

The agent looked at Parker as if he thought she might be protesting too much. His question came out in a whisper. "What *do* you know, Miss Lacey?"

Parker fought to keep calm. "Nothing. I just know artists, and most don't like to be in public.

They are very private people. The creation of a work of art comes from deep inside and has to have a great deal of silence and alone time to bloom."

They exchanged a look during her spontaneous lecture.

"If you hear . . ."

"I'll call," she interrupted, suddenly in a great hurry to be rid of them. She'd read once in a mystery that the guilty always talk too much, and what had she just done but rattle on.

As they walked to the door she dropped farther behind, guessing there would be no goodbyes at the door. Neither man looked at the walls that were filled with beautiful works. Their lives seemed to have no room for color, and that frightened her far more than the badge or gun they carried.

The moment the agents left, Parker rushed back to her office and closed her door. She used the phone she'd bought a week ago when she'd been with Tori at the airport.

Tori picked up on the second ring.

"Hi, Parker," she said. "When you getting here? You wouldn't believe the light in this open land."

"I'm not coming for a while. I have to make sure I'm not followed. Stay safe, Tori. Lies seem to be circling and I fear your stepfather is encouraging them. Somehow he's even got the FBI involved."

Tori was quiet for a moment, then whispered, "You understand why I had to leave."

"I do. After having just been visited by the FBI, I have no doubt. No wonder you were so upset. You must have had very little privacy since your paintings became so popular. I'm going to do all I can to help. I'll call again when I'm on my way."

Chapter SEVEN

Crossroads

Yancy hung his new coat on the workshop latch and moved into his barn workshop. He didn't even look up at the loft. The woman he'd called Rabbit wouldn't be up there. She hadn't been for three days.

He knew because he came to check every night. He'd even walked over a few days on his lunch break, hoping she might have dropped by. No sign of her or of his coat.

He was beginning to believe she was only a figment of his imagination. Maybe wishing for someone his age to talk to had conjured her up. A man gets used to the loneliness after a while, but that doesn't mean hope vanishes.

What were the chances that a woman he'd never seen around town was hanging out in his workshop? She'd been pretty, real pretty, and he would have noticed a girl with beautiful blue eyes and dark, waist-length hair. He volunteered at half the things in town. He went to all the town-hall meetings and was always running to the grocery or the hardware store. He would have seen her somewhere.

Smiling, he remembered how her thick midnight braid had brushed her hips when she'd climbed down the ladder. If he was just making her up, at least he'd done a good job. Even her smile made him grin now, three days later.

"You up there, Rabbit?" he muttered to the silent barn.

A board above him creaked, making him jump.

"I've been waiting," she answered with a laugh. "I had to make sure you were alone."

Startled, he looked up and saw her lean over the edge of the loft. She was dressed, as before, in jeans and a flannel shirt, with his coat folded over her arm. Little Rabbit was so petite folks might mistake her for a teenage boy if they didn't see her long hair braided down her back and the gentle rounding of her chest that showed even in the baggy shirt.

Yancy tried to clear his thoughts. She was back.

"Well, come on down, Rabbit. We've got work to do." The rule came back to him. No questions. "I thought I might have dreamed you up, but dreams don't usually steal coats."

She swung a leg onto the ladder. "I'm sorry about that. I brought it back. But I'll have to borrow it again to wear home."

He watched her as her left foot hit the rung of the ladder and slipped.

An instant later she was flying down toward him, tumbling out of control like a bird with a broken wing.

Taking one step, he caught her in midflight. This dream he'd been thinking about felt very solid in his arms.

Without holding her too tight, he lowered her feet to the ground. She was real. Her heart pounded against his chest for a moment before he let her go.

"Thanks," she managed as she backed away. "I've always been clumsy."

"You didn't look clumsy," he managed to say as he fought the urge to reach for her. "You looked like you were flying."

She shoved a hand in the pocket of his coat and pulled out a bag. "I brought you cookies, but it appears they're only crumbs now."

He accepted her gift. "I love cookie crumbs. I'll share them when we take our coffee break, if you can stay awhile?"

"I can stay. The other night, when I worked here, I walked home and slept like a baby. So, what have we got to do tonight? I feel like a cobbler's elf."

"I'm putting together the hearth for the fireplace. I could really use your help." He pulled a tarp away from a long piece of wood he'd carved months ago. "It's a two-man job."

Her face lit up when she grinned. "One man, one rabbit, you mean."

"That'll have to do." It crossed his mind that the lady might be a little nuts to show up at night in a stranger's barn, but right about now in his life, a bubble off normal didn't sound like too bad a place to be. He liked watching her work. She had skills he'd probably never develop. Plain, old, ordinary wood became art in her hands.

As the night aged, he began to feel like he was half-drunk. She'd come back. The work seemed to go more than twice as fast with her help. When he made a mistake, alone he would have sworn, but together they laughed.

It was funny, he thought as he watched her; deep inside, he felt like he'd known her all his life. He'd read once about an old Greek myth that claimed humans were once twice as tall. When the gods decided to make males and females different, they cut all the humans in half. From that day on, people walked around searching for their other half.

An easy way of just being together drifted between them. They didn't need to ask questions or carry on small talk. Like they'd always been a part of each other's lives. Or like they were each other's missing half. Impossible, he thought. Men like him were loners, born to have no one care enough to last a lifetime.

She helped him carry the hearth through the darkness between the barn and the house. When he clicked on the construction lights in the old house, she squealed with pure joy.

Turning loose her side of the hearth, she circled the room. "Even in the shadows I can see the beauty of this place." The construction lamps made spotlights on the floor of the huge open room, and she danced in and out of their beams like a ballerina on stage.

Yancy didn't notice the beauty of the room he'd so carefully created. He was too busy watching her. "Take your time looking around. I'll just stand here holding this hunk of wood myself," he teased.

Her laughter filled the empty space. She ran back and helped him carry the hearth to where the bones of a fireplace waited to be dressed.

As he spread his arms wide to hold the frame in place, she moved between him and the hearth, measuring, taping everything in place. By the time she was satisfied all was level and balanced, he was no longer thinking, period. When she brushed against him, he seemed to be the only one who noticed they'd touched. She smelled so good. Like peaches and freshly washed linens. He could do nothing but stand perfectly still, holding the hearth in place and breathing in the nearness of her.

When she finally left to run back to the barn for the toolbox, he forced himself to relax and think of what they *were* doing, not what he would have liked to do. If he'd thought she would have welcomed an advance, he might have dropped the hearth and grabbed her. After all, he could rebuild the hearth, but he might never get another chance to hold her.

Only she might not welcome his touch. He wasn't the kind of man who knew how to come on strong with a woman. He guessed his shy Rabbit wasn't much more knowledgeable when it came to men and women than he was. She did love helping, though. A kind heart was rare in the world.

When she returned, she was all business, but the easy nearness, the light touches continued. He told himself she wasn't noticing what she was doing, but he was memorizing every brush her body made against his, every time her hand touched his shoulder, and loving the way she leaned near. If she was launching a gentle attack, maybe he should tell her that he'd gladly surrender.

An hour later, they both stood back and admired their work. The hearth was beautiful. A work of art, thanks to her cuts and finishing.

"Not bad," Yancy said. "We could roast marshmallows in a fire there."

She nodded. "If we had the wood for a fire, a few matches, some chairs to sit in and some marshmallows."

"Just details," he admitted, looking around. "I'm almost finished with the downstairs and I have no idea about furniture."

"You could make it."

He liked that idea. "I wouldn't need much. I got the bar to eat on. All I'd need is a stool and maybe a rocker by the fire."

She moved to the bar and leaned against it. "What about your guests? Where would rabbits sit?"

Without thinking, he circled her waist and lifted her up. "You could sit on the bar."

A moment later he realized what he'd done. He might have let her touch him, but this time he'd touched her. No, he'd handled her. Like she was a kid or a close friend. He didn't even know her name. He had no right. He didn't know much but one rule had always been clear. A woman could touch a man, but a man never handled a woman without an indication of the woman's consent.

Yancy stepped back and straightened. His eyes staring down at the floor like he'd done in prison when he was little more than a kid lost in a world of rules and punishment. He'd spent every day since he'd been out trying to act normal, trying to do what was right, but deep down he knew part of him would always be an ex-con.

The silence of the empty room seemed to throb with each heartbeat.

They'd had a great night working together, talking, laughing. But a woman who wouldn't tell him her name wasn't likely to welcome his hands on her. When he'd caught her as she fell from the loft, he'd felt her stiffen even as he lowered her to her feet. She'd been polite. She'd thanked him for saving her, but she'd moved away.

"Yancy?" Her voice echoed in the empty room.

"I'm sorry," he whispered as he forced himself to look up. "I didn't mean to . . ."

Her gray-blue eyes were smiling. "It's okay, Yancy. You didn't hurt me." She crossed her legs and put her elbows on her knees. "The bar may be a little high but the view is great up here. I can almost see your handmade furniture. Rockers by the fire. A writing table by the window. Bookshelves climbing along the wall to match the stair steps over there. If you build me a stool, make it a few inches higher than yours so we'll look directly at each other. I get tired of always looking up at people."

He leaned his head to the side, studying her as if she were an animal he'd never encountered. "You're not mad at me?"

"Why?" She watched him.

"I put my hands on you, Rabbit."

"You did that when you caught me. If you hadn't I'd have probably broken a few bones." When he just kept staring, she added, "I've made up my mind that you are a good man, Yancy Grey. I've not always been a good judge of men, but I'm learning. I am not afraid of you. I believe you won't hurt me."

"I wouldn't," he managed to say, knowing she had no idea what a gift she was giving him with her trust. "But most folks don't warm up to me very fast after they find out I've been in prison. I've done hard time, Rabbit, and they say that changes a man forever."

She looked more interested than afraid. "Wan to talk about it?"

He'd been asked before and always said no, but somehow this time he thought it might be all right. He jumped up to sit on the bar a foot away from her and began.

He told her of how he'd been caught stealing when he was nineteen and had turned twenty in prison.

She listened as he remembered details he'd spent years trying to forget. He had to be honest with her. She trusted him.

"The smells in the whole place made me half-sick most of the time. I'd go out in the yard, even on the coldest days, just to be able to breathe. Once, it was snowing and I was the only one to step outside. I just stood, looking up at the snow, and listened to the rare sound of silence while I breathed in the smell of nothing but winter."

She covered his hand with hers without saying a word.

"I used to lie awake in my tiny cell listening to the sounds around me, wishing I were somewhere, anywhere else. Sometimes I'd dream of getting out and just living a normal life, but prison is still there in the back of my mind. No matter how hard I breathe out, there's still a little bit of the smell left in my lungs."

Her stormy-day blue eyes were full of compassion.

"It's been seven years and I still feel the pressure to do everything right. Like I have to watch myself every minute. If I do one thing wrong I'll somehow wake up back in prison with all the bad smells and the sound of men crying and cussing. If I say the wrong thing. If I don't tell people the truth about where I've been, then I'm hiding. If I do, I'm afraid of how they'll react."

Lacing his fingers in her small hand, he added, "I wouldn't be surprised if you disappeared, Little Rabbit. If you do, I should tell you that tonight was just about the best of my life. Even if I never see you again, I don't think I'll ever forget working beside you. It was nice, real nice."

He'd had this routine before with women he'd met. They acted like it didn't matter that he'd served time, but if he called for a second date, they were always busy. He expected it. He hadn't blamed them. He wouldn't blame her. She'd probably just disappear as if she'd never been there and he'd have no idea how to even look for her.

She pulled her hand away and he let her go without protest. "Help me down, Yancy. It's late."

He nodded and jumped off the bar. Carefully, he circled her waist and lifted her down. She didn't meet his eyes as she looked around the room.

"What are you building next?" she asked, changing the subject.

"The banister." He answered in a dull voice, knowing this must be her way of saying goodbye. "I thought I'd make the rails out of the same oak that I used on the hearth, then have the top done in wrought iron to make it more modern."

She moved into the shadows where the stairs climbed the north wall. He heard her feet take the first few steps. "I can see it. It'll add warmth to the room and last forever."

"I'm thinking my lifetime will be enough. I don't have any relatives to pass this place along to." He walked to her and glanced up into the darkness, where no lights warmed the second floor.

She came down one step so that they were at eye level. "I have to go," she whispered—as if there were anyone to hear but him. "Start the rails. I'll be back to help shape and stain them."

Studying her, he wondered if she were lying. "Fine," he managed, wishing he had the nerve to ask her just one question before she disappeared.

He waited for her to come down the last step.

She didn't move. The house was pure, snow-flake silent.

"I didn't mind you touching me." She moved one step closer. "Would you mind if I got a little closer to say good-night?"

Before he could answer, her lips touched his. When he didn't move, she leaned against him and put her hands on each side of his face. "Kiss me back, Yancy," she whispered against his mouth. "Please, kiss me back."

Something deep inside Yancy broke. Maybe it was reason. Maybe it was the door to his own private prison.

He pulled her against him and kissed her full on, like he'd always wanted to kiss a girl.

After a few moments, he felt her fingers gently brushing against the sides of his face, as if she were calming him down. When he let her go, he realized he'd been holding her so tightly she probably couldn't breathe.

He'd kissed her too hard. Too long for a first kiss.

His hands dropped to his sides, but she didn't pull away. He wouldn't have blamed her if she ran. She had to think he was some kind of wild animal. It would probably be no surprise to her that he'd had very few girlfriends.

But she stayed so near he could feel her breath as she whispered, "Easy now, Yancy. Let's do it again. I'm not going away. You don't have to hold on so tight. I'm right here in front of you, wanting very much to kiss you. Do you think we can try again?"

He moved his hands gently up her body and held her as tenderly as he knew how as she kissed him a second time.

This woman with all her secrets and closed doors kissed him with an openness unlike anyone had ever kissed him. She wasn't just going through the motions, waiting for what happened next, but there was tenderness, caring, as if she'd held all her passion in check for so long that she had to explode.

This time he was the one who couldn't breathe.

Chapter EIGHT

Madison O'Grady was one of the best pilots Fifth Weathers had ever seen. It took him a minute to get used to the cramped space and the vibration of the chopper, but the view was beautiful, both the land outside and the woman so close she was almost touching him.

They flew low across Kirkland land, following the canyon and riverbeds as if running with the wild horses. The landscape took his breath away, and when he glanced at her, Madison smiled as if she understood how he felt.

Finally, he calmed enough to explain how a cowhand had reported seeing a car far down in a gully where not even a truck could go. The canyon was too steep for the cowhand to get his horse close to the car, so he'd called in to the sheriff's office.

"We might not have checked out an old car," Fifth added, "but for the last week we've been getting info that a woman is missing. We don't have details, but if she was passing through this area and was kidnapped, whoever took her might have wanted to make the vehicle disappear."

Madison looked down at the treeless, rolling land. "That wouldn't be easy to do in this country. An abandoned car would be easy to spot."

"Right," he said. "Short of digging a hole and burying it, the best way is to sink it in water. Only, if a flash rain comes, it'll swell the gullies and drag the car along in a sudden flood. A few hours later, it could be miles from where it was dumped and above water or damming up a creek."

Much as he hated to brag, Fifth did feel like an expert on the subject. "The one animal, besides man, that does the most to change the lay of the land is a beaver. One den, built on a stream, can end up changing water flow for miles. So, even if it's simply an abandoned old car, someone has to deal with it."

"So we're looking for beavers?" She made a face.

"No." He laughed. "We're looking for a car that might have done the beaver's job. Someone reported seeing our missing person driving a red Chev. If we find it and there is a body in it, that's where the law comes in. Of course, there have been other apparent sightings of this missing lady. One report said she might have taken a bus from Oklahoma City. Another claimed to have seen a hitchhiker near Dallas who fit her description. Right now we have no idea which ones are true. All I know is she's missing and someone is in a real hurry to find her."

They flew for almost an hour, with Fifth marking off their route as they went. Now was a good time to note the flow of streams for future reference. The sheriff liked to walk the land, but Fifth preferred using a computer when he could. Madison was saving him several days of work. Some of the terrain could be reached only on horseback, and that would have taken a week.

No old car appeared. Maybe it went back underwater. Maybe the guy who spotted it was wrong on his location. But, thanks to his mapping, the flight hadn't been a waste of time.

When they finally landed and she cut the engine, he leaned back and said, "Thanks. I can't wait to get all this data into the computer. We might not have found the SUV, but I have a much better sense of the flow of the streams around these parts."

She grinned. "You are welcome, Deputy Weathers."

He collected his notes. She picked up her satchel. They walked back to the headquarters in matching strides.

"I'd like to offer to buy you lunch, but I'm afraid you'd think I meant it as a date." Fifth fought the urge to step out of range as he asked.

"I'm starving. I might go if we both understand it's only a thank-you lunch." She pointed to where the sheriff's cruiser had been parked. It was missing, along with Staten's huge black Dodge. "Looks like everyone left us."

"There is a big meeting in town. Didn't they tell you? We may have wind turbines coming in across this part of Texas. Some say it'll double the size of the town. If I know the people of Crossroads, they'll talk it to death before deciding."

She nodded. "Quinn mentioned it. I'm staying over for a few days, so she said we'll have lots of time to catch up. I grew up around here, but my parents moved to Granbury when I started college."

Opening the car door, he added to the offer. "If you have lunch, I promise to bring you back to Kirkland's place. I'm guessing you don't have a car and you won't want to wait in town for the meeting to end."

Madison hesitated. "You're right, but I don't know about a lunch date. Small town. Crowd in town, half of which will know me. All probably know you. They'll have us engaged before we order dessert."

"Well, then, we might as well do it right here. How about in the back of my cruiser or on the grass? We could skip lunch or dating or marriage. Let's just . . ."

"Stop it. I get the point."

He laughed. "Don't tell me you're shy?"

"No, I just don't like crowds."

He understood. They would stick out by about a head. "I know just the place that will be perfect for lunch, or whatever you have in mind. Trust me."

She looked like she was about to say "not a chance," but instead she folded into his cruiser without a word.

He lifted a brow. That was easy.

The conversation was stilted all the way back to town. When he pulled through the Dairy Queen and ordered, she relaxed a little. Five minutes later, when he parked in the empty museum parking lot, she smiled.

"I remember this place. There's a seating area overlooking the canyon."

"Our table is waiting. No crowds. Only the wind and ants."

She laughed as he handed her two root-beer floats while he got the burgers and they headed toward the picnic area.

Within a few minutes, they were talking like old friends. She told him stories of being in the air force after college, and he told her about wild car chases and arrests that he'd only heard about.

They figured out that they graduated from high school the same year, but she seemed to have had hundreds more adventures than he had. She'd traveled the world and been in combat once when she'd flown a rescue mission. He'd traveled Texas and had pulled his service weapon once in two years.

Both shared stories of being the tallest in every class picture and the problems they both had dating.

In the end, when he drove her back to the Kirkland Ranch, Fifth felt like he'd made a friend.

Maybe they'd work together again sometime. Maybe she'd call him the next time she visited her relatives, but he saw no sparks between them when she said goodbye.

As always, he was in the friend category.

The only problem was, this time he wasn't sure he wanted to be.

Chapter NINE

Crossroads

Rabbit didn't come back for two nights, but Yancy went to his barn and worked late. He'd planned the stairs to be his next project, but found himself looking for excuses not to work on it. Finally, on the third night, as he cut the wood for the rails for the staircase, his mind drifted repeatedly to how she'd felt in his arms.

She was small, but after holding her, he had no doubt that she was a woman fully developed. He liked the way she felt and the way she smelled, but most of all, he liked the way she wasn't afraid of him. She trusted him. Maybe not totally, but enough to build hope on.

He worked. He'd wait.

When he heard the creak of the door, he dropped his tools and turned toward the sound. She blew in with the first raindrops from a midnight storm.

She met his eyes briefly, and then she was running toward him as if she had missed him as dearly as he'd missed her.

He opened his arms and caught her as she jumped. For a while he just held her, feeling her body shake slightly. At first he thought it might be from the cold, but then he realized she was crying.

Backing up a few feet, Yancy leaned against a sawhorse so he wouldn't seem so tall. Her face moved between his throat and shoulder and he felt her tears as they soaked through his shirt.

His shy little rabbit was hurting. He patted her back lightly, wishing he could take her sadness away.

A hundred questions came to mind, but he remembered their one rule. He'd have to wait for answers. All that mattered now was that she was safe here in his arms.

He kissed the top of her head and moved his hands comfortingly across her back.

She snuggled against him and cried softly as though her gentle heart was breaking.

"Are you hurt?" he finally whispered.

Shaking her head, she pulled away enough to look at him. "Promise me you'll never tell anyone about me. No matter what happens, no one must ever know I'm here. I've vanished, you see, and I'm not ready to go back. For the first time ever, I'm living my own life. If this time ended, I'm not sure I could bear it."

"I promise." Whom would he tell? Yancy thought. No one would even know to ask. Besides, he'd sound nuts telling anyone he'd spent all these nights woodworking with a woman he called Rabbit but hadn't asked who she was or where she came from. "I'll keep your secret, if it will keep you safe." He pushed a tear off her cheek. "I'd do anything to help you."

She leaned against him and finally stopped crying. "Thanks," she whispered as she kissed his lips feather light.

He returned the kiss. Just a touch, not an advance. Her lip trembled slightly, but she didn't move away.

He held her, loving the nearness of her, wanting to help, needing to know what was wrong, but afraid to ask more. For now, it was enough that she was safe and unhurt. It didn't matter what she was running from—only that she was running to him.

He brushed what felt like dried paint from her temple. "You been working in someone else's workshop, Rabbit?"

"No. I was just playing around with oils today. I tried to mix the colors to match the sky at dawn, but I couldn't get it right."

"So, you paint." He held his breath, fearing she'd think his statement was a question.

"Not much," she answered. "Not lately."

"Maybe I'll give you a chance to do it again." He smiled at her. "I found an old rocking chair at a yard sale. It needs work, but I could repair the broken pieces of wood and you could paint it red."

She nodded. "I'd like that. I've always wanted to paint a rocker." She fought down a giggle but he saw her smile.

The sound of a car passing on the road fifty yards away made her jump, but she didn't leave his arms. When they heard the car pull off the road and head toward them, Yancy held her tighter. He could hear rocks crunching and winter-dead weeds snapping as the tires moved down the rut of a path to the house that no one ever used.

A beam of light flashed through a crack in the door.

They were about to have a visitor and there was no way out except through the barn doors. Yancy felt her panic as he moved his hand across her back trying to comfort her.

He knew she wanted to run, but from the sounds outside, the car couldn't be more than five feet from the barn door.

Without hesitation, Yancy picked her up. With one step onto his toolbox and another on the table, he was high enough to lift her into the loft. "Get back behind the boards and don't move."

"But—"

"Go, Rabbit. I'll stand guard. No matter what happens, don't come out."

She scrambled up. A car door opened somewhere outside. Yancy jumped from the table and ran the few feet to the loft ladder. He swung it down and shoved it beneath the table, where it blended with a pile of loose boards and scraps of materials he'd planned to trash.

As he picked up his hammer, he moved so that he faced the door, the table now between him and whoever might be showing up at this hour.

A car door slammed and footsteps sounded, coming closer, making no effort to be silent.

Yancy raised his hammer. If trouble stepped in through the barn doors, he could throw the tool and have another pulled from the wall behind him before the stranger could react. If someone were coming for the woman in the loft, they'd have to get past him first.

The door creaked and cold air rushed in as if the barn were inhaling.

"Yancy?" a low voice called. "You in here?"

Yancy was so relieved that he almost dropped the hammer. "Fifth," he answered as Deputy Weathers stepped through the opening. "You scared the hell out of me, man."

The tall officer smiled. "Sorry, I tend to have that effect on people. It's hard for me to sneak into a place. I've tried lathering my whole body with lard because someone said it was shortening, but it didn't work."

"Very funny." Yancy tried to calm his nerves, but they were still jumping under his skin. "Sounds like a joke one of the old retired teachers would tell."

"It is. Mrs. Ollie told it to me the other day."

Yancy forced himself not to look up at the loft. Rabbit wouldn't come down, and he had to act like it was just an ordinary night. "You must be helping Mrs. Ollie practice so she can get her driver's permit back. She always tells jokes when she's nervous."

"Yeah, she's doing better with her driving than she is with her stand-up comedy career. Drives fine, just can't remember if she should be in the right or left lane. Which complicates things on all these two-lane roads."

Yancy nodded. He'd ridden with her once. His life had flashed before him so many times he thought it was in permanent reruns.

Normally, he would have visited, but tonight all he could think about was saying goodbye to his friend. "What brings you out this late, Deputy? Coming in from a date or on official business?"

"No date. I was just driving home and saw the light. Don't usually see you working this late. Thought something might be wrong."

"No," Yancy said, "I'm just finishing up a project. I get out here working and forget about time."

The deputy pulled off his hat, leaned against one of the other tables and crossed his arms. He appeared to be planted there for a while. "I almost had a date a few days ago. One of the O'Grady clan. Tall and lean with the prettiest red hair you've ever seen. We had a lunch date."

"Really?" Yancy tried to act interested.

Weathers shook his head. "I think I just wanted it to be a date. She was something, but I didn't get any signals that she was interested in me."

"Why not ask her out again? Maybe you'll grow on her." Yancy added, "She's still staying out at the Kirkland place."

Weathers laughed. "This town is way too small. How'd you know?"

"Cap Fuller's grandson waited on you at the window of the Dairy Queen. He told Cap you had a tall redhead with you. Anyone in this county with reddish hair is probably an O'Grady and the only one visiting is Quinn Kirkland's niece. Kirkland told his grandmother when he visited her that she was staying with them."

Fifth frowned and Yancy laughed.

"That does it," Fifth swore. "I'm asking her out and taking her across the county line to eat. Nothing ever happens in this town that everyone doesn't know about." Weathers put his hat back on and headed toward the door. "By the way, this is going to be one fine house when you get it done."

"It keeps me busy." The last thing Yancy wanted to do was talk about his work, but he couldn't exactly tell the deputy to leave. Fifth was not only a lawman, but he'd become Yancy's friend. "This is late for you to be out, Fifth. Don't you have to be in the office by eight?"

"Sure, but I'm working on a missing-person case. You haven't seen a woman around? Small build. Long black hair. Midtwenties."

"Nope," Yancy lied. "What'd she do?"

"Nothing. She's just missing. Has been since the end of January. Left her car at the bus station in Liberal. Woman matching her description bought a ticket to Santa Fe, but never made it there. Bus driver thinks she must have left the bus somewhere in Texas. He said he had a crowd riding that night and barely remembered her. Once she made the missing persons' list, we've had reports of her buying a SUV in Waco and getting drunk in a bar near Amarillo. That's what happens when someone puts out a quarter-million-dollar reward. She gets more sightings than aliens do."

"If it's illegal to get off the bus, I'm a wanted man, too." Yancy kept his voice low and even, but it bothered him that someone was offering money for her. It made her sound like an outlaw.

What if the missing woman was his Rabbit? There were lots of small women in their twenties who had dark hair. Hundreds. Thousands in Texas.

The deputy shook his head. "She's not wanted, just missing. I don't know much about her except there are a hell of a lot of people looking for her. They're calling all the places where the bus stops, asking for information. Even got a few big-time private eyes tracking her, I've heard."

"There are dozens of bus stops in Texas." Yancy wanted to ask more questions, but he knew Rabbit was listening.

Weathers shoved the door open. "That's why I'm not wasting too much time looking. If I were on that Greyhound route, this town would probably be the last place I'd climb off the bus."

"Maybe it was dark. The view of the water tower is better then."

Both men laughed as the deputy moved out into the night. "Don't work too late, Yancy."

"I won't," he answered. He stood at the door and

waved as Weathers backed out. The moon was up and the rain had stopped, leaving a shine on everything. Folks laughed about how plain the land was here in West Texas, how the wind seemed to turn everything to shades of brown, but locals saw the beauty.

Yancy closed the barn door and threw the latch from the inside. Something he'd never done before. "You can come down, Rabbit." He kept his voice low, knowing that she could hear him.

She looked over the edge. "No ladder?"

"I'll catch you."

And he did.

If he held on to her a little too long, a little too tightly, she didn't complain.

When he set her down, she took her time moving away. She was growing used to him being near and Yancy knew without a doubt that he was growing addicted to her.

They worked in silence for an hour. He had a dozen questions, but he didn't ask a one. She showed him a way to cut the poles that would become a railing along the staircase. The cuts were all different from each other, shaping the poles at various angles, and at first he thought they were mismatched. Only when she laid them out in a row he saw the pattern flowing like a wave up the stairs.

"It reminds me of the way the wind makes the tall grass dip and flow," she said then bit her lip as if suddenly unsure of her work. "You can change it if . . ."

"I love it." He'd never seen anything like it. The staircase seemed to move and flow as he crossed the room. "I'll have a work of art in my house thanks to you."

"We've still got a lot of work to go before they're sanded and stained."

"How'd you learn to create something so beautiful out of blocks of wood?" The question was out before he thought.

"My dad taught me. I had a playhouse with a staircase like this."

Yancy smiled, glad he hadn't upset her with his question. "I had a box in the vacant field next to our apartment once. I called it my hideout, until some homeless guy took it over."

They both laughed.

When she picked up his coat as if it were now hers, he knew their night was over.

"Sorry about crying," she said. "And for stealing your coat, which I'll give back as soon as the nights warm."

"No problem." He moved to unlatch the door. "One thing I have to ask, Rabbit. Are you safe when you leave here?"

She nodded. "I stay in the shadows of the trees when I walk. I have a safe hideout to live in with no homeless folks nearby."

"I hope it's not made of cardboard."

Standing on her toes, she kissed his cheek. "It's not. See you tomorrow night."

Yancy turned and let their lips touch, making the kiss more than a peck, but just short of passionate.

He felt her tremble again.

Without moving, he whispered against her moist lips, "You'll always be safe here."

She moved away, but he saw the truth in her rainy-day blue eyes. She believed him. Maybe she wasn't afraid of him. Maybe she was more afraid of being close to anyone.

Standing in the open doorway, he watched her disappear into the night. He'd broken a rule tonight. He'd lied to the law and he didn't care. He'd do it again and again if the lies would keep her safe.

He had no idea why she wanted to step out of her life.

All he knew was that he was glad she'd stepped into his.

Chapter TEN
Mauve Monday's indecision

For the next few days, Parker tried to come up with a plan to get to Tori without anyone following her. She worried that her gallery needed her at the helm, but deep down she knew that wasn't true. She left it often to visit artists and to travel with some of her collection. She went to other gallery shows all over the world. She'd set up the place to run as smoothly without her as when she was there.

Tori needed her. She had to find a way to get to the farm near Crossroads. The talented painter, like many gifted people, needed someone else to help her work through the everyday problems. Parker knew this firsthand—she had lived with an established sculptor her first year out of college who could demand six figures for his work, but couldn't remember to pay the electricity bill.

They hadn't worked out as lovers, but he'd given her the direction for her career. She'd loved the business part of the art world. She was fascinated with the details it took to put a show together, with discovering new talent and directing their careers. She sometimes thought of herself as the director and the artists were the actors. They got the spotlight, but deep down, she knew that a little part of their success belonged to her.

This she could do. Organize. Polish. In a way, it was a safe career. She didn't have to prove her own talent; she simply had to show off others'.

But with the travel and the late nights, she'd never had time or any real desire to develop friendships or keep a lover longer than a season. Now, when she could really use someone she could trust, there was no one to call.

Tori must have felt that way in the airport that night. Parker knew she could be the artist's friend, only who would be Parker's friend?

Each night she watched the news. There must not have been much going on, because a few of the stations were doing nightly updates on Victoria Vilanie's disappearance. They had experts saying it was obviously a kidnapping. They interviewed Victoria's high school teachers and her first art instructor in college. All said that Tori was shy. One of the anchormen said that Victoria was one of the best young painters in the country and the world couldn't afford to lose her.

Parker watched, knowing that when she disappeared to go check on Tori, no one would mention her on the news. More and more, she realized she had to step up and be a true friend. If she didn't, the public would eat the shy little artist alive if they found her.

So, to be that friend, Parker had to make sure that no one followed her. No one would think that she also was vanishing. She had to make her leaving look like it was simply a business trip, nothing more.

As she planned, she forgot about how her leg felt weak and how her back often hurt. She forgot how sad the young doctor had looked when he'd stared at her. He hadn't said she had cancer. He hadn't had to. Parker had always known some-day the curse of the Lacey clan would find her.

"I don't have time to die right now," she said to herself. "I've got too much to do."

She thought of calling Dr. Brown and telling him he'd just have to wait a few weeks before he "made her comfortable," but she guessed he would have figured that out when he'd returned to her room and found she'd gone. She'd seen his number on her list of missed calls, but she refused to call his office back. Right now she had to convince her staff that she was traveling for work while she made plans to get away totally unnoticed by anyone who might think that she had a connection to Victoria Vilanie.

To disappear, she'd need some help from someone who either knew nothing about what she was doing or could be trusted completely. A saint or an idiot, she reasoned.

Slowly, she began compiling a mental list of all the people she'd called friends over the years. One by one she made calls.

Her lab partner in college didn't remember knowing a Parker Lacey.

Her college roommate was eight months pregnant with her fourth kid and said she didn't have time to chat.

Two old lovers wouldn't take her call.

Her former boss had died two years ago.

The only neighbor she knew had moved a year ago, and Parker hadn't noticed.

Parker paced the room like a caged lion. Surely,

in thirty-seven years, she'd made one friend. She didn't need a kidney; she only needed a favor. Someone to loan her a car or pick her up from the airport after one of her staff thought they were taking her to catch a plane.

Someone she could trade IDs with, maybe? No, that would be too much like a spy novel.

Even someone to give her a ride would be nice. Surely she knew a friend who would do a favor without asking too many questions.

As the days passed she realized she was being watched. If she didn't plan carefully, she'd lead the FBI—or worse, the press—right to Tori.

Only Tori wanted her to come. Parker had to find a way. Once they were on the farm, they'd talk. Parker would help Tori plan; after all, planning was what she was good at.

Parker thought about how the brooding cowboy on the adjacent farm would react if press crews pulled up next to his land. He barely talked to her—or anyone else—the day she'd bought her farm.

The good thing about living next to a loner like him was that she didn't have to worry about him spreading rumors of someone living at her place. She doubted he'd even noticed Tori there. If he had, he would have thought it was none of his business.

That one trait just might classify him as a friend in her book.

Chapter ELEVEN

Galen Stanley pulled the truck he'd rented in Liberal, Kansas, into the motel just outside Crossroads, Texas. The twilight rain was threatening to freeze over. He'd been driving for hours and was ready to stop.

The trail was cold.

His body felt every bit of his almost fifty years as he climbed from the huge rig. He could have slept in the back of the cab, but tonight, this close to the town he grew up in, he needed silence and a roof over his head.

He'd taken this assignment not because it was easy or had much chance of being successful, but because when he'd seen one of the locations he'd be checking out, he knew it was a sign telling him it was time to go back.

Back to the place he'd run from over thirty years ago. He'd been a traveler ever since.

As much as he hated to admit it, his gypsy blood sometimes whispered through his veins. He believed in signs and curses. In the past thirty years, he'd cheated death one too many times to not know that it would eventually find him. Maybe this place where it all began would be the place it all ended.

The loneliness that always weighed on his broad

shoulders seemed heavier tonight. Maybe it was the knowledge that there would be no one to come home to. Not before, not now, not ever.

When he walked into the motel lobby, a sleepy old man in overalls climbed out of his recliner and limped the five feet to the counter. He didn't look too happy at being pulled from his TV program.

"You got a room?" Galen didn't bother to smile.

"Sixty a night for truckers. Breakfast is included."

Galen nodded and pulled two hundreds from his wallet.

"Name?" The old man moved to a computer that looked twenty years old. "And I'll need ID, address and an email if you got it."

"Gabe," Galen lied, as always. "Gabe Santorno." He passed him a driver's license with that name, along with an address in Denver that was simply a mail drop.

"One night, Mr. Santorno?"

"No. Two." He hadn't been this close to Crossroads in years. It was time he stopped working long enough to look around.

The old man chuckled. "You planning to take in the sights, stranger?"

Gabe raised his head and looked directly at the man. His gaze hardened. Fear flashed in the clerk's eyes.

The old man lowered his gaze first. "Just making conversation, mister. Your business is your own."

Gabe took the key and rolled his shoulders, forcing himself to relax. "Call me Gabe," he said in a low tone. "And no, I don't want to take in the sights. I just want to sleep. Tell the maid to skip my room." The place didn't look like it would have turndown service anyway.

"Then have a good night, Gabe." The clerk was trying to act as if he wasn't bothered, but he kept his head down. "If you sleep through breakfast, there's a café in Crossroads a few miles down the road that's worth eating at. Some say it's got the best chicken fried steak in the state."

"Thanks. I'll remember that." Gabe turned to leave, then added, "Old man, you were smart not to reach for that gun you've got beneath the counter."

"What makes you think I've got a gun?"

Gabe smiled. "You'd be a fool not to out here on this lonely stretch of highway, but I mean you no harm. I'm just a trucker passing through."

As he walked away, he heard the old guy whisper, "You're a hell of a lot more than that, Mr. Santorno, but it's none of my business."

Gabe parked the truck on a side lot and walked back to his room with his one suitcase. All he owned, all he needed was in one bag. It had been like that since he was seventeen. He'd wanted it that way.

Once inside, he locked the door and checked the windows. Then Gabe tried to relax. He stood in the shower until the water turned cold. He had a week's worth of stubble, but he didn't bother to shave. A man with a bit of scruff is more forgettable, he decided. And that was exactly what he wanted to be. Forgettable.

Standing wrapped in a towel, he forced himself to stare into the mirror. Scars crossed over his body like lines on a road map. Some were more than thirty years old, and some were from his army days. One, on his left shoulder—a souvenir from his last job—wasn't quite healed. He didn't care about any of them. He'd given up caring about anything or anyone years ago.

An army sergeant told him once that he fought like a warrior angel in a hurry to get to the afterlife. Maybe he did, but hell didn't want him and heaven didn't seem ready to take him in. He'd be fifty on his next birthday, and his black hair was salted with gray. One day soon, he'd lose his edge and the warrior would fall.

Gabe laughed. When that day came, he wanted to be buried in the Crossroads cemetery. Maybe that's why he took this assignment. Maybe it was time to visit what would someday be his last resting place.

He slept until ten, then dressed in black and slipped from the back window of his motel room. The rain had stopped but the road would still be slick. As he jogged the two miles to the little town, Gabe tried to push aside the last time he'd been in Crossroads, but the memories kept flooding back.

He'd been barely seventeen and dumb enough to believe in love. Jewel Ann Grey had been a year younger and even wilder than he was. He'd loved to say her name as if it were one word.

Even though there had been bad blood between the Stanleys and the Greys for years, he and Jewel Ann had run away together one night, full of dreams for their future. Their only crime that night was loving each other.

A few hours later, her father, leading a small caravan of pickups, caught up with them. He'd brought a truckload of relatives set on teaching Gabe a lesson for thinking a Stanley boy could marry a Grey girl.

As Gabe ran on the gravel beside the road, memories of that night pounded across his mind. He'd compacted them into short blasts, like hits to his heart. The details were gone, but the pain was still there.

It had been dark and rainy, like tonight. He'd pulled over when her relatives flashed their lights, thinking he'd talk to them. Only his own dad had been just behind the Greys and there had been no talking to either man that night.

It was probably the only time the two families had ever got together. Jewel Ann's father pulled her away, not caring that he ripped her clothes as she fought.

Gabe's dad had shoved her relatives aside as he came after his own son with a bat.

Two of Jewel Ann's uncles held him while his old man beat him. Her screams, as they forced her to watch, hurt worse than the blows. His dad had always been a cruel man, and he proved it that night. Once Gabe started bleeding, his old man put his hand against the wound, not to stop blood, but to make sure it flowed over his fingers. Then he took a break from the beating so he could spread blood over the girl's breasts.

She'd screamed until she passed out. Even her father's slaps wouldn't wake her.

They took her home, but his dad stayed long enough to cuss his son and tell Gabe that if he ever came back he'd kill him. Even after Gabe could no longer move or even try to fight, the blows kept coming, breaking skin and bones.

His dad left his only child in the ditch, covered in blood and mud. In his mind his son had dishonored the family, and there would be no coming back home.

Gabe knew he'd die if he didn't move, and pure rage made him get to his feet. Slowly, he limped to a truck stop a few miles down the road. It was almost dawn by the time he reached the place. There was no one to call, no use in reporting the crime. Everyone in town was afraid of his dad—even Gabe's mother.

He hid in the back of a truck with Colorado

tags and slept as it drove north across three states.

When the trucker found him later that night, he dropped Gabe off at the hospital. When the doctor realized how much blood he'd lost, he said it was a miracle Gabe was still alive. He had broken ribs, a broken arm and a concussion. And after they sewed up his cuts, he also had forty-seven stitches crisscrossing over deep bruises.

It wasn't a miracle he'd lived, Gabe thought. It was determination. He'd spent the days in the hospital changing, hardening, so nothing would ever hurt him again.

In the midnight moonlight Gabe reached the Crossroads cemetery and pulled out his flashlight. The trees that he remembered as being small were overgrown now and permanently bent by the wind.

The Stanley family graves were there, near where the canyon dropped down off the flat land at the back of the cemetery. It wasn't an ideal spot—on rocky ground and hard to get to by car. But Gabe always thought it had the best view of Ransom Canyon.

The facts about his parents were carved in the headstones: His father had died a few months after he'd beaten his son almost to death. His mother had died ten years later. There were no other graves in the family plot, even though it could have held a dozen more. To his knowledge, there were no more Stanleys. Only him.

He moved to the Grey family plot, looking for one name: his one love, Jewel Ann. Even in his mind, when he said her name, he said it fast as if it were one word.

There were six Grey graves dated the same year he'd been beaten. Two were names of the men he remembered holding him down that night. Jewel Ann's uncles. No new graves since. What was left of the Grey family must have moved on. After all, both families had roaming in their blood, so it would have been unusual for them to stay on this land for so long.

Jewel Ann Grey's grave wasn't there. If she was dead, she hadn't died here. Somehow that gave him comfort.

Gabe liked to think she'd married someone acceptable and moved on, but that night had probably damaged her as much as it had him.

He clicked off the flashlight and walked along the canyon's edge, knowing one missed step on the shadowy edge might be his last, but he'd walked this close to danger so many times it felt comfortable.

Below, he saw a few lights from a little lake community. He remembered there being only a few houses near the water, but now the shadows of homes surrounded the lake and spread up the valley almost to the north road.

As he climbed above the cemetery, he could see the lights of town. Crossroads had grown, maybe even doubled in size since he'd left. It slept so quietly, Gabe had trouble believing anything bad could ever have happened there. The high school was twice the size it had once been, and there was a huge sports complex that had been only a grass field when he was in school. The main street had another block of businesses, and what looked like new housing ran along the east side.

Gabe veered onto the north road and shifted from a jog to a run. He wanted to see if his home was still standing. The place had had three generations of Stanleys who'd lived in it before he did. His dad had never repaired or painted anything, so it looked terrible when he'd lived there as a kid. Now it might only be rubble.

He saw the trees that had been big years ago. They now framed the house on three sides, hiding it from the road almost completely.

As he neared, Gabe was drawn to a sliver of light coming from a building behind the old house. A barn that hadn't been there in his childhood.

Silently, he moved closer. The house might be dark and look like the perfect setting for a horror movie, but there was movement from what appeared to be a new barn.

For a while he stood watching the inside of the barn through the sliver of light. A young couple worked side by side. The man was tall and lean with dark hair. The woman was small, but it didn't take much to realize that she was more skilled than the man.

He couldn't tell if they were even talking. He only saw them cross the light as they worked. They were obviously comfortable with each other, for they often moved close together.

He knew he should go, but something drew Gabe to the light. These people were on land that he'd once thought would someday belong to him.

Finally, the woman laughed and lifted her head. Long black hair swayed past her waist. Something clicked in Gabe's brain.

He'd seen her before? But where?

Then she turned and he saw her face. The pieces tumbled together in his mind.

He recognized her, not from having seen her in person—but from a picture.

She was the woman he'd traveled halfway across the country to find for his contact back in Detroit. They wanted to know where she was. They were offering good money. Dead or alive. The people who hired him to find her said they didn't much care which.

He should finish the job and move on. Grab her, tie her up in the truck's sleeper if she wouldn't come peacefully and take her back. It wasn't his job to worry about what happened to her after that.

But Gabe didn't move. He simply stood in the darkness and watched.

Chapter TWELVE

Periwinkle starlight

Parker dug through old boxes of files that should have been thrown away years ago. It was almost midnight and she was running out of time. She had to find the name of the cowboy who'd sold her that farm in West Texas. He might be her only chance.

She'd never bothered to remember the names of people who weren't in the art world. After all, there were hundreds of gifted and brilliant people worth knowing, so why bother with those who don't even have a membership to a public gallery?

Parker realized she sounded like a snob. She *was* a snob. Her parents had been snobs. They'd sent her to all the right schools where snobs send their children. And she'd also learned young never to be too open, never to trust completely, never to get involved in other people's lives or let them too close to you.

But now she did need someone to trust, and after three days of looking, she had come up with no one.

The cowboy seemed to be the last on a short list of people who might help *and* keep quiet about it.

Finally, she found the deed. The amount she'd paid for the farm made her smile. She remembered the guy had been taller than she was, bone-thin, dust-covered, and had had dead eyes. If she'd offered him half the price, he probably would have taken it. Neither of them had bothered to try to make conversation when they'd signed the papers. He hadn't even removed his hat. He'd just sat across the table, his arms folded over his chest like the world could end any moment and he couldn't have cared less.

Parker didn't like the idea of having to call him. Even his name sounded like it should be a character in a Western. Clint Montgomery.

She walked to the window of her town house and peeked through a tiny break in the curtains. The beefy guy who'd claimed to be an FBI agent was still there on the corner, circled in pastel blue light. He had been for several days, either him or someone who looked just like him. If she drove away, she had no doubt they'd follow. If she booked a flight or took the bus, they'd probably be in the seat behind her. She might not be much of a lead to finding Victoria, but she might be the only one they had.

Parker had thought of calling the FBI and asking if they were really watching her, but she decided if they didn't suspect her now, they would after the call.

No calls. She had to follow her play. Convince

the office she was out scouting for new artists while losing this guy outside.

Sitting down, she stared at the cowboy's number. She was about to do the very thing Tori had done ten days ago. Ask someone she barely knew for help.

She dialed the number and waited.

Two rings. Three. Four.

Parker closed her eyes. This might not even still be his number. Montgomery might have moved—after all, it wasn't like he'd call her and tell her if he did.

Six, seven, eight.

Logic told her to put the phone down, but this was the one person she could think of who knew no one in her world. Even the beefy guy on the corner wouldn't put them together. If she drove her Jaguar, they'd spot her on the lonely roads. The bus had worked for Tori, but the odds of it working again weren't good.

"Pick up, cowboy," she demanded.

Nine, ten . . .

"Yeah, what do you need?" a low male voice growled into her ear.

"Mr. Montgomery?"

"You got me, but I'm not buying."

"Wait! Don't hang up. This is Parker Lacey."

There was a long pause. "Who?"

"Your invisible neighbor."

"I remember. The lady who buys a farm and

then never steps foot on it." He didn't sound too friendly.

"Right, that's me." She needed to rush on before he disconnected. "I was calling to see if you might be coming to Dallas anytime soon?"

"Look, lady, I'm knee-deep in calving right now. Could you call back in a month or so and we could have a chat about my travel plans?"

"Don't hang up," she said again. "I need a favor. A big favor."

"Can't you call a friend? Or family?"

"I have no family," she admitted, "and I have no friend I can trust." In fact, if she asked anyone she worked with to help, it would be discussed at length in the break room even before she could finish packing. Plus, if they knew she was helping the famous artist Victoria Vilanie, they'd probably be texting the media while they gossiped.

"I'm sorry for that, lady." He didn't sound sorry at all or even interested in talking.

"Stop calling me *lady*," she snapped, then realized that being rude to him probably wasn't the best road to take. "I just need you to drive to Dallas. Pick me up at the north exit of the Galleria Mall. You know where that is?"

"Nope," he said. "Anything else I can do for you?"

"Yes." Parker fought back tears for the first time in years. "Don't tell anyone. Not your buddies or your wife or your priest. Just pick me up and drive back to your ranch. I'll walk over to my place from there."

He was silent for so long she decided the guy had probably fallen asleep. For all she knew, he was Crossroads' resident nitwit. She'd thought of a dozen possible ways to get to her farm, but any other plan left a path that could be followed.

Finally, the cowboy cleared his throat. "I can't tell a priest—I'm Baptist. I don't have a wife. She died a month before you bought the place next door. As far as my buddies, it would be a waste of time to tell them a secret. After a few beers, it'd fall out of the back of their heads."

She didn't know whether to laugh or cry.

"Can you pick me up or not? Can you keep it a secret?"

"What time?"

"Noon tomorrow. Remember, north door of . . ."

"I got it, lady. I'll be there."

"I'll be happy to pay you."

He swore. "Don't insult me. It's a favor you asked for. I'm not looking for a job."

"How will I spot you?"

"Blue pickup. You can't miss me. I'll be pulling a trailer-load of hay."

"Thank you, Mr. Montgomery." She whispered, after she heard him disconnect, "You don't know it, cowboy, but you may have just become my best friend."

94

Chapter THIRTEEN

Crossroads

Yancy carried two huge bags to the gypsy house and put them on the bar. The late afternoon sun streamed into the wide living space through the cracks in the boarded windows, making the room seem like it was glowing. The outside of his house might still look ugly as coal, but the inside was definitely polishing up like a diamond in the rough.

Last night he and Rabbit had worked late, but tonight they'd complete another project. One more step toward being finished.

He pulled objects out of the bags he'd brought in: a picnic quilt he'd borrowed from Miss Bees. Two camp stools he'd found in the storage room at the retirement center. Coat hangers he'd straightened. Three pieces of wood he'd picked up in the alley. A book of matches. And last, marshmallows.

Tonight they'd put in the banister, then celebrate, maybe talk for a while. And they'd kiss one more time. He liked that part of the plan the best. She was starting to mean too much to him to rush her. Yancy told himself just being near her, working together, talking was enough.

He checked, making sure all was in place, before he crossed to the barn. Rabbit wouldn't be coming until later, but he wanted it all ready.

Tonight, when the stairs were finished, the house would seem like a home. His grandmother's house, the house where he was born, was taking shape. But something else was happening inside him. Yancy, for the first time in his life, was falling in love.

It made no sense. He didn't even know her name. But he swore he could see her soul, and it was beautiful, just like Rabbit was on the outside.

He smiled as he laid out his tools on the worktable. Nothing in his life made much sense, but he knew Rabbit was a blessing he hadn't even known to wish for.

His childhood had been a struggle to survive. His mother had cared more about her drugs than she had about him. By the time he was in his teens he was running wild in the streets. He'd gone to prison before he thought of himself as a man. When he'd been released, he'd stopped in Crossroads because he'd heard his mother mention the place. Yancy had no idea that the old house at the edge of town had been left to him in an unknown grandmother's will.

He'd read a book once about gypsy lore: the book said that, according to these beliefs, a man can damn his offspring. Yancy had never known his father, but he must have been bad, because his mother never mentioned him. Once, when Yancy had insisted that she tell him one thing, she'd simply said that he'd died a horrible death.

When he'd learned about the house, Yancy couldn't help but wonder if the grandmother, his father's mother, had left Yancy the place in an effort to say she was sorry for something that had happened long before he was born.

After learning that his father had died tragically, Yancy didn't ask any more about his family. If it hadn't been for the Franklin sisters, he might never have known that the gypsy house was his. If he hadn't remembered his mother saying that she'd lived in Crossroads, he might never even have stopped in the town.

If somehow his life did have a plan, Yancy hoped Rabbit would be a part of it. When he worked beside her, he felt whole. That he might find his place after drifting in the wind for so long.

But he didn't forget that he *had* landed in Crossroads with nothing worth keeping in a back-pack and enough money only to buy breakfast. That day had changed his life. He'd decided to walk over and help two old men trying to trim a tree and they'd taken him in, given him a job and a place to stay. He'd worked for the Evening Shadows Retirement Community ever since, loving caring for the old folks as he learned from them.

A tap on the barn door made him jump. It was barely dark. Rabbit wouldn't be dropping by so early. Plus she never knocked.

Hesitantly, he shoved the door open.

A man about his height stood just outside. He was unshaven and had salt-and-pepper hair, but nothing about the guy looked lost or homeless. He wore a wool fedora and a bulky black coat. The kind that cost hundreds of dollars and would easily conceal a weapon.

Instinct—and a life spent hanging around the wrong kind of people—put Yancy on full alert. Hitchhikers sometimes got dropped off in Crossroads, but something told him this guy wasn't just drifting.

"Sorry to bother you, mister." The stranger tapped the brim of his hat in greeting and pushed his glasses up on his nose. "I was just wondering if you knew who owns this house."

"I do," Yancy answered without putting his hammer down. "I'm remodeling it."

"I can see that. Peeked in the window before it got dark. Hope you don't mind. You're doing a great job. This house looks like it's been on this spot for a hundred years." The man glanced back at the place. "Might fit in nicely with some research I'm doing."

"It has, and thanks for the compliment." Yancy wanted the man gone. He didn't care about research. Rabbit wouldn't come anywhere near the barn if she saw this guy, but Yancy couldn't be rude. It wasn't the way of folks from these parts. "I'm not that skilled a carpenter. I'm kind of learning as I go, so don't expect to see the project finished anytime soon."

The stranger straightened slightly. "I was thinking of retiring and settling here in Crossroads. You wouldn't want to sell this place, would you? Save yourself a lot of work."

"No." Not for any amount, Yancy almost added. While growing up, he never remembered having a real home, just trashy apartments and run-down back rooms of wherever his mother found a job.

"I could give you a good price," the man said.

"Not interested."

The stranger rocked his head. "I understand, but you see, I used to know the family who lived here."

"So did I." Yancy decided he didn't like the stranger. The hat's brim shadowed his eyes but he still had the feeling he was being studied. "There is no family left around here. A widow lady named Stanley used to own it, but she died over twenty years ago. House went to ruin after that."

The stranger nodded. "Stanley, right. I remember that was the name. Gypsies, if I remember right."

"Like I said, all gone. Moved away or died off years ago. Folks say the Stanley clan was cursed."

"Your name wouldn't happen to be Stanley,

would it? With that dark hair you could have a few drops of gypsy blood." The stranger moved a few inches closer.

"Nope. I told you, as far as I know, there are no more Stanleys." Yancy had said it three times now, but the stranger acted as though if he asked enough times the answer might change.

Yancy took a step backward, not liking the man being too close. "I wish you luck on your house hunting, mister, but I need to get on with my work. You might ask the Franklin sisters about what happened to anyone you remember. They own the bed-and-breakfast in town and do a good job of keeping up with folks."

"I'll do that." The man pulled his hand from his pocket. "Thanks for your time. I'm Gabe Santorno. Hope to be living in Crossroads when I'm not down in Austin."

Yancy gripped his hand. "Yancy Grey."

Gabe Santorno's grip tightened, and for a moment, he looked a little lost.

"You okay, Mr. Santorno?" Yancy, being in charge of a retirement center, was always on the lookout for signs of a stroke or heart attack. This guy didn't look old enough, but something about his on-guard stance made Yancy think that he'd had a hard life.

"I'm fine. I'd best get back to my motel. It's been a long day."

Gabe Santorno moved away so fast he seemed

to melt into the night. One second he was standing right in front of Yancy, and the next, he was gone. Shivering, Yancy moved back to his work. He had an eerie feeling, like someone had just walked over his grave.

But he didn't have time to worry about some stranger wanting to buy a house. He had a surprise to get ready for Rabbit tonight.

Chapter FOURTEEN
Joy

Tori walked in the shadows of trees along the road. It was earlier than usual, but she wanted to be with Yancy. She liked working with him. At first she'd thought it was because the feel of the wood and the smells in the shop reminded her of her father when she was a kid. Before fame found him. Before work consumed him.

Only now she came because of Yancy. He had a kind heart and a gentle way that drew her. There was a goodness in his soul, she decided.

Her thoughts drifted to the few men she'd met since she'd left college and started working full-time on what her stepfather called her "Great Collection." He and her mother had introduced her to a few—mostly older—men; the ones nearer her age just stopped coming around. Once she moved back home friends from college called less and less and never stopped by. She was always too busy to go out anyway with her career climbing. Her stepfather warned her that new friends were only interested in what she could do for them and her mother panicked when Tori stayed out past dark.

After a while, she began to realize that her villa behind her mother and stepfather's estate was her own private cage. They'd told her they wanted to protect her. Then she was too successful to go anywhere alone. Even when she occasionally flew to an art show by herself, they took her to the airport and picked her up. They always hired a driver and assistant to meet her at baggage check and not leave her until she'd passed security on her way back.

Tori was pulled out of her thoughts suddenly. She darted behind a tree as a car passed. Even if she had to be cautious when she walked at night near town, she felt so free here in Crossroads. It felt as if not only her body but her mind was free of being constantly observed.

As she froze, listening for the car to slowly disappear at the bend in the road, she realized that the lies she told herself formed the worst prison of all. She'd made herself believe that her mother and stepfather would look out for her and her interests. That it was better to be alone than to be a misfit. She'd convinced herself that they were somehow shielding her from harm by keeping the world away.

The night settled into silence and she began moving toward Yancy's barn. She might be into her twenties, but there were gaps in her. Holes. She'd studied painting but she'd forgotten to study life.

When she slipped into the barn, Yancy was walking from the house. Silently she disappeared behind the worktable.

"I saw my coat duck in here," Yancy said, laughing as the door creaked. "I know you're here, Rabbit."

She popped up. "I wanted to surprise you."

Walking near, he kissed her on the head. "You always do. You take my breath away. The fact that you show up here always surprises me."

She put her arms around him and would have kissed him, but he pulled away. "We've work to do, Rabbit. Don't go getting me distracted."

"You don't want to kiss me?"

He touched his forehead to hers. "I do. More than you know, but I think we should save the best until last."

Acting disappointed for a moment before winking at him, she teased, "I don't mind waiting, but that doesn't mean I won't be thinking about your lips on mine."

"Me, too," he admitted.

Tori knew he probably wanted to know more about her, but he'd been true to his word and hadn't asked. "Yancy, I haven't dated much."

Yancy looked up from his toolbox. "This is a date? No one told me."

She giggled. "It is."

"Great." He winked at her. "To tell you the truth, I haven't dated enough to recognize one. Before I went to prison, no one wanted to date a kid living on the streets, and then once I was behind bars the pickings were slim. A nurse in her forties at the infirmary did grin at me once, but every other tooth was missing in her smile."

"I can't believe the ladies in Crossroads don't hunt you down. After all, you're rich. You own the gypsy house. You're handsome in a shaggy kind of way." She messed up his already unruly dark hair.

He didn't argue. "I am rich, but my house is haunted, they say."

"Really?"

Yancy crossed his heart with the screwdriver in his hand. "Really. I got so many dead relatives floating around upstairs I may have to have the Baptist preacher do an exorcism."

"Don't you mean a priest?"

"No. I asked him. He said if he cast out all the ghosts in this county he'd lose half his congregation."

They began to work, talking about ghosts and things that go bump in the night. She didn't care if ghosts roamed the place or not. When she was with Yancy she felt alive.

Chapter FIFTEEN

Gabe stood in the trees and stared at the old house where he'd grown up. He could see Yancy Grey working in the barn. The same man he'd seen last night through a sliver of light. The man he'd talked to briefly just before sunset.

Yancy had told him all the Stanleys who'd owned the old house were gone. He couldn't have known that the man he was looking at had once been a Stanley.

"Yancy Grey," Gabe whispered in the darkness. Impossible. Yancy was part of Gabe's old name: Galen Yancy Stanley. Very few people knew that. Jewel Ann, his first love, and his mother. They had both claimed to love the name Yancy. His dad had hated the middle name. Said it sounded like a cowboy name.

Somehow, Yancy Grey had to be connected to Gabe. He tried to put the pieces together, only the path to the truth didn't seem to make sense.

But the man he met in the barn had his middle name, Gabe kept silently whispering in his thoughts. What were the odds? Yancy couldn't be a part of his family; they were all dead. The few aunts he'd had were long past childbearing when he'd left town, and, because of the old feud, none would have married a Grey anyway.

It had to be just a coincidence. A Stanley man's middle name and Grey for a last name. Not likely, but possible, Gabe decided.

If Jewel Ann had lived and gone on to marry, she might have named her son Yancy, but why would his last name be Grey? Jewel Ann was already a Grey. She wouldn't have married her kin.

The answer circled through his mind, telling Gabe that the impossible was real.

The proof had stood right in front of him. Not a vision of what might have been or a nightmare of what would never be, but a real, flesh-and-blood man. A man who bore Gabe's middle name and Jewel Ann's last name. If she'd got pregnant the night they'd run away, Yancy Grey was about the right age.

The puzzle fit together and he saw the picture it painted in his mind.

Only that would mean something good had come from the worst night of his life. Gabe had trouble wrapping his head around that.

If she'd lived? If he had a son? He would have known.

All these years, he thought Jewel Ann dead or that she'd blocked him from her mind. He'd never tried to find her, because he thought she'd never want to be reminded of what had happened. The love he'd shared was forever blackened in blood.

All the men who had beaten him had left him for

dead that night in the ditch. The last time he saw Jewel Ann's father, he was lifting her head by her hair. She'd finally stopped screaming and had passed out, but she was still tied to the hood of the car they'd eloped in. Tied like an animal that had been staked and killed. She still had blood smeared across her bare breasts. His blood.

Her old man had shaken her head back and forth as he jerked her hair. He'd slapped her, trying to wake her, until blood dripped from her nose and mouth. She was limp as a broken doll but still he slapped her, hard, as if angry that she was missing the beating. Gabe had heard him tell her he planned to take her home and beat her every day for shaming the family. He'd laughed as he finished the bottle in his hand while other men cut her free and wrapped her in a blanket.

Gabe remembered thinking that she was already dead. Hoping she was, because sweet young Jewel Ann would never be able to stand the pain, the shame. He'd told himself he would have come back if he'd had any hope she was alive. But he never came. He'd let hope die that night.

Only somehow, Yancy Grey was there at the old house. If he had been born and carried their names, she must have lived long enough to give birth to him. Maybe she'd raised him. Maybe she was even still alive.

Gabe kept saying Yancy's name over and over in his mind. The Greys wouldn't have welcomed a bastard grandchild, especially not one conceived with a member of the Stanley clan. Or maybe she'd run when she'd found out she was pregnant. There were places that would have taken her in. She would have realized she was pregnant about the time Gabe's dad had died.

Gabe remembered his mother as a mouse of a woman who was always afraid, but never unkind. If Jewel Ann's parents had kicked her out, his mother would have taken her in after Gabe's dad had died. She would have cared about a child her only son had fathered.

Emotions had been dead in Gabe for so long, he was having trouble dealing with them now; they hit his heart in one tidal wave after another. All the years of being in the army and thinking he had no one back in the States to return to. No one to care about him. No one he cared about. All the years of drifting, of not allowing himself to think about what might have been if he hadn't stopped his car on that lonely road. He should have known better than to stop. Her father was a mean old drunk and his father used to laugh while he beat Gabe. His mother never stepped in to help Gabe, but maybe she'd helped Jewel Ann. Why had he stopped that night? Why had Gabe thought they would listen or that they'd understand love? He should have known better. He should have kept driving, raced away. At least then they would have had a chance.

Gabe hated the men for what they'd done, but he hated himself even more. He'd stopped the car when he should have run, and he'd been running ever since. The guilt felt like bullets to his heart.

Standing still at the tree line, he watched as the small woman he'd seen the night before darted into the barn. She wore a man's jacket and a funny stocking cap that made her look like an elf. She looked like she'd walked the darkness before, like she was comfortable in the night the same way he was.

Gabe leaned against the tree and listened.

The night carried their voices, but he couldn't make out words. They were working on something on the table. Laughing and talking. Once, she stood in the light and looked out. She couldn't have seen him, but again, he recognized her as the famous artist whose picture had been plastered on the front page of the Detroit papers. There was no doubt she was the woman he'd been sent to find.

When the night aged, Gabe ventured a little closer to the house. Not for a better look at her, but to see the man called Yancy one more time.

His son! The man in the workshop might be his son!

Gabe couldn't turn away. He watched as they went back to the barn to carry more carved wood to the house, circling again and again like ants preparing for winter.

Finally, as the construction lights glowed in

the house, Gabe moved almost to the porch, watching them put a staircase railing together. As they worked, Gabe noticed again that they were flirting with each other, as well. Touching often. Leaning close to whisper as if they weren't alone.

Theirs was the gentle game Gabe had never allowed himself to play after Jewel Ann. He'd had a few women over the years, but they'd known that love was no part of what they did.

Gabe knew he should turn away. This moment did not belong to him. Nothing, not the house nor the man inside, belonged to him. He was just a stranger passing through—a man hired to do a job, a modern-day bounty hunter. Yancy probably wouldn't want to know his father was still alive. Gabe was not a father Yancy could be proud of.

The young couple moved to the fireplace, and the woman laughed and clapped her hands with delight as Yancy lit the logs that were stacked there. Like two kids on their first campout, they roasted marshmallows and huddled close to each other. Yancy laid his arm over her shoulders —protecting her, warming her, treasuring her.

Gabe turned away. As he walked back to the motel, he tried to tell himself this was all a big mistake. Maybe it was just a coincidence that the young man's name was Yancy. Maybe he'd just bought the house for back taxes.

At dawn, he checked out of the motel, drove to Lubbock and traded his truck for an old van. He could never change the past, and his son would never know about him, but maybe Gabe could make one thing right for Yancy: he could make sure no one found the girl whom Yancy was obviously crazy about. Dumping the truck was the first step. Changing himself would be the next. He needed to step out of the darkness and into town, and he needed to do so without making anyone suspicious.

Victoria Vilanie just got her own personal guardian angel.

Gabe was determined that whether Yancy was his son or not, he would get his chance to love.

Chapter SIXTEEN

Sepia Tuesday

Parker spent the next morning working in her office as if it were an ordinary day, but the colors of her brilliant workplace seemed faded, like an old photograph. As she sat in a staff meeting, she ran through the lists she'd made in her mind.

The meeting at the hotel in the Galleria had been written on her calendar for a month: it was a casual lunch, a planning session for an artist who valued himself far more than the world seemed to. He blamed everyone but himself for his work not doing as well as expected. Not enough advertising. Poor placement in the gallery. Bad lighting.

This was not a meeting Parker minded missing.

She'd even tried to change the time once because it was too far from her art gallery. Last week she'd tried to cancel it because she was going into the hospital for tests and wasn't sure she'd be out in time, but she hadn't been able to get in contact with the artist and his lawyer kept putting her on hold.

So, now she had somewhere she had to go alone and she knew no one would try to contact her for at least an hour. By then, she'd be out of Dallas.

As she left the meeting and walked back to her office, she made sure she'd canceled her appointments for the afternoon.

Her secretary, Minnie, walked beside her, nodding that she'd called each one as Parker recited the list. She'd told Minnie she wanted to catch an earlier flight and asked her to cover all meetings that came up for the next few weeks.

Minnie was so excited to be taking charge, she didn't question why Parker seemed in such a hurry to leave.

"I'll cover here," Minnie said. "I know you want to explore new galleries. That is the reason you're such a success, Miss Lacey. You venture out, all alone on these scouting trips."

Parker smiled. "I'm tempted to skip out on this last meeting."

Minnie almost giggled. "Do it. I'll cover for you with the artist and his lawyer. I'll call and reschedule whether they like it or not."

Parker Lacey hadn't missed an appointment in years. She'd already planned to miss the meeting, but she'd never tell Minnie. No one could know that she was using the noon meeting to slip away. "Great idea, but I'll try to make it."

If the beefy guy saw her leave, he would think it was simply for a meeting. He'd never know about the two outfits she'd packed in her huge Coach purse. She also carried a briefcase, no longer filled with papers.

Minnie stopped as they reached Parker's office door. "If I don't see you before you leave, have a safe flight and stay in touch."

"I will." Parker smiled and closed the door, her mind already full of what she'd do when she got to her farmhouse.

From the first she'd wanted the house near Crossroads to be her own little secret hideaway in case she ever needed it. Now she was going there to help a friend, and no one would know where she was or that she was with Victoria Vilanie.

Parker wondered if it were really just the invasive press that had made Tori want to disappear. Was it something more, like blackmail, a violent ex-boyfriend or death threats? Parker wondered why she'd helped Tori in the first place. This was

the first time in her life she'd really helped someone—become personally involved, instead of just
making a donation or something. She wasn't the
type to listen to anyone's problems, much less
blindly help a woman she'd met in person only
once.

But Tori's cry for help had sounded like the
opening to a great mystery novel and Parker
loved mysteries. For once in her life she wanted
to be in one, if only as a bit character. She wanted
to help. Deep down she knew it was also something more. Tori had reached her. Parker wasn't
sure how she knew it, but she believed without a
doubt that the artist's sanity, and maybe her very
life, depended on her escaping. For once Parker
could not stand on the sidelines. She had to help.

It was 11:20 a.m. Time to put her plan into action.

Parker slung her purse over one shoulder,
picked up her briefcase and cane. Confidently
she walked past the main desk, ignoring the pain
in her knee and the ache in her back. "Is my car
here? I don't want to be late for the meeting."

"Yes, Miss Lacey," the company guard named
Floyd said. "Your driver will get you through the
traffic and delivered in plenty of time."

Parker smiled and handed Floyd her briefcase
loaded down with toiletries, cash she always
kept on hand for shopping emergencies and the
phone she'd bought.

Floyd walked out with her, as always. "You

have a good meeting at the Galleria, Miss Lacey."

A touch of guilt prickled her skin. Minnie and Floyd were loyal employees, but Parker could not share this secret. The guard was retired police and might feel the need to report if he had information concerning a missing person. If Minnie had been in on any details, she'd already be talking about it.

As she climbed into the car, she thought she saw two men in suits bolt for their car to follow. *Good luck following us on the crisscrossing highways,* she thought. They might eventually trail her, but they'd be a few minutes behind. That was all she needed.

Whoever these men in suits were, they must want Victoria desperately to waste time watching her. Parker had to be a long shot. She wasn't Tori's friend, or she hadn't been until that night at LAX. Either Tori had very few friends or someone was spending a great deal of money on every slim lead.

She frowned, knowing that she'd talked too much when they'd interviewed her that night. She should have said nothing. Then they might not be following her.

Parker didn't want to think of another possibility. Floyd had called out where she was going. The suits might be closer than she thought. Floyd had also been the one to let them in the night the suits came to talk to her. He'd said they were FBI, but she hadn't made the call; Floyd had.

Parker tried to remain calm. She was over-thinking this. Floyd had been with her for five years. She closed her eyes, trying to think of anything he'd ever done that was out of line.

One thing. Yesterday he'd asked to see her business phone. He'd said his had stopped working. She'd thought it odd when he'd dis-appeared around the corner to make a call. She'd even checked her log. If he'd tried to call someone it hadn't gone through. No record of a number.

Parker let out a nervous laugh that held no mirth at all. Maybe she'd read too many mysteries? Maybe she wasn't cut out to keep secrets? Maybe her phone was bugged?

Thirty minutes later she entered the Galleria Mall's south entrance and dropped her business cell phone in a flower arrangement just outside the small dining room doors. If they tracked her phone, the suits would think she was in the meeting, and she had little doubt they would be doing exactly that. Thanks to Floyd.

It took her five minutes to cross the hotel and walk out of the busy north door. Her knee felt like it might buckle but she kept marching. Ignoring the pain, she took a deep breath and walked outside. An old blue pickup was parked between the rows of cars. Not illegally parked, but easy to see.

He didn't get out to help her in, but he did lean

over and open the door when she knocked on the window. It wasn't easy climbing up with one bad knee, but she made it. Her cane tumbled to the floorboard, and she ignored it.

The cowboy just watched. He looked so blank she feared for a moment that she might be climbing into the wrong blue pickup.

Clint Montgomery didn't bother with questions; he simply pulled out of the parking lot.

They were twenty minutes down a back road when he finally said, "Looks like no one is tailing us. I assume that was what you wanted."

"Right. Thanks." She felt the muscles in her shoulders begin to relax. So he'd figured out that she was escaping. It didn't matter. He'd have no one to tell.

He tapped his wedding band on the steering wheel. "I have to drop this load of hay off north of Grapevine. It won't take long."

She nodded and he kept driving. Finally, she said, "I guess I owe you some kind of explanation."

He finally looked at her and she noticed a touch of gray at his temples. He wasn't bad-looking in a hard, cowboy kind of way. Strong jaw, dark eyes, solid build.

"Look, lady, you don't owe me nothing." His voice was low and indifferent. "I'm just doing a neighbor a favor. In fact, if it's all the same to you, I'd just as soon not know what you're up to. If you're running from a husband or boyfriend, knowing would make me spend too much time looking over my shoulder. If you robbed a bank, as long as I don't know, I can't be arrested as an accomplice. If you're running from taxes, get in line."

She laughed. Apparently Clint was also a list-maker. He'd had a five-hour drive to think about it, and he'd decided that he simply wanted to stay out of her problems. She liked that.

They pulled into a run-down gate with a sign that said Equine Stables and Rescue. Without a word, Clint parked by the barn and started unloading bales of hay. She waited in the cab, watching clouds gathering above and feeling pleased with herself. She'd made it this far. She'd escaped. It would all be downhill from here.

Parker wasn't sure what she was supposed to do, but getting out to help never crossed her mind. Within minutes several men and women ran from the barn to offer Clint a hand. They were laughing and talking to him as if her cowboy was a welcome sight.

She studied him. Older now, of course, and he looked healthy. The touch of gray at his temples would have made him look distinguished if he'd bothered to comb the unruly mass of chestnut brown. Chestnut, she almost said aloud. Just like his eyes. The coloring didn't seem to fit such a hard man.

When Clint finished he climbed back into the truck, dusting pieces of hay off his well-worn shirt.

"You sell hay?" She sneezed.

"No, I gave it away. This place helps mistreated and abandoned horses. I had extra in the barn, so I figured, since I was making a trip this way, I might as well bring them a load."

"Oh." That was nice, she thought, and added, "I always pick angels off the Salvation Army Christmas tree at the mall and buy needy kids clothes and the gifts they always list on the back."

"Oh," he said like she was speaking a different language. "You want a Coke?"

She almost said an espresso would be nice, or even a cappuccino sounded great on such a cloudy day, but she didn't want to confuse him. "That sounds wonderful."

A half an hour later he pulled off at a truck stop and used the drive-through window to order two thirty-two-ounce Cokes. An hour after that she asked if he could stop for a minute.

He raised an eyebrow in question, then said simply "Oh" as he pulled into a truck stop that looked just like the last one they'd stopped at.

She jumped out and ran to the ladies' room as fast as her high heels would let her.

When she came out, he was waiting for her just outside the door. Without a word, he offered her the cane.

"I don't really need it," she lied. "I just use it for protection." Dumbest reason ever, she thought, but it was all that came to mind.

He walked a few steps and tossed it in the bed of his truck.

When she didn't comment, he asked, "You mind if we stop for lunch here? I'm starving. This place has a buffet, so it'd be quick."

"All right." She walked without limping toward the eating area that was packed with truckers and traveling families who all seemed to have the required three screaming kids. "I'm a little over-dressed." That was putting it mildly, she thought, as an entire family walked by wearing matching T-shirts, pajama bottoms and bunny slippers.

He looked her up and down. "Take off your coat."

"Yes, that might help." As she tugged off her jacket, she noticed that her blouse was wrinkled and almost put the jacket back on.

Before she could act, though, he handed her a sweatshirt off a display and said, "How does this fit?"

It was two sizes too big, had Don't Mess with Texas painted on the front in bright red and clashed with her coral-colored skirt. There were so many things wrong she didn't know where to start.

"It's fine," she lied, thinking anything was better than pajamas and bunny slippers.

He smiled like he'd thought of something brilliant and she forced down her objections. She knew she had to blend in, and the cowboy was trying to help.

At the counter, he paid for two buffets and the sweatshirt while Parker just stood frozen as she looked down twenty feet of steaming food, all on her never-eat list. Every kind of fried food she could think of. Even fried okra and pickles. Huge buckets of potatoes cooked different ways and a big dish of gravy. The last five feet were desserts.

"Looks good, doesn't it?" he said over her shoulder. "You can always trust a place where the truckers eat."

I'm in hell, she thought, but nodded and said aloud, "Do you think they have salmon?"

"They could probably fry you up one."

She caught the glint in his eye and realized he was kidding her. Laughter bubbled up from deep inside her. No one kidded her.

He smiled; his eyes now seemed dark chocolate brown and nothing about them was dead.

"There's a salad bar over there." He pointed with the hat in his hand. "I think I'll hit it first."

She followed. When they found a table, he waited until she sat down before he lowered in the seat across from her. They were halfway through the meal before he finally said anything. Then it was simply to ask for the salt.

Parker usually ate alone and guessed he did also. Neither was used to company.

By the time they headed back to the pickup, a slow rain was falling and thunder rumbled from the north. Without a word, he put his arm around her waist as they ran for the truck. The light touch steadied her.

When they neared, he reached ahead and opened her door. Then without warning, he swung her into the bench seat.

Parker was too shocked and cold and wet to speak. As he started the engine, he grinned. "It's getting cold. I should have brought a jacket."

"I could go back in and buy you one of these sweatshirts. Then we'd match."

Clint pulled onto the highway and headed northwest. "No, thanks. I'll dry."

When she started shivering, he pulled a blanket from behind the seat. "The heater may take a while to work. Cover your legs with this and turn sideways in the seat. You can shove your feet under my leg."

"You've got to be kidding. This blanket smells like a horse and I don't believe I know you well enough to . . ."

"Suit yourself, lady." He sounded more irritated for caring than mad.

Parker spread the blanket over her legs and twisted to put her feet on the bench between them. She used her Coach bag as a backrest against the door. One of her shoes had slipped off, so she kicked the other foot free. Right now, she was too cold to care.

The cowboy was right. The blanket wasn't long enough to cover her feet. Without a word, he raised his leg a few inches and she slid her cold toes beneath his denim-clad thigh.

"Thank you," she said, feeling her feet warm.

"You're welcome." He turned on the radio, and they listened to the forecast of a storm moving in. When he rested his arm over her knees, she could feel his warmth even through the blanket.

She cuddled against the leather seat and closed her eyes. Her last thought before she fell asleep was that she hadn't thought about dying all day.

Her adventure had begun.

Chapter SEVENTEEN

Deputy Weathers stumbled down the stairs at the bed-and-breakfast, as usual. He blamed his clumsiness on the six-inch steps and not on his fourteen-inch feet.

"Morning, Fifth," both Franklin sisters chimed as if his daily tumble was his morning doorbell.

"Morning," he said when he rounded the corner, ducking at every doorway. "I hope I made it in time for breakfast this morning."

They both giggled. Most of the time, Fifth was

their only boarder. How could they forget him? If he overslept, they'd leave half a dozen muffins in the microwave for him, and if he worked late, they left milk and cookies by his bed.

Fifth had thought about getting his own place; after all, he'd been here almost two years, and the bed-and-breakfast was probably twice as expensive as an apartment, but on the downside, if he moved, he'd starve. The sisters fed him breakfast, always left breads and fruit on the up stairwell table, packed him a lunch if they knew he was going to be on the road or out on patrol. If they served beer after five this place would be paradise.

He grinned, remembering the day the sisters had driven the highways, looking for his cruiser, because he'd forgotten his lunch. The sheriff had given him a hard time about it until Fifth offered to share.

To be fair, Fifth thought, in return for the extra food, he helped them move things up and down from the attic and around the yard. They were always trading one old piece of furniture out for another and they decorated for every holiday. Plus, he ate whatever they cooked, with no requests and no complaints. He cleaned his plate, just like his mother had taught him, and he had sense enough to compliment them on the meal.

Fifth was almost to his usual seat when he noticed another guest sitting at the table.

A man in tinted glasses sat at one end of the table by the bay window. The stranger was on the thin side. Tanned, even though it was winter. Scar on left hand, and another that moved from his collar into the hair just behind his ear. He looked to be in his late forties or early fifties.

The stranger glanced up from his paper and smiled. "You must be Deputy Weathers," he said politely. "The sisters have been telling me about you."

Fifth couldn't quite catch the accent. Not foreign, but not from around here.

Fifth offered his hand.

The man's handshake was weak, almost limp. This guy probably hadn't done manual labor one day in his life.

As Fifth took the chair at the other end of the table, he made another observation: the stranger had brought a book to the table. Which probably meant he carried a book everywhere.

The man cleared his throat. "I'm Dr. Gabriel Santorno. I'm here doing research on early families in Texas for a class I teach at the University of Texas down in Austin."

Fifth grinned. "Well, Doc, you came to the right place. The Franklin sisters know everyone around these parts." When Daisy put down the juice, nodded at both men and left the room, Fifth leaned closer. "She dated Sam Houston, I've heard."

The professor laughed into his napkin. "That's impossible. She's a hundred years too young."

"She's older than she looks." Fifth wanted to like the professor, but as always, the lawman part of his brain reserved final judgment, and there was something that bothered him about Santorno. Maybe it was the accent he couldn't place. The man had an easy way of floating through conversation and very proper table manners. His glasses weren't dark enough to be proper sunglasses, but they made it impossible to see more than the outline of his eyes.

"I'm sorry about my glasses. I'm highly sensitive to light," the professor said, as if he'd read Fifth's mind.

Fifth nodded as he buttered his roll.

"Where are you from, Dr. Santorno?" Fifth kept the question light.

"Oh, a little town north of Austin."

Fifth tried again. "Your accent doesn't quite have that Texas twang."

The man nodded several times. "Oh, that's probably because I grew up traveling. My father was a photographer. I don't think I ever went a full year in one school until I moved out and attended college. My father mostly did shots for real-estate sales. Wherever the housing market was growing, we moved to. Mostly across the Southwest."

Fifth shifted. The answer was long, but it

occurred to the deputy that people often over-embellish when they are lying.

Before he could ask more, Daisy Franklin hurried in with breakfast: egg casserole with pigs in a blanket on the side.

"Oh my, my," the professor said. "I thought that fine muffin and the fruit was the meal."

Fifth chalked up one plus for the professor. He pleased Daisy so much she blushed.

Ten minutes later when the man asked Fifth about his duties here in Crossroads, Fifth decided he'd asked one too many questions for someone just trying to make conversation. What time did he have to go to work? What area did he cover? Whom did he call for backup if trouble came?

When he started asking the sisters about the old gypsy house, Fifth considered taking a few minutes when he made it to his computer to check the man out.

As he drove to the office, Fifth tried to figure out just what it was that bothered him about Dr. Santorno. Maybe it was that the professor had taken the only chair in the dining room that could see both doors. Law enforcement tended to do that, but there was nothing about his stance that hinted Gabe Santorno was, or had ever been, a lawman. He seemed thin and looked like a man whose only exercise in life had maybe been walking.

When Fifth reached the office, he'd barely got

his computer booted up when Madison O'Grady marched in.

Near as he could tell, she was dressed the same as she had been a few days ago, but so was he. Those blue eyes were storming again. Damned if he wasn't lost again. Something about an angry woman turned him on.

He stood. They'd been all polite and friendly when they'd had lunch, and since then, he hadn't been able to stop thinking about her. Correction—about how she'd suggested they do it on Kirkland's dining table, or better yet, the couch. He'd even envisioned them upstairs in one of the bedrooms, and he'd never even seen the upstairs of Kirkland's headquarters.

A slow smile spread across his face. "Did you change your mind about the sex, Madison? The sheriff won't be in for another half an hour. We could do it right here on my desk."

She laughed, obviously assuming he was kidding. "I need more time than that."

"I could lock the door." Fifth was bluffing, but he was starting to worry she'd call his bluff.

"All right. The desk looks good, but you might want to move the computer."

Fifth fought the urge to rake the desk clean. If she was serious, he was willing and ready.

To his surprise, she backtracked, closed the door, then walked straight toward him.

"That door really doesn't have a lock," he said.

"Then I'll have to settle on a quick ride." She moved so close he could feel the warmth of her body.

Then she laughed, breaking the tension.

Fifth didn't know if he was disappointed or relieved. "Don't tease me like that, Madison. You'll give me a heart attack."

"Sorry. I just came by to say that I'm leaving. I have to get back. We're flying some training missions—you know, just in case someone invades Wichita Falls. Except for that first part, I really enjoyed working with you, Deputy Weathers."

He tried to relax. "Same here. I have a feeling I'll remember you for a long while. No woman's ever asked me to do it on the dining table before. Any chance you'd kiss me goodbye?"

She laid her arms on his shoulders. She wasn't hugging him, exactly, but pressing against him, and he loved that she was tall enough to run the length of his body.

He wasn't sure what to expect. She stared into his eyes and slowly moved against him as if they were slow dancing.

He put his hands on her waist. "You feel so good," he whispered, pulling her closer. "How about we forget about the *just be friends* part for a few minutes."

"Fine with me. I've always liked breakfast passion." Her lips brushed his ear as she whispered, "And midnight passion, for that matter. Wish I could stay around. There is something about you, Deputy, that draws me."

Her lips touched his and he was lost. They could have been standing in the center of town where both highways crossed and he wouldn't have been able to let her go. The kiss was white-hot, the best he'd ever had. Give it ten more seconds and he wouldn't care if the door was locked or wide-open.

Then, just as suddenly as they'd kissed, she pulled away. "I really do have to run," she said, as if what they'd just shared hadn't fried half the brain cells in his head.

"If I came back . . ." She took a step toward the door.

"When you come back," he corrected. "Make time for us to have a real date."

She was five feet away. "I'll try, but my schedule is unpredictable."

He moved at a speed that surprised him. In a few steps, he was reaching for the doorknob first. The door was still closed. He was still alone with her.

"Before you go." He had to think fast. Obviously this was all play to her, but he wanted her back here in Crossroads more than he'd ever wanted anything. "I've got a person of interest who I'd like you to check out."

"I'm interested."

"You need to see him. He's one of those people who—well, the parts don't all seem to fit together. You know, the kind folks say was a real nice guy and then find out he's a serial killer."

"I'm interested," she said again. "I'll do some digging if you'll get me all the facts you can. I'll call when I'm back in Wichita Falls. You think he might be somehow connected to the missing-person report?"

"He could be," Fifth lied. "The professor looked like the kind who'd report a missing cat on a 911 call."

She patted Fifth's chest. "Send me any info you find and I'll see if I can locate more. If you need me, I can be here in an hour."

He thought of telling her how he needed her right now, but he'd probably scare her off. Fifth wasn't the kind to come on strong.

But she was. Chances were she was the type who'd frighten him.

Chapter EIGHTEEN
Cadmium-yellow dawn

Parker woke to the beat of an old country song playing so low she thought, for a moment, it was in her mind.

She didn't open her eyes. She'd heard people say that they slept the sleep of the dead, but she'd never believed it until now. Not even a dream had interfered.

Last night the storm had slowed Clint down after they left I-20, making them arrive late into the night. He'd wanted to drive her to her door but she'd insisted he drop her where the road turned off to her land. After all, it was only a few hundred yards for her to walk.

She swore the man growled and glanced down at her left leg, but he didn't say a word. He'd done as she ordered in her business *I'm the boss* tone.

"It's still sprinkling. You'll get wet, lady," he had grumbled as he watched her scramble for shoes she hadn't worn for over a hundred miles.

They were back to *lady*. So much for first names.

"At this point I don't think I'll even notice the rain." Not wanting him to know that she already had a houseguest, she added, "I need to do this alone, Mr. Montgomery. I don't expect you to understand or care if you do."

"Good," he said. "I don't."

When Parker climbed out of his truck, she noticed that the road was in good shape, but she was too tired to thank him for that. He'd had to spend the money she was paying him on something. At least he kept the road up, and even in the cloudy night sky a dark outline indicated her house was still standing.

She should thank him for that, but Parker had been too tired to say another word last night.

The irritating man had sat in his truck and flashed his brights on her until she finally made the curve in her drive where an old oak seemed to shiver in the wind. Suddenly, she stepped from the light into total darkness. Parker heard him turning around and backtracking the quarter mile to his entrance.

Parker had realized then just how dark it was in the country. Dark, dark. Can't-see-your-hand-in-front-of-your-face dark.

She'd just stood in the middle of the road for a few minutes, her briefcase in one hand and her Coach purse in the other. Both seemed to weigh twice what they had at noon, and gravel roads were not made for heels.

Slowly, the details of her house materialized. It was a small, two-story building with an attic banked in dormer windows. By the time her eyes had adjusted fully to the night, she was at the steps. She took them one by one, like an aging drunk maneuvering to the front door. Her left leg ached, but the sense of being free overcame all else.

The place was unlocked, thank goodness. She'd never find the single key in the huge purse, in the dark.

Parker had stumbled in and dropped her bags. The next time she bought a big Coach bag, it better come on wheels.

It had been too late to wake Tori. She must

have been asleep upstairs, or a few lights would have been on. Tori had said that she worked and slept at odd hours, never knowing when the muse would find her. The last time they'd talked, Parker had promised she'd call when she knew she was arriving, but until she saw the cowboy's pickup, she wasn't sure she was really on her way.

Parker had taken three steps in and bumped into a couch.

Furniture?

She remembered that ten years ago the cowboy had said the furnishings went with the house, but she couldn't recall much being inside the place, and what had been there was dull, dirt brown.

Pulling off her heels, she collapsed on what she believed was a leather cushion. She hadn't slept in what felt like days, and the constant rain beating the windshield for hours had driven her com-pletely mad.

Now, in the cool morning air, she lay perfectly still, letting her body wake up one muscle at a time. She must have fallen asleep sitting up and then tumbled over like a fallen tree. One shoe was off, and the other felt like it was still on.

She moved her fingers, figuring she'd have to come alive slowly or the shock would kill her.

Warm wool brushed her hand.

Hesitantly, she opened one eye. The first thing to come into view was the long windows, framing a cloudy day with wood that was a shade of light aspen pine, making the room feel almost like a cabin. Thunder rumbled in the distance as musical tings of raindrops tapped the windows and formed tiny rivers down the glass.

She opened the other eye and the full room came into view. Western, she thought, but not overdone. Sagebrush-green walls. Buckskin leather furniture. Open space, making the room look bigger than she remembered. Absolutely nothing on the walls.

Sitting up, she whispered, "My house?"

Laughter shattered the silence. "I hope so, or I've been squatting on someone else's property."

"Tori?" Parker turned and saw her little artist friend sitting at a bar behind her. With no makeup and her hair in a long midnight braid, the famous Victoria Vilanie looked totally different.

Something else was missing, Parker noticed. There were no dark circles under Tori's blue eyes, and her pale face had tanned. She no longer wore Goth black, but a red-and-white-checked shirt and jeans rolled up at the ankle.

The girl jumped off the stool and walked toward her, carrying two mugs. "I hoped the music would wake you. I didn't think you'd be in until today or I would have left a light on."

All at once they were both talking and hugging like long-lost friends. Parker gave details of her adventure and Tori gushed about loving it here in the silent, pure light.

Finally, when Tori took a breath, Parker said, "We did it! We ran away."

"We did." Tori smiled. "Just like you said. We fell off the face of the earth."

The worry that had weighed on Parker was gone, and she could see peace in Tori's eyes, as well. She didn't seem to realize that half the world was looking for her. She was happy.

"Are you painting?"

"Come see." Tori grabbed her hand and they ran up the stairs to the attic like two kids.

The small attic room with two huge windows was unfinished. Paint tarps lay on the floor. A table, made of sawhorses and lumber, leaned against one low ceiling. Paint and brushes were scattered across it and test blobs spotted the unfinished boards. Creativity seemed to have exploded in the room.

Parker circled. "They're beautiful, and so different from anything you've ever done." A few were oils, and others were sketched out on paper. If Tori hadn't been standing in front of her, she could have never believed the same artist whose dark, moody paintings were in her gallery had also created the calm scenes before her.

"I know. I didn't paint the first week. I just walked and thought. I feared I might never paint again, but lately it's like I can't paint fast enough. None are finished, but I wanted to get my ideas down."

"You had enough supplies?"

Tori grinned. "No, I'm pretty much out. Thinking of cutting up the sheets for canvas."

Parker laughed. She knew art and this work was good. Very good. "Before I left the office, I had two huge boxes of supplies shipped to the neighbor. He should get them today or tomorrow at the latest. I meant to tell him about them, but we didn't do much talking."

"You didn't leave a trail?" Tori asked nervously.

"No. I paid cash for the supplies and asked the art store to ship it all as fast as possible. Apparently overnight takes two or three days in this part of the world. The kid who waited on me wasn't too excited about the idea of boxing everything until I handed him a few extra bills, and then he said he'd pack it special."

"I can't wait. But I'm running out of room up here. If you hadn't arrived soon, I was thinking of taking over the other bedroom."

"I could cover the walls in the main room with these. With the right tools, I could even make frames. I used to do that when I started the gallery."

Tori smiled. "We'll have such fun, and I know just where to find the tools. Make a list of what you need and I'll borrow them from a friend."

"You made a friend? Does he know anything?" Parker voiced her own concern. Meeting even one person out here could be dangerous for Tori.

"No. I just happened on a man working on an

old house. I offered to help. He doesn't ask questions and I make sure he doesn't follow me when I leave his place," Tori explained. "It's been nice to work with wood again. Before people decided I was gifted, I used to help my dad with his woodworking. Yancy reminds me of that time." She giggled. "He thinks my name is Rabbit."

Parker didn't like that anyone knew Tori was here, but if the artist trusted the man, that was good enough for her.

As Tori showed off piece after piece, Parker studied the paintings, which were full of light and movement. "I think a very simple frame that doesn't take anything away from the work would do best." She'd love to show the new work in her gallery, but somehow here, in this little farmhouse, seemed just the right place for it, at least for now.

"Let's move back downstairs and I'll make some coffee."

"Tea," Parker corrected. "I rarely drink coffee." She thought of adding "or Coke," but yesterday she had downed thirty-two ounces.

Tori shook her head. "Out of luck there. Now that you're here, maybe you can call the housekeeper with grocery changes. They're due to drop by next week. Tell them no bologna or white bread. No cereal. Yogurt would be nice. Some kind of fish other than canned tuna and double the supply of fruit."

"Has anyone been by to check on you?"

Tori shook her head. "The cabinets and refrigerator were stocked when I got here. Housekeeper left a note and a dozen moon pies on the counter. I'd never had a moon pie, but they're like crack—eat one and you're hooked. We'll need boxes of moon pies if we're to last another few weeks out here. I'll get you hooked."

Like two old friends entwined in each other's lives, they talked about art and how this escape felt so right. Parker sensed that Tori didn't want to talk about what had frightened her or made her feel so trapped. She was glad that Tori had trusted her enough to let her help. The rainy day seemed a great deal brighter.

Something hit the porch with a thud, and both women ducked behind the bar. The sound of an engine pulling away on the gravel road rustled through the thunder, then was gone.

Tori tiptoed to the door. "Probably the mailman?"

"Has he come before?" Parker leaned to look out the curtainless window, feeling foolish for being so jumpy.

"Nope. Like I said, not one person has dropped by." Tori slowly opened the door and poked her head out a few inches. "The rancher next door yelled at me one evening while I was walking on the county road."

Parker followed Tori a few feet behind. "What did he say?"

" 'Get out of the road, kid.' " Tori laughed. "Plus a few cusswords. Real friendly. I can see why you didn't talk to him on the drive from Dallas." She walked across the porch, and a moment later, she was back carrying a beat-up old box.

"Mail?"

"No. Just a box." Tori put it on the bar, and they both unfolded the untaped top.

"Doughnuts!" Tori squealed as she pulled a bag out. The moment she opened it, the smell of hot chocolate doughnuts filled the air.

Parker tugged the second bag out while Tori ran for plates. It was nothing fancy, just a plain plastic grocery bag. One box of tea and two pairs of socks inside.

Tori's eyebrows rose. "Strange gift."

Parker looked at the tea. It was the kind she'd asked for at the buffet last night. Peach chamomile. Written in black on the paper holding the socks together was simply "Maybe these will keep your feet warm until I'm around again."

Tori read the note over Parker's shoulder. "Looks like you have an admirer, or maybe a stalker with a foot fetish? Who do you think sent them?"

Pulling one pair of socks free from the paper, she tugged them on her cold, bare feet. "The box is obviously from our neighbor. Apparently, no one ever mentioned to him that flowers or candy might be nice."

Tori gratefully took the other pair. "Socks, tea and doughnuts. You ask me, he's a keeper." She took a bite of the first doughnut. "He can yell at me on the road anytime as long as he delivers doughnuts."

Parker shook her head. She didn't have time to keep any man. She just wanted to live the days she had left. Really live. Then, when she went back to the hospital where they could *make her comfortable,* she'd have an adventure to remember.

It occurred to her that her back didn't hurt this morning and the pain in her knee that always ached was barely noticeable.

She smiled. This wouldn't be a cane day, she thought, even if she had the cane that was probably bouncing around in the back of Clint Montgomery's pickup.

Chapter NINETEEN
Crossroads

Yancy decided to drop by his house while he was out running errands. He pulled into the drive, thinking soon he'd be doing this every day when he came home from work. He'd be like everyone else in the world, coming home to his own place.

When he unlocked the back door, the house was silent, as if napping in the afternoon sun.

He loved just looking at the staircase he and Rabbit put together. It was not just beautiful; the design looked like it belonged here. A magical, one-of-a-kind piece.

He walked through the rooms picturing how everything would someday blend together. One project at a time. One night of work at a time. A few minutes later when he unloaded boxes of tiles that would eventually become the backsplash behind the sink, he glanced up and thought he saw movement on the second floor of his house.

Yancy froze. There was still a part of him that believed ghosts walked the earth. He blamed it on his gypsy blood. Folks in town had told him how there were stories about the old house. Stories of people seeing shadows and spirits drifting past the windows on cloudy nights.

He stood rooted in the afternoon shadows beside his back door, trying to think of what to do. Telling himself he wasn't afraid, Yancy tried to decide if he was imagining things or if someone really was in his house. Maybe that man with the fedora had come back, hoping to talk him into selling the house.

Maybe kids had broken in and were just poking around inside. There had been break-ins before. Once four teenagers got hurt when they went inside. Part of the flooring gave way, sending a few of them to the hospital.

When a blink of a shadow crossed one of the

upstairs windows, Yancy decided not to rule out a ghost as the third possibility. From what he'd heard about his relatives, they weren't the type to rest in peace.

He set the tiles down and grabbed his best hammer from the tool wall. Whoever, or whatever, was inside his house, they hadn't been invited.

As he slipped in the back door the thought crossed his mind that he should have called the sheriff. Only backtracking didn't seem like a good idea. And *calling the police* was too new to his vocabulary to feel natural.

Crossing the kitchen, he headed up the stairs, for once not taking the time to admire his work. Raising the hammer, he moved slowly into the first bedroom. The floor had been repaired when he'd rebuilt the ceiling of the first floor, but on the second floor the boards were still rough and unpolished.

They creaked as he moved across the room. "Whoever's up here is trespassing."

He heard a giggle and relaxed. "Rabbit?"

"I saw your car parked by the barn and decided I had to come save you. Yancy Grey, you are a workaholic. I'm taking you to rehab." She moved slowly out from behind a broken closet door, looking more spirit in the shadows than real.

"Okay." He surrendered without a fight. He'd follow her anywhere. "How about we break away for a while? I've got the afternoon off. Let's go for a drive."

Five minutes later they were on the open road, heading east. The afternoon sun was warming and he had a full tank of gas. Life didn't get any better than this.

"Did you have a good day, Rabbit?"

She stopped playing with the radio long enough to answer. "You bet. We had doughnuts for breakfast."

Yancy didn't like the sound of "we," but he knew he couldn't ask. This was the first time she'd ever mentioned being with anyone. "I'm happy to see you, but I'm surprised you're out before dark."

"Me, too," she answered. "But I ran out of supplies, and more won't come till tomorrow. I thought I'd just go over and explore your house. I didn't think you'd be there. You never have been before."

"You mean you've broken in on other occasions?"

"It's not that hard. The key to the side door is on the windowsill less than a foot away from the lock."

He laughed. "Oh, so you're a regular prowler in the neighborhood?"

"Nope, just in your house. I've explored every inch of it." She laughed again. "And, by the way, I found that hand in the basement that kids used to say crawled across the floor all by itself."

"I'd believe you, honey, but my house has no basement."

They talked about things she'd been afraid of growing up. Slowly, she volunteered a few pieces of information, and mile by mile, he learned tiny scraps about her life. She hadn't been able to sleep without a light after her father had died. She'd never had a pet. She'd never had a brother or sister to talk to. She hated Halloween and dreamed once that every day was Halloween, where people wore masks and tried to frighten one another.

He told her about also growing up as an only child and she said she understood totally and had hated it, too.

Before, they'd always been working and their discussions were usually about the project, but now conversation flowed as the miles passed by. He loved the way she saw the world, the way she got excited over things he'd passed a hundred times and never even noticed. For her the earth was a canvas and nature the painter.

When they saw an old billboard, she made him turn around and go back for a second look. A hundred signs must have been glued onto the boards over the years. Then the weather had peeled off pieces again and again until no one advertisement stood out, only a patchwork of ads. Tiny scraps of posters slowly weathering, slowly blending.

She tried to reach high enough to touch the sign. "There is every color of the rainbow here. Bright colors, water-washed colors, some muted and faded by the sun. It's the most beautiful thing I've ever seen."

Yancy tried looking at it sideways, then backing away for the big picture, but he couldn't see it. "Tell me more," he said, hoping her vision would show through.

"Don't you see? It's like a whole town of people. Young and old. Bright and faded. Withered and twisted. Each scrap looks different as it stands against another."

"Oh, I see what you mean," Yancy lied.

"Individually, they're just scraps of paper, but put them together and you have a work of art." She smiled. "If I had any money, I'd buy this for you."

She'd finally said something he understood. "Rabbit, if you're broke, I could loan you whatever you need. I have plenty, you know."

She shook her head. "Thanks, but I'll be fine."

"I'm not kidding. I got seven thousand, three hundred and seventy-two dollars in my checking account. If you need it, it's yours."

"I need enough to buy more doughnuts. Could you loan me that much?"

"Sure. Next town we hit we'll buy as many as you want. We can go shopping in the junk stores, too. You can find anything there."

146

"I could use a coat. And rain boots. I've never had rain boots."

An hour later they'd found her two coats and a pair of rubber boots that were yellow with ducks on them.

"I need to buy Parker some boots, too."

"Parker?" Yancy didn't realize he'd said the name out loud until she looked up. "Who is he?" Yancy wasn't sure he wanted to know.

Rabbit seemed to read his mind, and for a moment, he thought she was feeling sorry for him. Then she took a deep breath and whispered as if the guy at the desk might care enough to wake up. "Parker is a woman. She's my friend. I have no idea what size her feet are, but she could use some cowboy boots. Since she arrived she's worn nothing but socks."

Yancy relaxed. "Is she tall or short like you?"

"A head taller than me, but thin." Rabbit touched his shoulders. "Almost your height, but not as wide."

Yancy looked over at the pile of worn boots and, for the first time he could ever remember, decided to waste a little money. "Let's get one pair two sizes bigger than you wear and one four. Then we'll buy boot socks. Put on a few pairs and you can wear the little ones if they are too small for her."

"They make socks just for boots?"

"Sure. Doesn't everyone know that?"

Rabbit was already into the mountain of boots. Finding sizes was easy; finding a pair proved more difficult.

As they walked back to the car, loaded down with clothes and boots, she asked to drive. He didn't really want her to, but he couldn't turn her down.

"I'll pay you back," she said when they shoved the bags in the back.

"Don't worry about it." It was worth ten times what he'd paid to watch her wander the store and discover things. She'd bought a sweater that hung to her knees, a scarf that looked like it would go with nothing, socks for both her and Parker, and those ugly yellow rubber boots.

She leaned near and kissed his cheek. "I will pay you back someday, Yancy."

She surprised him by being a very good driver, though she did like to go fast. He didn't mind. He sat close enough to put his arm around her shoulders, almost holding her.

He was enjoying himself until a highway patrol car pulled them over.

Yancy tried very hard to act normal. He pulled his driver's license out and his proof of insurance. He even mentioned that Fifth Weathers was a friend of his, but the patrolman didn't seem to know the deputy or care.

When he asked Rabbit for her ID, she pulled out a small wallet from her jeans. In the lights of the dashboard he noticed all she seemed to have inside the wallet was her driver's license and a ticket stub. She hadn't lied about not carrying any money.

"I'm just giving you a warning, miss," the officer said as he shone his light in on her face.

"Thank you. It won't go on my record, will it? I've never had a ticket."

"No, miss." The highway patrolman handed her back her ID. "You folks have a safe night," he added as he disappeared into the night.

Yancy wished the guy had said her name. He felt cheated. This cop, a stranger, knew her name and Yancy didn't.

When he looked up, she was watching him and he guessed she'd figured it out, because she whispered, "My friends call me Tori."

He nodded. "What about me? What do I call you?"

"I've gotten used to Rabbit, but if you like you can call me Tori. I'm vacationing at a friend's house and she joined me this morning. That's all I can tell you. The rest is all boring."

Yancy smiled. "That's enough. I thought you were on the run."

"I am. I'm hiding out, on the run, lying low."

Yancy brushed her hair out of her face. "I'm very fond of outlaws. Especially ones who get excited about ugly yellow duck boots."

She drove the car back onto the highway and

they talked about outlaws and the Old West as they drove.

An hour after dark, they stopped and bought a dozen tacos. They drove down another dirt road and ate them while they watched the stars. Then they laughed as they both tried to remember how to get back to the main road. It took them half an hour, but neither seemed to care.

It was after ten when he neared Crossroads. "I can take you home," he said.

They'd been listening to the radio and he wasn't even sure she was awake. "Tori? Did you hear me?"

"I heard. I just didn't want the night to end." She curled up against his arm. "I'll walk home from your house, but you have to promise not to follow me. I can't explain, but it's very important no one knows where I'm staying."

They were back to playing the no-questions game. He wanted to tell her that she could trust him, but he couldn't push.

He pulled in beside the barn and cut the engine. "If that's the way you want it." He opened the car door and started to step out.

"It's the way it has to be," she whispered and climbed into his lap.

Her back was against the steering wheel and her front was pressed against his chest.

Yancy smiled. "You can't be very comfortable there, Rabbit."

Resting her head on his shoulder, she whispered, "I just want to be close to you. I don't think I could ever be close enough to you, Yancy."

Suddenly the answers to his hundred questions didn't matter. He just wanted to hold her. He slid the seat back a few inches and pulled her against him. He wanted to breathe her in, feel every part of her as close to him as skin.

He wanted her to know how much she mattered to him. How he was falling in love with her. How she was changing the very core of him. But Yancy didn't know the words to say.

He just held her tightly.

And the miracle of it all was that Tori seemed to be holding him just as tightly.

Chapter TWENTY

Saffron sunset

The afternoon turned sunny as Parker found herself napping on her own porch. It still seemed so odd to think of this as a real place, her place, when it had always been more like a house she saw briefly once but moved in only in her mind.

Tori had vanished a few hours ago saying that she needed to walk and think about what to paint when the new supplies came in.

Parker knew that artists needed their quiet time. She also knew what she had to do.

She hadn't thanked Clint Montgomery for picking her up and now it was time to ask him for another favor. He might not be friendly, but she didn't think he was mad at her. If he had been, he wouldn't have delivered doughnuts and socks. Of course, not being mad probably didn't extend to talking to her any more than he had to or even doing her another favor.

After putting on one of the two outfits she'd brought in her bag, a pair of leggings and an oversize silk shirt, she waited until late afternoon to cross to his place.

The tennis shoes she'd brought weren't really made for wilderness walking, but they'd be much better than heels. The road would have been the easiest way to go, but she'd be far less likely to be seen if she crossed the field. All she had to do was climb over one barbed-wire fence. She could see the roof of his place from her porch.

Maneuvering across her land wasn't difficult; it was like walking through a park. The tall grass served almost as a carpet. She loved the fresh, clean air and the sounds of nothing but nature. If it were any cooler it would have been jacket weather, but with the sun in her face, all seemed just right.

Her knee hadn't ached all day, but then, she hadn't been walking the gallery in four-inch heels for hours. She'd been lying around like a fat house cat.

Once she got to Clint's land, it took her several minutes to find a break in the fence big enough for her to slip through between the wires.

A barb managed to catch her across the back of her shoulder, cutting her as she twisted through. She couldn't reach or see the cut in her shoulder, but it didn't feel deep.

Once on his property, it got far more complicated. Now she was on land that had been grazed, the ground was more uneven, far more muddy and was spotted with cow patties. She stepped in one while trying to avoid another.

When she finally made it to his barn, her cowboy wasn't even there.

Great! Just empty corrals and overgrown peach trees by the back fence.

His truck was parked out front of a low, mission-style home, so he couldn't be far. If she waited long it would be nightfall, and she'd never make it home after dark. If she left, she'd just have to make the journey again tomorrow morning.

Parker climbed up onto a wide porch that ran the front of the house. She was thinking maybe she'd just leave him a note. That should be enough. She'd say thank you and mention the supplies coming. He'd probably be happy not to have to bother to talk to her.

Funny, she couldn't think of exactly what he'd said during the drive from Dallas, but she remembered his touch. His arm had been strong and steady across her back as they'd run from the truck stop to his truck in the rain. He'd lifted her up as if she'd weighed nothing when he'd set her inside. His arm had rested over the blanket across her bent knees as she'd tucked her toes beneath his leg.

His touch had been gentle even though his words were cold.

She looked around, thinking that his home might help explain the man, but she saw few clues. The house was built flat to the ground and spread out, becoming almost part of the earth. She wasn't surprised to find the door unlocked. So, taking a deep breath, she decided to step in. After all, it wasn't breaking and entering if you didn't break anything coming in.

The home was silent, with dust dancing in the slices of light coming from the windows. Not one color spoke to her as she looked around. Beiges, tans, pale blues, dull greens, all faded by time. The front room was still, lifeless, like a morgue. Like nothing lived there, not even the man she'd called "cowboy."

Blinking, she tried again to really see the room. Books were stacked everywhere. Mail piled high on a bar he obviously didn't eat at. A small, boxy TV layered in dust. A desk that faced the wide windows that ran across the front of the house.

Tugging off her shoes so she didn't track mud into the cowboy's home, she moved to the desk. Unlike the rest of the room, it was organized, but void of many personal belongings. It held a computer, a cup with pens and pencils stuffed inside. Folders, trade magazines, stock reports were scattered in no order, and there was an old rotary phone that looked like it had come from the '60s and a stack of sun-faded notes with the initials *CM* in the corner.

She picked up one sheet and turned it over, thinking about what a different life the cowboy lived compared with hers. She could never live in such a bland room, looking out a window that showed only farmland and blank sky. His world must be so insipid, so lifeless.

She wanted to thank him, tell him about the shipment of supplies coming in and then leave. She didn't belong in his world any more than he would fit in hers. Their even trying to be friends made about as much sense as a turtle and a roadrunner dating. They were too different.

She heard a soft jingle, almost like a tiny wind chime, and looked up.

Clint stood in the doorway, the late afternoon sun seeming to fight its way around him. He didn't look any more friendly than he had before. Only now he was obviously dressed for work.

Chaps, stained and worn. Muddy boots. A thick chambray shirt and a wide, worn black Stetson.

"Afternoon, lady," he said as if they were passing on the sidewalk. "Want to tell me what you're doing here?"

"I was leaving you a note." She held the piece of paper up as if it were evidence.

He shifted, and she saw the rifle in his hand.

Parker straightened slightly. "I suppose you shoot trespassers?"

"Ones without shoes, I do." He didn't look like he was kidding.

"I came to thank you. I wanted to tell you I gave your address for a shipment that should be arriving in a few days. I thought I should thank you for delivering the tea and the doughnuts. That was very thoughtful."

"That all you came to say?"

"And the socks. That was nice, too." She wasn't sure what else to say.

He was making no effort to keep up a conversation. She almost felt the need to explain the rules to him. He'd talk. She'd talk. He'd . . . Oh, never mind.

She walked toward him and let a breath out when he propped the rifle up by the door. "Well, I'll be going now. Unless you have something to say, Mr. Montgomery. A short 'you're welcome' would be nice or maybe 'How you been?' No, that might be too much like a conversation."

He just stared at her like she was a broken windup Christmas toy stuck on "Jingle Bells."

"It was nice seeing you again." She was almost to the door. He needed to move one direction or the other so she could pass. "If you ever need anything just call on me. I owe you a favor now." She was almost to his nose. "I'd best be getting along."

"There is one thing." He watched her as if he thought she might jump suddenly in fright. "If you've no objection, I'd like to kiss you."

"Why?" The word was out before it passed her brain.

"Just something I've been thinking about and I'd kind of like to get it out of my system. I'm forty-three."

Parker didn't know if she was the cure or the disease. Or what his age had to do with anything. Maybe he was just picking up scraps of conversation trying to put a thought together.

She'd never had anyone say anything less sexy to her in her life. He wasn't telling her he was attracted to her or even interested. If this was his way of romancing a woman, it was no wonder he lived alone.

"Never mind," he said, shaking his head. "Dumb idea."

"No. I guess I have no objections. It's a small favor to ask. In fact, I should think of it as neighborly. I'm thirty-seven, in case you care."

She was starting to sound as crazy as he was. She thought of adding for him to go ahead and kiss her. Get it over with. How bad could it be? She'd kissed her share of frogs in her life and he was definitely not a frog.

She moved right in front of him, leaned her face up slightly and closed her eyes.

What she'd expected was a hard, closed-lip kiss on the mouth.

What she got was a very soft brush of his lips against her cheek.

She heard the slight jingle of his spurs as he shifted.

Then another light brush of his lips and another as he moved toward her mouth. Gentle encounters, almost shy. He made no effort to hold her. It seemed enough for him to just be so close to her she could feel the warmth of his body.

When his lips did finally brush over hers, she felt his breathing slow and knew he was relaxing. As he did, the kiss turned tender. Not a payback for a favor. Not an attack on her senses, but something with meaning.

Her body mutinied to the other camp and she moved closer. When her blouse brushed his shirt, his hands slid around her waist, deepening the kiss.

Her last thought before her brain melted was how did her cowboy, out here in the middle of nowhere, learn to kiss like this? She'd been kissed by men who bragged of having many lovers, but none could compare to this one tender kiss.

Suddenly she was hungry for something that, a moment ago, she hadn't even known she wanted. Her hands moved into his chestnut-brown hair and pulled him closer, demanding more.

He lifted her off the floor, her body pressed against his. The man felt like he was made of rock, only he was warm, so warm she felt like she was melting into him and loving the feel of being so close.

When he lowered her slowly, without breaking the kiss, she almost wanted to cry out that she wasn't ready for this to be over.

Only he wasn't ending anything yet. Apparently, he was just getting started.

His big hands moved up her sides, slowly warming her through the thin layer of silk. When he reached the edges of her breasts, he pulled back slightly, almost touching her, almost caressing her, far more intimately than a friendly kiss might allow.

Parker let out a sigh, wishing he'd be bolder but loving that he hesitated.

As his hand moved over her shoulder, he froze, then pulled away so suddenly she cried out.

"You're hurt," he said as he turned her in his arms. "You're bleeding."

"It's nothing. Just a cut I got on the wire."

She kept protesting, but he pulled her to the

159

bathroom and tugged a first aid kit from the shelf.

Parker took quick gulps of air, feeling the loss of his warmth as she wondered what had happened to the man she'd just kissed. He couldn't be the same man standing before her now swearing under his breath.

"Take off that blouse," he ordered as he washed his hands.

"I will not." Didn't the man know that no one ordered her around? She was Parker Lacey. She was a self-made millionaire. She was thirty-seven.

Oh, wait. He already knew that.

"Take it off so I can see the cut. It could get infected. Every animal on the prairie has probably rubbed up against that fence."

The thought grossed her out. She didn't even like the idea of people having pets that sat on the furniture. The possibility that a cow and her open wound might have brushed the same fence turned her stomach. She might contract rabies or foot-and-mouth disease or who knows what else.

She unbuttoned the first few buttons of the blouse, and he tugged it over her head.

Parker kept her eyes closed as he cleaned the cut and applied ointment. So he was seeing her back. Big deal. His voice was gruff, almost as if he blamed her for the accident, but his touch seemed caring.

"It's only a little cut," she said more to calm herself than him.

"It's deep enough to bleed."

She opened her eyes and looked into the mirror at his worried expression.

Then she realized all he had to do was look in the mirror to see her front because her lace bra hid very little. When she met his gaze she thought she saw a smile at the corner of his mouth. He'd read her mind.

"I'm sure you've seen a bra before," she snapped.

He spread a big Band-Aid over her cut and whispered close to her ear, "I wasn't looking at the bra."

He stepped back. "I'll get you one of my shirts to wear home."

She thought of saying "no, thanks," but the idea of putting on a bloody shirt really wasn't appealing. "It will be too big," she finally answered.

"So was that one you had on. I don't know where you buy your clothes, but your shirt must have belonged to a giant and those jeans you got on are way too tight. Plus, you don't seem to own a pair of shoes you can keep on."

"They're leggings and I don't need help with dressing."

"I wasn't complaining, just observing." He handed her a denim shirt. "I won't mind helping with the undressing if you ever need it."

"Thanks. Fat chance," she added, but he had already backed out of the bathroom. Parker took the time to wash her hands and run his comb through her hair. He'd been right to doctor the cut. It felt much better. Her hundred-dollar blouse would have to be tossed. Cuts in silk never patched.

The soft denim shirt felt warm against her skin. *Another reason to thank you, cowboy,* she thought.

She found him on the porch, scraping the mud off her tennis shoes.

"You don't have to do that," she said. "I'll just get them muddy again on the way home."

"No, you won't," he said without looking up. "I'm taking you home. I don't want to take a chance on you bleeding all over my good barbed wire again."

"But . . ."

"But nothing, Parker. I figured out why you wouldn't let me drive to your door last night. You thought I didn't know about that woman living at your place the past few weeks. Hell. I see her out walking almost every day and I nearly ran over her once when she was jogging down the road after dark. I can see your attic light on every night. She must be afraid of the dark. Half the time it's still on when I get up at five."

"You're watching her?"

"No. I don't care about her. It's none of my business. Maggie and Flip told me about you having them stock the house, so I figured you'd invited her."

162

"Who are Maggie and Flip?"

"Your housekeepers for the past ten years. They gave up trying to reach you years ago and just call me when something needs fixing around the place. Flip says you send a check every January to cover their work. Other than that, they weren't sure you were real."

"I thought their names were Margaret and Francis?"

He looked up and rolled his eyes. "Really, you think an old cowboy would go by Francis? I've known him all my life and no one ever calls him Francis more than once. His wife does the cleaning. He takes care of keeping the place up. Built the flowerbeds last fall."

"I hadn't noticed."

"You will, come spring. He seeded them with wildflowers."

Parker stared at him. "You told him to do that, didn't you?" It wasn't a question. She already knew the answer.

"We talked about it and figured you'd like the flowerbeds to match the walls in your rooms inside. That is, if you ever decided to visit."

"You two didn't have to do that."

He shrugged. "One way or the other I figured it needed doing."

"I'll remember that." She slipped into her shoes. "I'm ready to go home now."

The sun was almost touching the horizon as they

walked toward his truck. When he went right past it, she was confused, until she saw the horse tied to the back.

"You mind riding?" he asked, as he began pulling the reins free.

"I don't know how."

He laughed. "I know how, and so does the horse. Two out of three will be enough." He swung into the saddle and offered her a hand. With one tug, he pulled her up in front of him.

"Relax, Parker. You're safe enough." Without another word, they moved toward the road at a slow pace.

She watched the sunset, loving the orange and gold as it spread across the land. Halfway between his place and hers, she asked, "About that kiss?"

"What about it?" His voice was low, near her ear.

"Did you get it out of your system?"

"No," he answered. "Maybe we should try again."

His hand moved across her middle, holding her secure, caressing her. Logic told her she should end this now, but she couldn't seem to get the words out.

There it was again, she thought. That gentleness he could show but couldn't seem to voice. That call to an adventure that she couldn't turn away from.

"I'm not looking for forever." She always believed in being honest at the beginning of anything with a man. That way, she wouldn't waste time dreaming, and he wouldn't spend time fantasizing.

His laughter came hard. "I don't even believe there is a forever, lady. But if ever there was a woman who needed kissing, I'm thinking it's you. I've seen a lot of pretty girls but you are downright beautiful and haven't been kissed near enough."

She tried to stiffen. Compliments wouldn't work. "So you were simply offering to kiss me as a way of helping me out?"

"Nope. But I'm offering that and more if you're interested." His fingers moved from her shoulder to where her hands gripped the saddle horn. As he crossed over her, he'd lightly brushed her breast . . . by accident? . . . on purpose?

His voice was low in her ear as his hand warmed hers. "No relationship. No strings. No forever. Just you and me maybe making a memory we'll both keep."

Parker closed her eyes and tried to think. Was she willing to take the first wild adventure of her life, that would probably also be her last?

"When?" she whispered.

"I'll be waiting at the end of your drive at sunset tomorrow. I'll bring you back before dawn."

"I don't have forever, but I might have a night."

"Fair enough." His hand slid beneath her shirt and brushed the bare skin just above her waist as he kissed her temple. "One night with you might just last me long enough."

Then he was lowering her onto the side of her porch. He touched his fingers to the tip of his hat and was gone before she could say another word.

Chapter TWENTY-ONE

When Gabe stepped from the shower, he heard his cell beeping. Grabbing a towel, he crossed the darkened hallway to his rented room and picked up his phone.

"Santorno here," he answered, knowing no one ever called him except on business and this time of night only one man managed the office.

"We got a lead on Victoria Vilanie." Charlie Watts didn't waste time on greetings. "A highway patrolman stopped her about fifty miles from your present location. The guy obviously didn't recognize her, but I picked up his log while I was scanning all reports. Unless someone stole her license, she's in the area."

Gabe stood perfectly still, letting water drip around him. "Can you send me the paperwork?" He lowered his voice, not because he thought someone might overhear, but out of habit.

"Will do," Charlie snapped back, "but according to the report, she wasn't alone, so watch yourself."

Gabe moved toward the desk lamp and flicked it on in case he had to find pen and paper. "So maybe she didn't go nuts and run away from her loving family. Maybe she's just having a wild affair. Sounds like something a twenty-four-year-old might do." He'd already figured out she wasn't nuts or high from watching her work with Yancy, but he wasn't about to admit that to the home office.

Charlie, far too old to take assignments, manned the night phones at the agency. He was like an old firehouse dog. He wanted to run with the bell, but age and four hundred pounds kept him planted behind a desk. "I've been talking to her family every day, Gabe. The stepfather's upset because she's due to ship new paintings next week and she hasn't finished them. He's mentioned twice that he has to know where she is, dead or alive. Sounds like if he gets her back, he's got his workhorse. Of course, if she's dead the value of her work will skyrocket. Either way he wins."

Gabe liked talking to Charlie Watts. The old guy had seen a great deal over the years and had a bloodhound nose for BS. "What about the mother?"

Charlie hesitated. "She missed the second conference because she had a hair appointment she couldn't break. That pretty much told me what I needed to know. Rich folks will pay big money to get their grown kids back. Then they send them off to private country-club rehab so they'll at least look normal and tanned when they get out."

"This one isn't a kid, even if she looks petite in the photos. Since she's managed to avoid us for weeks, I'm thinking she might have her head on straight."

Charlie snorted. "Stepdad mentions drugs every time he calls. Wants to make sure everyone, including the police, knows she's a druggie. He says she's messed up bad. Has been since her real father blew his brains out in front of her. The guy said he had to take over being her legal guardian before she became an adult herself. Said she tried to kill herself once."

Gabe thought of the sweet girl Yancy seemed to treasure. She didn't look like the type to off herself, but then, he'd thought of ending it all a few times, too. The only thing that kept him from it was figuring that he'd end up in a worse hell than here.

"Charlie, does the office know about the report in Texas?"

"No. It came in after hours. I just thought you'd like to be the first to hear."

"Thanks. How about sitting on this info for a few days?"

"You know there are others looking? I think we're billing for six in the field right now. They're spread out pretty thin from Kansas to New Mexico."

"I know. I also know some won't care how much they frighten her, or hurt her, for that matter. I saw a girl Burt and Lee brought in last year. They'd hauled her in the trunk of their car for over five hundred miles. Bruised, bloody and throwing up from coming down off a bad high, she looked more dead than alive when she climbed out. If she wasn't crazy when she ran away, she was by the time they handed her back to the arms of her parents, who wouldn't even touch her."

"I remember that one." Charlie added, "Burt and Lee should have faced charges for it, but the parents wanted it all kept quiet. No cops involved."

Gabe kept his voice level. "I don't want that happening to this woman."

There was a long silence on the other end of the call. "Tracking people down isn't an easy business. Years ago it was mostly bad guys jumping bail or cold killers who someone wanted caught more than the police did. I even handled a few for the mob. They paid good and I didn't ask too many questions. But now . . ."

"I know." Gabe closed his eyes. It was getting harder to tell the good guys from the bad. "If I can find her, maybe I can talk her into coming back. That estate she lives in with her parents is like a hotel. She couldn't have it too bad in a place like that."

"And if you can't talk her into going home?"

"If I find her, I'll bring her back where she belongs. Like you've told me before, we're not the judge—we're just the deliverymen. But, Charlie, give me a few days. I'm close. I can feel it."

"It'll cost you, Gabe."

"I figured." Gabe smiled. "Best steak in town and all the beer you can drink."

Charlie took the bait. "I'll call you when and if that police report gets found but don't think I'm doing you a favor. I saw that girl's face on the flyer. I don't want to see it all bruised up from being bounced around in the trunk of a car."

"Me either." Gabe ended the call.

His chest ached so badly it felt like he was having a heart attack. He was starting to care again and it hurt too much. Somehow, he'd find a way to talk to the girl Yancy called Rabbit. If she didn't want to go back, that was up to her. This time he'd worry about what was right, not what was profitable.

Then, suddenly, he had a more pressing problem.

Miss Daisy had walked past his open door and screamed when she noticed him, almost naked, standing by the desk lamp.

Gabe grabbed his shirt. When the towel tumbled, he dived behind the bed. Cusswords rumbled, but Daisy didn't hear him. She was too busy shrieking.

Fifth Weathers came running from his room

with his gun drawn. For a few moments, chubby Miss Daisy and the deputy tried to get past each other in a hallway wide enough for only one.

Miss Daisy kept yelling, even though all she could see was one bare leg sticking out from the corner of the bed.

Gabe had nowhere to run. Two people were already blocking the only exit.

When the deputy finally got the larger half of the Franklin sisters to move along, he closed Gabe's door and said calmly, "You can come out, Professor. I told Miss Franklin to go down to the kitchen and make herself some tea. She's got to calm down or she'll explode."

Gabe stood up and quickly slipped into his clothes as well as his character. "I've never been so embarrassed, sir, I assure you. I can't believe that poor woman had to see me in the bare. It's intolerable. I'll never be able to face the sweet lady again." He kept shaking his wet hair. "I'm afraid I'll have to have a bit of brandy with my tea, if she'll even let me go down to the kitchen after this."

Fifth holstered his weapon. "Way I see it, Professor, if the sight was so horrible she wouldn't have stood there and kept screaming while she kept looking. You seem in good shape for a fellow your age. I'm thinking she'll get over the fright."

Gabe fought not to crack a smile. "So, Deputy,

if I apologize, do you think maybe she'd let me stay?" Gabe suddenly raised his hands. "Oh my Lord. I've exposed myself to a lady. I've committed a crime. If you allow me to dress, I'll go down to headquarters and confess." Gabe did his best to look like he might cry. "Oh, no. I'm sure I'm prison-bound. I don't think I'll do well incarcerated."

Weathers looked confused. "We don't have a headquarters, just an office, and I doubt very much that Miss Daisy wants anyone to know of your crime. Plus, I heard your phone about the time you turned off the shower. You must have darted out of the bathroom to answer the call. Who knows what Miss Daisy was doing up here? She's told me at least twenty times that this short hallway is the gentlemen's quarters and she only enters it when cleaning."

Gabe acted like he was distraught. "She saw me in the buff, sir. It must have been very upsetting."

Fifth shrugged. "When I was growing up my mother used to say she'd never go see a male stripper because she already lived with a dozen. I had one younger brother who I don't think wore clothes until the day the school bus picked him up for kindergarten."

"Maybe I should go down and try to calm the poor lady," Gabe offered.

"Good idea, but you might have to strip again because after two years of living with the Franklin sisters I can tell you for a fact that Rose is not going to be happy that Daisy saw something she missed."

"Maybe we should keep this incident to ourselves, Deputy. It might save the lady some embarrassment."

"I agree." Fifth stepped back, letting Gabe go first. "Wouldn't want to tell me where you got all those scars on your back, would you, Professor?"

"Car accident in my youth," Gabe murmured.

"Really," the deputy added as he followed Gabe down the stairs. "I would have sworn a few were bullet holes."

Gabe laughed. "Then I'd really have a story to tell, wouldn't I, Deputy?"

"I guess. If you lived, of course." Both men laughed. "That many shots to the chest I'd have to think would kill a man."

Gabe shook his head. "The accident was bad enough. I missed a whole semester of school. It was torture, Deputy, pure torture."

Chapter TWENTY-TWO

Panic

Tori paced the attic room. It was late, almost dawn, but she couldn't sleep or paint. All she could think about was that she'd handed her driver's license to the highway patrolman. What if he recorded it somewhere? Parker had said there were people looking for her. The FBI even feared that she'd been kidnapped or killed, according to a report Parker saw.

Tori was in trouble. Big trouble. She'd known her parents would look for her, but she never dreamed it would make national news.

Logic told her that they'd been more than an hour away from Crossroads when the patrolman stopped them. There was little chance she could be tracked to Crossroads, and if she was, no one, not even Yancy, knew where she lived. Even if someone did find Yancy, he wouldn't tell anyone about her. He'd already proved that. Even if the police knocked on every door for a hundred miles and found this farmhouse, Parker would never give her away. She felt safe here. For the first time in her life, she had friends who would protect her.

Six years ago, when she'd realized her mother wasn't letting her grow up and become independent, she'd almost killed herself mixing drugs with alcohol. Her stepfather made a big deal about her being disturbed. She needed protecting, nurturing, watching. All that had changed was that she'd lost even more of her independence. They'd moved her to a house in back of the big place so she could be closer to her work, and they'd taken her car for months.

She'd felt like a prisoner. Her only escape had

been to paint, and her canvases were as dark as her mood.

It had taken years to finally be allowed to fly alone to art shows and drive into town to shop. And even then, the trips were monitored, allowing her no extra time. Drivers, handlers, bodyguards were always near when her parents were too busy to travel with her.

Finally they'd grown bored with the weekly shopping trips where Tori spent hours just looking around. They let her go alone to the small town near their home.

Tori hated shopping, but she went every week just to get away. After a while, she'd stopped spending the cash she always took. No one noticed. They'd only watched what time she left and grown angry if she was not back for dinner. Eventually, they'd even sold her car, and the one she borrowed each week was in her stepfather's name.

Her stepfather told everyone that he had guardianship over her because very creative people have trouble with the real world. Even if he didn't have legal guardianship he did have power of attorney. His name was on everything she owned. He could freeze her funds.

For a long time her only revenge was the hundreds she dropped in her real father's old toolbox when she returned from her shopping trips. When she'd left almost a month ago, she'd packed thousands in her last purchase on her last shopping day. A backpack.

The backpack had been stored under her bed at the farmhouse. If she had to run again, she might need every dime.

Tori pulled out of her dark thoughts. "Not every dime," she whispered. "I'll pay back Yancy." If she could she'd keep her family away, far away, from the kind man who'd offered her all his money.

She'd gone along with her stepfather for so long, he believed a few harsh words were all it took to rein her in. That and her mother's rants about how she'd die if her only child turned out to be as insane as Tori's father. He'd been gifted, too, and Tori's mother swore that that's what had driven him to suicide.

Tori knew she'd let them rule over her for far too long. Maybe she wouldn't have been such a great success so young if they hadn't pushed or had the right connections. Maybe she wouldn't have been able to double her fortune in investments as her stepfather claimed he had. But she could have still painted. She could have lived a normal life.

In the shadows, her paintings surrounded her like close friends. Tori remembered how happy her father had been the summer they'd built her playhouse. He hadn't cared about being rich. He'd never wanted fame, but it had found him and eventually devoured him.

"Tori?" Parker's voice came from the bottom of the stairs. "You all right up there?"

"I'm fine," she answered.

"Want some cocoa?"

"We have cocoa?" Tori almost ran to the door.

"My secret admirer dropped off another box a few minutes ago. Best oatmeal cookies I've ever tasted, cocoa and fruit."

Tori almost danced down the stairs. "It's not even light and he's delivering food. I love this guy." She stopped suddenly, frozen in midstep. "You don't think he could possibly be the grumpy neighbor who picked you up in Dallas?"

Parker grinned as if she had a secret. "He might be. Maybe I'll try talking to him one more time."

"Great. Tell him you love spice cake and are addicted to moon pies."

Parker had a funny look on her face when she shrugged. "I'll tell him if I see him."

They giggled and talked until all the cookies were gone, then both decided, since it was full light, they might take a nap. Tori grabbed a blanket and decided to sit outside until the sun grew too warm.

But an hour later, she was sound asleep when it started raining. She cocooned into her quilt, smiling even in her sleep. Her mind might not know it yet, but her heart did. A butterfly was awakening within Tori, ready to fly.

Chapter TWENTY-THREE

"Madison, is that you?" Fifth whispered, hoping the walls of his bedroom at the bed-and-breakfast weren't too thin.

"Of course it's me, Fifth. You dialed my number. Who do you think would answer my phone?"

He closed his eyes, swearing he could see those icy-blue eyes flashing. "I wanted to see what you found out."

"Why didn't you call before five?"

"I wanted to have a private conversation."

She laughed. "Next you'll start breathing heavy and asking me what I'm wearing."

"What are you wearing?" Fifth hit himself in the head with his cell phone. If he got any dumber the sheriff would send him back to middle school. "Sorry about that. For a minute I forgot this was a professional call."

"Well, remember that from now on, Deputy," she snapped. "If you want to talk personally, hang up and try again. And while we're at it, I would have already called you if I had any news about Gabriel Santorno."

Fifth disconnected. He needed to start over. For once he needed to get it right. Madison didn't suffer fools lightly; hell, she didn't seem to suffer them at all. Which probably left her out of ever being invited to any of his family reunions.

He punched Redial.

She answered on the fourth ring.

"Hello, Madison. What you wearing?"

She giggled in surprise. "No, you go first."

He leaned back. She was talking to him now and not sounding angry. "Unfortunately, I've still got my uniform on," Fifth said, then hit himself again with the phone. That wasn't right either. He should have said something cool like "nothing but a smile while I'm thinking about you" or something like that. He thought of hanging up again and starting over, but he wasn't sure she'd answer the next time.

"Well, if you're dressed, go downstairs and look out the bay window off the dining room. When you look up, think of me."

Fifth gripped his phone tightly as he stumbled down the stairs and moved into the shadowy dining room. Maybe she had something romantic planned, like they'd both look at the moon at the same time. He never thought of stuff like that, but he bet women did. Hell, he'd never had phone sex. All he knew was that it started with "What are you wearing?" She'd have to carry the rest of the conversation.

His oldest brother had told him that women were always thinking, even when you weren't looking. He'd said his wife not only thought about everything she wanted to do, but about what she wanted him to do, too. She claimed it was a real time-saver for him. He should be able to do a lot more because he didn't have to think about it ahead of time.

Fifth moved to the window. Madison seemed more one who acted than one who thought. He might be safer just to ask for a date, drive to Wichita Falls and take her out.

He'd book a hotel room before he picked her up, just in case she had roommates or lived on the base. No, that might be too forward. But if he didn't, and she was interested in him, he'd feel awkward signing in for a room while she waited in the car. She'd have time to think about why being with him was a bad idea.

He looked out into the backyard; it usually made him think of what gnome heaven must be like. Last Christmas the Franklin sisters had even put out a policeman gnome by the birdbath. They'd said it might not be a deputy-sheriff gnome, but it would still remind them of him.

Only tonight he didn't see anything but Madison standing in the grass.

For a moment, he just stared, fearing that he was losing his mind and imagining her. After all, he had taken a few more blows to the head than usual lately.

She was so beautiful with the moonlight shining off her dark red curls. He could be happy just standing right here staring at her all night. He took a deep breath as he watched her lift her hands. Slowly, she touched the collar of her white shirt. Her fingers began to unbutton the top button of her blouse. Then the second. Then the third.

She was far enough down that he could see she wasn't wearing a bra before he made it outside.

"Madison! What do you think you're doing?"

"Getting your attention."

"What if someone saw you?"

"The fence is seven feet high. I saw the two sisters who run this place leave and your professor slipped out the side door looking like he was going for a walk."

"All right, Madison, you have my attention. Now what?"

"I decided to fly up and hand-deliver this report to you. When you called, I was walking in from the field where I landed. How about we go somewhere we can talk?"

"You can't just land a helicopter anywhere." Fifth wasn't sure exactly what law she'd be breaking, but there had to be one.

"It's in my cousin Mike's field. He hasn't farmed in years."

Fifth looked down at her open blouse that showed the valley between her breasts. "You going to button up?"

She grinned. "Does it bother you?"

"Not at all. Your skin is so creamy white. If you don't mind me looking, any objection if I

181

feel it, too? Two senses are better than one for memorizing, and I never want to forget the sight of you in the moonlight."

"Weathers, I think you're a romantic at heart, but you're not touching my creamy skin until we're finished with business. We talk first. Then we'll negotiate the touching policy."

All he cared about was that she hadn't said no. So he opened the back door to the bed-and-breakfast and invited her in. She opened her satchel and started spreading out papers while he made coffee and counted down the minutes until the negotiations.

When he turned toward her, he simply stood there holding the two hot cups of coffee, watching her move. Her blouse opened slightly as she worked, as if playing peekaboo with him. He decided whatever the terms of the negotiation were, he'd give up. It would save time.

When he set the coffee beside her, he tugged at one of her wild curls.

She batted him away. "I had to dig deep, but what I found is a patchwork puzzle with gaps. Gabriel Santorno died almost forty years ago in Denver. He was six years old. His grave is in Fairmount Cemetery."

"Common name, maybe. Different person. Two Gabriel Santornos in Denver wouldn't be that rare, I guess."

She held up a piece of paper. "Same Social

Security number. Apparently, our Gabe Santorno had to wait to be sworn in at the army recruiting station in Denver until they got the number. For some reason it took him three days to find his birth certificate and Social Security card."

"How'd you find that out?"

Madison pointed to the corner of a printout of the original enlistment application. *Waiting on ss number or birth certificate* was scribbled beside where the date had been changed from March 3 to March 6.

"Everything on his application was the same as the dead Gabriel Santorno. No middle name. Same birthday, Social Security number and birthplace. So, who is buried in Fairmount? Or maybe a better question is, who is in Crossroads? Recruiters don't usually check names on death records since a live body is standing right in front of them."

"Do you have his army records? If he got in and served, there will be records."

"Yes. Active duty for twelve years. A ranger. Deployed three tours of duty overseas. Qualified as an expert in a dozen different fields, both combat and interrogation. The guy's got more medals than he could probably wear on his chest. Three Purple Hearts and several stars. He must have seen action many times."

"Bullet holes to the chest," Fifth whispered.

"Why'd you say that?" she asked.

"I saw the scars." Fifth's instincts were right. The professor was far more than he seemed.

"So you already guessed we weren't dealing with a sweet little tea-sipping professor from the University of Texas." She pulled one sheet of paper. "He even had a pilot's license, but looks like he never renewed it after the army. In fact, when he walked away from Uncle Sam, he fell off the earth for a while, and even within the past ten years he's been spotted about as often as the Sasquatch."

"What are you saying?" Fifth could tell she wasn't finished.

"The man's got more than one ID. To disappear off any records like he does, he may have a dozen."

"So why'd he use this old one here in Crossroads? He couldn't have been much over eighteen when he picked up Santorno's name off a grave."

Madison shrugged. "Maybe he's going back to the beginning here."

Fifth shook his head. "No, he's new to Crossroads. The sisters would have remembered him if he'd been here before."

Fifth thumbed through the information. "The guy's permanent address is a post-office box in Denver. He didn't appear to own a car. He'd been arrested under this name twice in the past ten years and charges were dismissed both times due to lack of evidence.

"Other than that, he's more of a ghost than a man. No credit cards. No bank account I could find. Hasn't applied for army or government assistance. Hasn't checked in at the VA. It's like after the army he lived underground. Never bought a house or owned a business or applied for a marriage license. At least not under this name."

She leaned her chin on Fifth's shoulder. "Doesn't it strike you as odd that a guy who was a warrior for a dozen years doesn't even own a gun?"

"A registered one, anyway." Fifth added, "The sheriff told me once that men who pass too close to death never go out unarmed. I'm betting our professor has more than one weapon on him right now as he's taking his walk."

Madison leaned back. "Any more questions?"

"Yeah," Fifth said. "What in the hell is he doing in my town?"

Chapter TWENTY-FOUR

Hunter green shadows

Parker walked out her door at sunset. She still wore Clint's shirt, but she'd changed into jeans.

All day she'd thought of his proposition. If a man in Dallas had said such a thing in a bar, she'd think it was just a line. But her cowboy hadn't been flirting with her. He hadn't spent time flattering her or trying to talk her into anything. He'd just made her an offer, then rode off, as if knowing she'd need time to think about it.

One night. No promises. No forever.

Exactly what she needed. One night to remember when she was in the hospital. One memory of being loved by a stranger as if she meant something special to someone.

In the twilight, she could see his pickup parked at the end of her lane. Waiting.

Maybe she should walk down there and tell him she'd changed her mind. Wild affairs, or whatever this was, were not her style. She tended to have short relationships, where she spent six months trying to make it work, trying to make it right, and then another three months trying to figure out how to end it without shattering pride or furniture.

She began strolling toward the road, thinking about what she'd say. It would be easy; after all, they weren't in a relationship. They hadn't even begun one. They'd kissed. That was all.

He probably didn't care one way or the other. Who knows—maybe he regretted making the offer in the first place. Maybe he realized that since they couldn't even seem to carry on a conversation, they weren't likely to spend all night together.

Unless they slept. Why would they do that? Both had beds they could sleep in alone. Both were obviously used to sleeping alone.

Maybe she'd go down the lane and have a talk . . . maybe a few kisses, and see where it went from there. Whenever she got tired, she'd have him bring her home.

She was *not* spending the night.

Probably not having sex.

Definitely *not* having sex.

He climbed out of the truck as she neared, adjusted his hat low against the dying sun and just watched her.

The man looked near perfect in his boots and jeans.

Parker lifted her chin. She would thank him for the offer. It was flattering even if all he seemed to be offering was a one-night stand.

Yes. She would be polite but firm, then say good-night, she reasoned.

Well, maybe one kiss. Or two. The cowboy did know how to kiss.

Parker frowned. Her thoughts were like a game of Ping-Pong. Her sex life apparently had become bipolar.

She was five feet away when she saw him smile. He was even more handsome when he smiled. Who was she kidding? Clint Montgomery would be handsome sound asleep.

"Good evening," she said formally.

"Evening, Parker." He held his hand out as if inviting her to join him.

"I thought I'd come . . ." She put her fingers in

his and forgot what else she'd been about to say.

He tugged her toward him until she stood an inch away. Then, without a word, he lowered his head and kissed her.

One kiss, as soft as a midnight breeze. A beginning. A hello kiss.

When she melted against him, he turned her gently and pressed her back against the truck door. His body felt so good as he leaned into her and began lightly kissing her throat as if he thought his lips belonged there.

She knew she needed to set a few rules. She needed to take control of the evening. He needed to understand.

She'd interrupt him in a minute or two. They'd talk then. After he finished silently saying hello.

He finally pulled away and looked down at her. "How about we don't talk more than necessary? No promises. No lies. You say stop and I bring you back right here."

She nodded. That seemed like enough rules. End of a debate that hadn't started.

He took his time kissing her the second time, letting her know that he wasn't going to hurry. Then he straightened and helped her into the truck.

He drove with his hand on her leg. He wasn't holding her, just lightly touching her as if she might need calming.

Maybe she did need calming. Every cell in her

body was jumpy, and she swore her blood was running double time through her veins.

When he passed the entrance to his place, she opened her mouth to question. Then she remembered the rules.

A few minutes later, he turned off on a dirt road. When he stopped to open a gate, she thought of sliding beneath the wheel and driving away.

What was she doing out here with a man she barely knew? With her luck, this was where he buried the bodies. This way, he didn't have to drag her out to Nowhere, Texas, to kill her. She was coming along silently, of her own volition, with Prospective Victim written on her forehead. If this were documented on one of those crime shows, it wouldn't last long enough to be interrupted by a commercial.

When he climbed back in the cab, he shifted into first gear and put his hand back on her leg like it belonged there.

He got out again to close the gate, and her last chance to escape was gone.

"You all right?" he asked when he slid back in.

"Yes," she lied.

"There's something you got to see." He drove down a road that was no more than two worn lines in the grass. The world grew darker and darker until the two beams from the headlights were all the visible light.

In the silent dimness of the pickup cab, he took

her hand and laced it in his. Then his thumb began to move slowly over her palm.

That touch again, she thought. That tender touch.

After five minutes, they pulled onto a ledge above a canyon so dark it looked like a black river twisting through the land.

He cut the engine and climbed out, tugging her along with him.

"Watch your step," he said as he pulled her closer to the edge.

"I can't see anything."

"Just hang on to me." He stepped behind her and circled his arms around her, pulling her against his chest as he leaned his back on the front fender. "You'll be safe right here, Parker. Don't worry."

She settled into his warmth and closed her eyes, listening to an owl calling from down into the canyon. His cry echoed off the walls in an eerie kind of sound.

"Do you see it?" His words brushed her ear.

Parker opened her eyes and saw a huge moon rising along the opposite side of the canyon. In the silence, she watched as it climbed, casting light down the canyon in shades of pale blue and black silver.

"It's beautiful," she whispered.

As the moon rose, she couldn't stop smiling. No artist could ever paint it so lovely.

When it hung above them, she turned in his arms. "Thank you," she whispered.

"You're welcome."

She closed the distance between them and kissed him.

For a moment, he didn't seem to know what to do. He just let her kiss him. When she tugged at his bottom lip with her teeth, he woke up.

He kissed her back with a hunger that delighted her. She'd never felt like she was someone's passion before, someone's irresistible desire. There was something wild in the way he kissed her, like she was a need he had deep inside and not simply a want.

In one movement, he swung her around and propped her on the fender of his truck, resting his face on her chest. She could feel his breathing against her throat and she brushed her hands over his hair.

"What is it?" she whispered.

"I can hear your heart pounding," he said as he tugged her collar open and kissed his way back to her mouth. "I'm having trouble believing you're real. If you're not, don't wake me."

Parker had never wrapped both her arms and legs around a man, but she did it now. She wanted to hug him, to hold him close.

He ran his hands over her legs as he deepened the kiss to fire.

For a long while, they stood in the silent night and got to know one another without words. His touch had branded every part of her body, and she'd done the same to him. For a woman who never lost control, she was in deep water now and loving the way it felt to let go.

They were both still fully clothed yet she felt she knew his body better than she'd ever known any lover. He liked his kisses deep and tender. His hands were strong, almost rough, almost demanding one moment and hesitant the next. He let her settle against his chest and relax as he gently kissed his way across her face. Then his need began to build and his kiss turned hard and insistent as his hands molded over her.

She took it all. The tender and the passion. This quiet man did something no one had ever done. He made her feel totally alive.

Finally, when the wind kicked up, he lifted her into his pickup. Without a word, he drove her back to where her lane began.

When she would have asked why he stopped, he turned toward her and cupped her face. The quick kiss was hard. Laced with need. She had no doubt that he wanted her, but he'd stopped. He'd brought her back from passion's edge.

"Why?" she finally whispered.

He pulled away and stared out into the night. "Because you're not sure and if we went any further I'm not sure I could stop. When you come running to me, Parker. When I know for sure what you want, then there will be no stopping."

She slid across to the passenger door and

jumped out. She didn't know whether to be angry, flattered or just plain confused. They weren't kids. They weren't even young.

Twenty feet down the path she heard him say, "I'll pick you up same time tomorrow."

"Don't play games. Don't lie. No promises. Remember? Don't wait too long because I just might not be coming. I haven't got much lifetime left to be hanging out with a cowboy who hesitates. I knew I should have been the one to set the rules. Not exactly what I thought would . . ."

His truck was already heading back up the road and she hadn't finished her rant. He probably hadn't stayed long enough to hear a word.

At least he'd followed one rule. No talking.

"I won't be waiting!" she yelled.

The moon winked at her as it passed between branches of the old tree near the curve in the path.

"Oh, shut up!" She pointed at the man in the moon. "Why don't you go over to the dark side?"

Then for no reason at all, she laughed aloud at her own joke.

Chapter TWENTY-FIVE

Gabe walked over to the gypsy house, moving silently in the shadows out of habit. Neither Yancy nor Tori were there. He knew it was early, but he was too restless to hang around the bed-and-breakfast and pretend to be studying. He'd played so many roles in his lifetime, pretending to fit in, that he'd become an expert in many areas.

Early on, when he'd been in the army, Gabe had studied the history of war. He'd even picked up a degree in history from a little college in South Carolina. Then, for a few years when he was wandering across the South, he'd studied the Civil War. In his thirties, he'd worked undercover for Homeland Security a few years in the arms trade and had learned all about weapons trading. He'd been paid well, but the government kept his work secret for his safety.

When he'd started working for the agency, he'd learned to fit in wherever he traveled. A Southern gentleman who raced horses, a stockbroker in LA, a landman in the Oklahoma oil fields. And each place he went, each person he tracked, he studied. Sometimes he knew the man he hunted well enough to have taken his place.

He was a wealth of useless information, but the constant learning kept his mind off living. Maybe that was why he liked disguising himself as a professor. People didn't consider professors threatening, and he knew enough to hold his own in conversations.

Crossroads, his hometown, had been interesting to step into as an outsider. He'd learned things most of the locals probably didn't know. Only he was careful not to ask about the gypsy house, or

Yancy Grey, too often. He had to be prudent with his questions. Keep his glasses on. Play his part completely.

If anyone who knew Yancy looked straight into Gabe's eyes, they might figure out his secret.

So tonight, after circling Yancy's house, he turned toward town. He'd heard the Franklin sisters say there was a big meeting at the county offices on Main. Talk was, the ranches around here were selling small hunks of pastureland to allow for wind turbines. Most folks were for it, but a few thought it might cause problems. There were already turbines whirling like giant pinwheels, but soon there might be whole fields of them.

Gabe decided to walk over and listen to what was happening. He wasn't really that interested in the meeting, but he wanted to check out the county offices. Weathers had said the sheriff's office was in the building. It had been a long time ago, but Gabe had once broken into a sheriff's precinct to remove evidence. He'd known it was a crime, but the evidence belonged to him.

As he stood in the back of the courtroom, surrounded by people, some he used to know when he was a kid, Gabe tried to imagine what it would have been like if he hadn't left. Would he have really tried to go to college and make something of himself? Or would he have turned out to be just one of the part-time oil-field workers like his old man, who worked only when money was low?

He'd never know. Life didn't offer reruns. Only even after all these years he could still remember Jewel Ann's face. They'd grown up not speaking to each other since their families had bad blood between them.

He'd watched her at school, loved the way her black curly hair flowed around her shoulders. He'd even caught her watching him a few times. He'd been a junior and Jewel Ann a sophomore when he'd offered her a ride home one night.

They'd talked. He swore he loved her before they made it home. After that, falling in love was a game they played having no idea what the consequences might be.

Gabe pushed the past from his thoughts. He couldn't bear to think of Jewel Ann the way he'd last seen her, knowing that what happened had all been his fault. The script of life couldn't be rewritten, but maybe he could make sure their son had his chance.

Gabe watched as Rose Franklin presented the Main Street Business Association's views on the new project. Before he'd checked in at their B and B, he hadn't thought of the Franklins in years. When he'd been a kid he used to help out on their family's dairy farm. Both girls had been a few years older than Gabe, but they'd been real nice to him.

He'd pushed every memory of this town so far back in his mind he'd forgotten that it all wasn't bad. Riding along with the Franklin sisters delivering milk had been fun.

When the meeting was over, Gabe caught Daisy alone for a minute and apologized for the tenth time. "It was inexcusable," he said. "A fine lady like you should have never been shocked like that."

Daisy smiled. "Now, don't you worry over it, Professor. The shock probably did my heart good, and to tell the truth, all I really saw clearly was your hair dripping the second you looked up and saw me. After that, you moved so fast it was simply a blur in the shadows of the room."

"I'm sorry, just the same," he whispered.

"You need not worry about it, Professor," she said again. "And I should tell you that you do look younger without your glasses, but I know you must wear them."

"I must. Any light bothers me. The only time I can go without them is when I'm walking in the dark."

She seemed to have got over seeing him nude and was now enjoying the attention of his constant apologizing. "I won't say more about what happened last night, dear lady, if you would allow me to buy you and your sister a slice of pie at Dorothy's Café."

Daisy shook her head, but Rose rushed over. "Of course, Professor. Only my sister hates the

197

cold draft in the café these cool nights. Every time we go in to eat the door is constantly opening and closing."

Gabe didn't mention doors opening and closing were probably a problem at every café.

Rose was on a mission and didn't have time for him to talk. "Would you mind if we bought the dessert and took it home? Dorothy does make a chess pie that we can't match. Also, we both prefer our own brewed coffee to the café. Cleaner cups, you know. Dorothy says she washes every cup but I swear I can still see stains."

After they'd picked up the pie and returned home, they sat at the little kitchen table and ate, the sisters doing most of the talking and Gabe thinking that they hadn't changed a bit over the years. He gently guided the conversation around to the families he remembered. Daisy's recollection was stronger and, he guessed, more accurate. Rose tended to fill in with creative license now and then when her memory failed her.

About ten o'clock the front door opened. All three sat silently as what sounded like two people tried to tiptoe up the front stairs. One laugh was definitely female.

"Who do you think that was?" Rose whispered.

Daisy lifted her nose. "Obviously Deputy Weathers. He's the only one besides the professor who has a key to our front door."

"But who was with him?"

"A very tall redhead," Gabe volunteered. "I saw them in the café."

"That'd be Madison O'Grady. I heard she was seeing our Fifth. They had kind of a date last week."

"Oh, that will never work." Rose shook her head. "She works for the government. I think she's in the air force or maybe I heard someone mention that she was an independent contractor now for them. Whatever that is. She lives all the way over in Wichita Falls."

A thud sounded from above and then another laugh.

All three looked up. Rose spoke first. "What do you think they're doing up there this time of night?"

"Well, I'm not going up to take a look. He's a deputy sheriff and she was a lieutenant, so that makes her a veteran. Both probably not only carry guns, but know how to use them." Daisy straightened as if about to say the Pledge of Allegiance. "I'm sure whatever they are doing is highly classified government business."

Gabe nearly choked on his last bite of pie. "I say we leave them to their work."

The sisters nodded. Daisy stood and refilled all three cups, and they went back to talking about everyone in town except the two giants upstairs.

Later, when Gabe passed the deputy's closed door, he realized his jaw hurt from fighting not to smile all evening.

Chapter TWENTY-SIX

Compassion

Tori hadn't been out of the house for two days. The supplies had shown up on their porch two days after she'd got the warning ticket. So instead of worrying about having left her first trail, she spent the entire time painting.

The work was all-consuming, as usual. Several times, if Parker hadn't brought up food, Tori would have forgotten to eat. Most people wouldn't have understood, but Parker did. Sometimes the work came in wave after wave, and Tori got lost in the current. She'd paint until she was so tired she'd fall asleep with a brush in her hand and then wake with ideas flooding her brain.

Even if she'd wanted to walk over and see Yancy, the rains kept her inside just as they seemed to keep Parker from walking to the end of her lane.

On the third night, the sky was still cloudy, but Tori decided Yancy would be worried if she didn't show up for at least a while.

She hadn't realized how much she'd missed him until she circled by his house and found both it and the barn dark. She tried to think of reasons he hadn't come. He said he never missed a town meeting, and he'd mentioned there was going to be one soon. Maybe he was at the meeting. He'd told her that he worried about the old folks he worked with. Maybe one of them was sick or in the hospital. If so, Yancy would be with them. He cared about every one of the residents of the Evening Shadows Retirement Community as if they were family.

She'd told him no details of how to find her, so he had no way of telling her what might be keeping him away. Maybe he'd come the past two nights and had worried where she was. He might have even worried that she'd disappear as suddenly as she'd appeared.

Closing her eyes, she tried to remember the feel of his arms around her. He never held on too tightly. He made her feel treasured; only sometimes, she thought he might think of himself as temporary, as if one day someone else might take his place.

She was midway through her twenties; she should have experienced so much more of life, but with Yancy, she knew that what she had was real. He wasn't just someone to hang around with until someone better came along. He mattered more to her every day and it was time she let him know.

On impulse, Tori pulled down a tiny sample jar of paint from a shelf in his barn and printed

Missed you. T on a rough piece of wood. That way he'd know that she'd tried to contact him.

She propped the note on his toolbox.

After looking at it, Tori tossed the board aside and started over on another. *Missed you. Love, Rabbit.*

When she saw Yancy again, she'd tell him who she was. He'd listen. He'd care. And probably he'd have no idea who Victoria Vilanie was to the art world anyway. All he cared about was a girl he called Rabbit.

The memory of him offering her all his money, of him saying he was rich, made her smile. He was richer right here in this little town with this old house than she'd ever be.

Taking one last glance at the note, she clicked off the workroom light and opened the door. As she stepped out into the night, she noticed that the rain had started falling again. Moisture whipped in the wind, so hard it seemed to be raining sideways. Tori pulled Yancy's coat close around her, wishing she were brave enough to walk into town and find him.

A shadowy figure moved slowly along the road about twenty yards away. The man carried a flashlight with a single beam lighting his way. His thin form blinked in and out between the tree branches. For a moment, she thought it might be Yancy. Same height, almost the same build.

Only Yancy didn't wear a hat and this man's

steps were slower, more cautious. Something about him looked familiar, like maybe she'd seen him out walking before. A night walker, like her. She'd noticed a few over the weeks, but they kept to themselves as she did.

Tori remained still, waiting for him to pass. If he'd seen the workshop light, he might be aware of her, but once she turned it off and stepped outside, she doubted he could see even her outline.

The stranger suddenly stepped sideways, as if avoiding something in the road, and tumbled down into the ditch that had been dug five feet into the ground between the road and Yancy's property.

Tori moved closer, staying well into the shadow of the house so the stranger wouldn't see her.

She watched as he tried—once, twice, three times—to get up in the shallow stream that ran along the ditch whenever it rained.

Something was wrong with his leg. It wouldn't seem to take his weight.

Tori watched him, feeling sorry for the man, but knowing she shouldn't get involved. He'd be fine, she told herself. He'd get his footing and move on. Parker had preached the importance of no one knowing she was here and Tori had said Yancy would be the only breach in their plan.

But the man didn't stand on his next try. He tumbled. She heard him hit hard against the side of the road and splash backward into the ditch.

A low cry whirled in the night. Like a wounded animal. Like a man in pain.

Tori moved closer until she could see his dark form half in the water and half in mud.

The stranger had curled into a ball, as if giving up.

Tori cried out, almost feeling his pain, not from the fall, but from the helplessness of his situation. The sides of the ditch had to be slippery, and if his leg were hurt, he might have little chance of climbing out.

She had to help.

"You all right, mister?" she shouted over the rain. "Do you need some help?"

He didn't answer.

She moved closer. Maybe he'd passed out? He wouldn't freeze out here in the mud, but if he was seriously hurt, he could bleed to death. If he died and she hadn't helped, she'd never forgive herself. If he died in front of Yancy's house, the people in town really would think the old house was haunted.

Five feet from the ditch, Tori stepped on the flashlight he must have dropped in the fall. She reached down and clicked it on as she pointed the light toward the man. The first thing she saw was his hat sitting by the road, as if it had been placed there just before he tumbled.

It wasn't easy getting a good look at the stranger; he was covered in mud. "Mister! Are you all right?"

He looked up into the light and all she saw was blood.

Tori moved closer, splashing her way through the water as she crossed the ditch. "You're hurt!"

The man rubbed his head, smearing blood. "I seem to be. I tried to stand, but I think I've twisted my ankle. The third time I fell over I must have hit my head." His voice was calm, almost as if he were logging the accident for a report.

Tori brushed her hand over his dark, wet hair. She felt the cool rain and the warmth of blood at his temple. He was wet and cold and appeared a bit lost.

"Come on. Lean on me. I'll get you inside."

The man put his arm around her shoulders and let her lead him to Yancy's house. He was dressed nicely—a dress shirt, a vest and a very muddy jacket—but blood kept dripping from his hairline and he kept apologizing, as if he were inconveniencing her.

Every other step she felt his weight and they both almost tumbled a few times before reaching the side door of the house.

Once she got him into Yancy's kitchen and cleaned off the wound with cold water and a clean rag, she saw that the head injury wasn't serious.

"It's not deep," she said with a relieved breath.

"Head wounds do tend to bleed. I'm sure I'll be fine," he replied. "I'm so sorry to worry you, miss. I'm afraid I simply took too long a walk tonight and the rain caught up with me. I'm so glad you were near. All I could think to do was curl up and wait out the storm."

"You could have drowned if you'd passed out in the ditch." Tori fought down a smile. She was sounding like this man's mother, and he was easily twice her age. The dear man looked even more helpless than she often thought she was. He didn't have an umbrella with him.

Tori cleaned him up and pressed on the wound until the bleeding stopped while he told her what seemed like his whole life story.

He was a professor at the University of Texas down in Austin. A widower, living alone for the past ten years. He was researching families in the area and asked if she'd lived in Crossroads long.

Tori distracted him by handing him his hat. He seemed so pleased it wasn't ruined that he forgot that he'd asked her a question.

"I'm staying at the Franklin Bed-and-Breakfast. Lovely place. You know the Franklin sisters, I'm sure."

"No. I'm afraid not." She almost added that Yancy was the only person in Crossroads whom she did know, but that would be too much information.

He laughed a silly kind of laugh. "I thought everyone around these parts knew the sisters. They run the only bed-and-breakfast in town a few blocks from here. When you meet them they'll ask all kinds of questions, and before you know it, they will have figured out how they are related to you."

"Oh," Tori said and changed the subject, asking him about his ankle.

The professor twisted to look at his foot and said he didn't think it was broken, but she could see that he was in pain. "I've been getting a little wobbly lately. Messed my knee and ankle up years ago, and sometimes it still seems they want to mutiny against the rest of my body."

"Maybe you should walk in daylight. If I hadn't been here no one would have seen you from the road this time of night."

"Good advice, but I like the night. It's as though I've got the world to myself. I can think. Plan my lectures."

"I know how you feel." She wrapped a rag around his ankle, hoping it might help keep the guy steady.

"You must be a friend of Yancy Grey's if you knew the key would be next to the door," he said. "I met him the other day. He was working in the shop, but didn't invite me into his house. My, my, he's done a great job with this place."

"Yes. He's a dear friend," she answered, figuring that was a safe thing to say. "Everyone knows the key's beside the door, he claims. He says he only keeps the door locked because he likes unlocking it."

"Even though I now think Mr. Grey may be a little nuts, he's a nice man."

"Yes, he is."

The professor nodded once. "Well, any friend of Yancy's is a friend of mine. I wish to thank you from the bottom of my heart for saving me."

"You're welcome. I don't have a car, but I'll walk you home when the rain stops."

"Thank you, dear. I feel like such a fool. I've read that being too sedentary isn't good for men my age, but exercise will probably kill me."

She noticed the professor was more interested in talking than listening. He didn't seem aware that she'd never introduced herself. If she could keep him talking, she'd leave him at the bed-and-breakfast knowing nothing about her except that she was a friend of Yancy's.

With the rain only a drizzle, she held on to the professor as they walked in the center of the road.

"What startled you earlier?" she asked when he paused.

He went into detail about how it must have been a snake or maybe only a twisted branch that looked like a snake. He was tumbling off the road before he got a second look.

"How long do you plan to stay?" Tori had the second question ready.

The professor gave her a detailed account of all his plans. She wouldn't have been surprised if he had the class outline in his vest pocket.

"Have you always loved Texas history?"

And on and on. She asked question after question until they were at the door of the bed-and-breakfast.

He was in the middle of inviting her in when the sisters opened the door and took over being Florence Nightingale the moment they saw the cotton strip around his head.

Tori vanished in the confusion. A block away, she smiled, realizing that she'd helped someone tonight. It felt good.

As she passed the Evening Shadows Retirement Community, she saw Yancy in a long office window with scattered chairs circled around him.

He was sweeping the floor of a front room, moving chairs into place as he worked. An ordinary task. Probably part of his job every night.

Tori neared the window and watched him. He was smiling to himself, almost dancing with the broom.

Tori placed her hand on the glass as though she could reach out and touch him. It was late. He'd obviously had a long day, but she couldn't turn away.

The second he noticed her, he was running out the side door and pulling her to him as if he hadn't seen her in months.

Without a word, he lifted her up and took her inside.

Tori laughed. "I'm not a toy you left in the rain, Yancy. I can walk."

"You're wet and covered in mud." He tugged his old coat off her and saw the blood on her shirt. "You're bleeding, Rabbit. What happened? Should I take you to a hospital? Were you in a wreck? I feared something had happened to you when you didn't show up last night."

"No. I'm fine. I just helped a man who fell down in that muddy ditch in front of your house. He was the one bleeding, but not hurt badly."

Yancy looked toward the flowerbed she'd been standing in. "Where is he?"

Tori looked into his eyes, trying to calm him. "I walked him to the bed-and-breakfast. He's fine." She cupped his face in her hands. "Are you aware that one of your eyes is more brown than blue and the other is slightly more blue than brown?"

Yancy calmed. "Of course I'm aware of that, Rabbit. I look at myself every morning."

He pulled her hands from his face and leaned back, relaxing, but he didn't turn her hands loose for a long moment.

"It must have been the professor, then. I've seen him pass here a few times." He tried brushing off some of the mud on her jeans. "You're wet and muddy and bloody. How about jumping in a hot shower? I'll toss your clothes in the washer."

"Sounds like a good idea. I've been so wet and cold I feel like my blood has icicles."

Five minutes later she was standing in a hot shower in a tiny bathroom. The water felt so good, but being near Yancy felt even better. As steam filled the room, she could smell him. The soap he used, the aftershave, even the clean smell of his shampoo.

When she finally stepped out from under the water, she dried off, wrapped her hair in a towel and slipped into a robe he said that one of the retired teachers had given him last Christmas. It would have circled her twice, and it went all the way to the floor, but she didn't care. It was warm.

As she moved into Yancy's bedroom apartment in back of the office and sunroom, she saw him heating up a can of soup on a hot plate.

He pulled the one chair out from his tiny desk and offered her the seat.

She leaned over and toweled off her long hair. When she raised her head, he was standing before her, offering her a comb. "The soup will be ready in a few minutes. Need anything else?"

"No. I'm fine."

When he handed her a hot mug, she had just tied her hair back in a loose braid. The room was cool, almost drafty, on this windy night, and each wall was painted a different color. The book-shelves along one wall were all different hues and none of the furniture matched. It occurred to her that he might be color-blind.

"I like your choice of color." She could not bring herself to ask the question.

"Thanks. I like it, but I didn't exactly choose the

colors. They were just left over from whatever I painted around here in the cottages. Now the residents just look at my place and say 'Paint my kitchen the color of your third shelf' or 'I'd like that color of green for my porch.' "

Tori laughed. "I can see how this room could help."

"Oh, it does. I brought home ten samples before I found the right yellow for Miss Bees's sunroom. I used up the samples behind the door. Some mornings I open my eyes and see the strips and I imagine the sun is coming up behind my door."

He sat cross-legged on the bed, mug in hand, and ate his soup while she studied the walls.

"I'm glad you came by," he finally said. "The teachers had a party tonight. It was over by nine, but I'd already decided you probably wouldn't be at the house on a night like this."

"What were they celebrating?"

He shrugged. "I don't know. I'm not on that committee. I just set the place up before and clean up afterward." He stood. "Oh, I almost forgot the best part of party nights. I get to eat the leftover desserts."

He disappeared and brought back a tray of cookies and two Cokes.

She moved to the other side of his bed and picked out her favorites. "I love cookies, but I hate ice cream. It makes my head hurt."

"Maybe you should eat it slowly."

She giggled. "Then it freezes my mouth." She picked two more cookies. "But I love every kind of cookie ever made." She took a nibble.

"You can have them all, Rabbit."

She shook her head. "I'm afraid of too much happiness at one time."

"Me, too." Yancy grinned. "Like now."

Nodding, she understood.

"Your clothes are almost ready for the dryer. Want to watch *Golden Girls* while we have dessert?"

"Sure." Tilting her head, she wondered why he'd pick that show.

As he had before, Yancy seemed to read her mind. "I love that show. Maybe it's living here, but I identify with it."

She laughed and cuddled against him. "You're an adorable man."

An hour later she felt him kiss her cheek, and she realized she'd been sleeping.

"Stay with me tonight, Tori. We don't have to do anything. Just stay with me."

"Do you have covers?"

He laughed softly against her ear. "You're lying on them."

"Good. Then I'll stay."

"What about Parker?" he asked. "Won't she worry about you?"

"Nope. She's out with the neighbor."

"Oh." Yancy lifted her gently and tugged the

covers from under her. Then, without hesitation, he climbed in beside her. "Do you snore, Rabbit?"

"I don't know. I've never slept with anyone."

He was so still she felt more awake. "Is something wrong?"

He kissed her forehead. "No. Nothing is wrong. Nothing at all."

She was almost back to sleep when he added, "We're only going to sleep. Just sleep."

"That's pretty much what I'm trying to do, Yancy."

"We're just going to sleep," he repeated.

"You already told me that."

"Tori," he whispered, not sounding the least bit sleepy. "When you say that you've never slept with anyone, does that mean you've never had sex or that you've never slept with someone? Because either way is fine with me. I'm just asking."

Tori was too tired to answer. She was just going to have to let him stay awake and worry about it.

Chapter TWENTY-SEVEN

Dusty-cobalt blue

Parker sat on the porch of her little house and watched the rain come and go in waves of twilight. She'd seen Tori walk out over an hour ago. She should have been back by now.

Smiling, Parker realized she sounded like a dorm mother. Tori was younger than her by over ten years. Maybe there was a mothering instinct in her. Maybe that was what had drawn her to the little artist that night in LAX.

They'd met at the art show. Talked enough for Parker to know Victoria Vilanie went by Tori. Then when she'd seen Tori crying in the airport all alone, she hadn't been able to turn her back.

But she'd do it again. She'd help Tori. At first it had given her something to think about other than the cancer growing inside her. She hadn't needed a doctor to tell her; she knew. The sickness that killed both her parents before they were forty was now growing in her. No one might be looking for her, but Parker knew that she'd run away from her world, too. Tori might want to live in the real world for a while; Parker just wanted to step away from it.

Eventually, she'd have to go back and have that talk with Dr. Brown. She'd have to allow him to put into words what he'd tried to say. She knew the drill. He'd give her all the right drugs, maybe tell her about tests going on and studies, but in the end she'd die, just as both her parents did. Laceys didn't live long. Everyone knew it, and the family plot and dates on the headstones proved it.

Parker rubbed her knee. The pain had been less since she'd been here. Maybe because she wasn't spending hours on marble floors. Her back didn't hurt at all. Was it possible to be in remission even before you were formally diagnosed?

A blue pickup pulled onto her lane. Parker didn't move. She knew who it was. Clint. He surprised her when he didn't stop at the entrance, but drove straight toward the house.

For a moment, she panicked, then remembered that Tori wasn't home. Not that it really mattered, because Clint had said he knew someone was staying at Parker's place.

Parker waited for him. After they'd parted a few nights ago, she guessed he wasn't coming to pick her up and drive her out to see the sunset. The man was impossible to read.

He parked in front of the stone walk she hadn't even remembered being there when she'd bought the house. He must have known it well, because he didn't look down as he headed right toward her, boots clicking in rapid succession on the slate.

"Evening, Parker," he said, removing his hat as he stepped under the roofline and out of the rain.

"Evening, Clint." Parker almost laughed. They sounded like two old farmers who'd been neighbors for years.

He just stood there, looking at her.

She had on her white silk pajamas with beautiful African lilies painted across the material in splashes of primary colors, and, of course, she wore the socks he'd dropped at her door the first morning she'd arrived. She'd washed her short hair and hadn't bothered to straighten the natural curls that always tried to ruin her fashionable bob.

"You want something, Mr. Montgomery, or did you just drop by to stare?"

He twirled his hat. "I came by to say I saw your houseguest in town. I thought you might be worried about her. It being dark and rainy and all."

"She's an adult. I'm not her mother. I'm surprised she is in town and, more important, that you feel the need to keep up with her."

He grumbled like a bear being poked. "I wasn't keeping up with her. I was having dinner at Dorothy's Café. I saw her standing in front of the glass wall at the retirement office across the street from the café. Yancy rushed out and picked her up. She looked like a mud man wearing yellow rain boots and a coat double her size."

There was no doubt. He'd seen Tori all right.

Parker was grateful he'd dropped by to tell her. Without a car she couldn't very well go look for Tori, and she *had* been starting to worry.

"So, you think she's all right?" she asked.

"She's with Yancy. She's fine. I'm guessing he'll bring her home if the rain keeps up."

"Fine." Parker needed to at least be nice, she decided; after all, the cowboy had stopped by to tell her. "I made brownies. You want to come in and have one?"

He stared at her as if he thought it might be a trap, then shifted as if preparing to bolt. Slowly, he finally said, "Sure."

He followed her inside. While she cut the brownies, Clint looked at the paintings on one wall of the living room.

"They really make the room come alive," she said, having no idea if the man was listening. "I'm building simple frames for them, but I wanted to hang them and see how they fit together first."

She poured two milks without asking if that was what he wanted to drink. "I called Maggie, the housekeeper, and asked her to pick up a few things in town for me. Since I don't have a car, I thought it would be easier to just call in groceries and have her deliver them when she collected the mail."

No answer. If Clint was listening, he was showing no sign.

"You're probably wondering what all those boxes are stacked up by the back door. Online shopping. I had them shipped to the post office and Maggie picked them up. We now have outfits and not just a few pieces we packed with us when we ran."

Finally he turned around. "You running from something or someone, Parker, or to something?"

"Both, I guess. From something I don't want to face and to a friend who needs me."

"Oh." He gave the painting his full attention

once more. She'd thought he'd ask why she didn't bring a suitcase before, but after a few minutes he added, "Why didn't you ship the boxes to me? I would have brought them over."

"Didn't think of it," she lied.

He walked over to where she stood in the kitchen. The room was little more than a corner of the bigger area and it seemed to shrink with him taking up half the space. Tall and lean, he was a man no woman would walk past without noticing. Right now, he was standing there waiting for the truth.

"I didn't want to bother you." She lowered her voice. After all, he was only about six inches away. "I didn't think Maggie would mind and she said she didn't."

He ignored the fork she'd set by the plate and picked up the brownie. He took a bite and studied her while he ate. He leaned against the counter, almost close enough to touch her, and said, "You bother me anyway, Parker, whether you're asking favors or not. Tell me, is what you got on an *outfit* or part of the pieces you packed in a handbag so you could run?"

"This is pajamas." He was staring at her pjs as if they were a housepainter's worn overalls. "I ordered them from Neiman's."

He took another bite of brownie and looked her up and down slowly. "I think those would keep me awake if I slept in pajamas."

"What do you sleep in, then?" The question was out before she thought.

"Nothing," he answered and finished off his brownie.

She sat down, picked up her fork and cut a piece off her brownie, but she suddenly wasn't hungry. How could such a simple conversation make her feel so nervous inside?

"Well, I got to be going. I've got work to do tonight."

She followed him back to the porch. He turned on the first step and looked back at her as he put on his hat.

"Night, Parker," he said.

"Wait." She came closer, her arms crossed over her chest. "Do you think we could talk sometime? You know, really talk. Like regular people."

"What do regular people talk about?" For once, he seemed interested in hearing what her answer might be.

"I don't know. Their day. Their work. What they like? How they spend their time? What they want to do?" It crossed her mind that she'd had very few normal conversations in her life. Maybe that might explain why lovers never stayed long.

Maybe she was the problem here, not Clint. That was a novel idea. She'd always thought the other half of every relationship she'd been in to be the weaker link.

His fingers were in his pockets as if he was

willing himself not to make the first move. "I don't really want to talk, Parker, but I wouldn't mind kissing you good-night if you've no objection."

"All right." Maybe that was a start. Talking didn't seem to be their strong suit.

He leaned over and brushed his lips over hers. He wasn't touching her anywhere else. He'd said a good-night kiss and he was holding to what he'd requested. He tasted of chocolate and she leaned closer, brushing silk against his starched cotton shirt.

Then something seemed to shatter in him, and his arms circled around her as if he was holding on to life in a storm. The kiss was pure need, so great it consumed her. He didn't have to say a word. She knew he was starving for her, and for once in her life, she didn't hold back. She let all the hunger built up in her go. She needed to be held. She had to know that somewhere, even for one moment, someone could need her more than air.

The kiss was deep and complete as his hands slid over the silk of her body, exploring, feeling and making her feel very much alive. Then his arms tightened, hugging her again, lifting her against him. How was it possible that this cold man could make up for all the warmth she never had in her life?

His mouth left her lips and he tasted his way down to her throat. When he returned to kiss her deeply, his big hand moved into her hair, tangling his fingers in her curls. A gentle tug tilted her head so he could kiss her just the way he wanted to. She felt like she was floating, loving the way he touched her. Marveling at how he kissed.

Finally, he raised his head, then returned to brush her forehead with a touch of his lips one more time. "I like your hair," he whispered as he brushed it back, away from her cheek. "I could even get used to those pajamas, but, lady, the socks are not sexy."

She laughed, feeling alive and a little light-headed. "I also have boot socks. Did you know they made boot socks?"

"Yes, and they are not sexy either."

Parker couldn't believe their first normal conversation was about socks. What was wrong with her? "What is sexy?" she asked.

"You are," he whispered as he kissed her just below her ear. "From the minute I saw you walk out of that mall, all proper in a suit and heels, I thought you were the sexiest woman I'd ever seen. You can wear any kind of socks you want—it won't matter. Whenever I'm around you, all I think about is getting closer to you. We need to spend a little time together—not talking—when you're ready."

She welcomed one more slow kiss, then pulled away. For her, his request was out of line. She didn't know him well enough. She'd never gone to bed with a man on a first date or a second. And she and Clint hadn't even had one date.

He didn't try to pull her back. "I'll pick you up tomorrow night and we'll have a conversation, if that's what you want. I think I've made it pretty plain what I want, but I'm in no hurry. We'll play by your rules."

She nodded, like it was all up to her, the brain-dead woman in silk pajamas. "Like we agreed before. No forever." There, at least she'd managed to make one rule clear.

"I'm all right with that." He turned and walked back to his truck.

She stood in the shadows of the porch and watched him drive away. The lingering feel of his touch still warmed her body.

She wanted him more than she'd ever wanted any man. She wanted one memory to keep her warm. In the last minute of her life she wanted to close her eyes and imagine his arms holding her as she said goodbye to the world.

Chapter TWENTY-EIGHT

Gabe limped downstairs as silently as he could. His knee and ankle still hurt a little, but the tumble had been worth it. He'd made contact with Tori.

The old Gabe, the one who didn't know he had a son, would have been proud of his work tonight.

Sometimes with the bad guys or the druggies, he didn't try to make contact. He just stormed in and told them they were coming with him. Most of the time the dopeheads couldn't think straight enough to argue. They just followed along, especially when they found out that Gabe didn't mind if they continued their habit in the car.

He didn't care. It usually kept them quiet, and delivering someone high was easier than dropping off someone in need of a fix. He'd even tell them that there would be someone where they were going who would take care of them. The druggies always thought that meant a dealer, not a parent or the police.

He liked to make the drop, collect his money in cash and be gone before the person had time to realize what was happening. He was a bounty hunter, not a buddy or a priest. He didn't care, as long as the money came in.

Only Victoria Vilanie was different from anyone he'd ever retrieved. She wasn't crazy or drugged up or wanted by the law. She wasn't a kid. Whoever had put out the call and offered a quarter million for her return wanted her back bad.

Bad enough to get the police involved and who knew what other government departments. It didn't take a genius to figure out why. She was a gold mine. As long as they had control of her, they were making big money.

The stepfather and mother whom Charlie Watts

had told him about over the phone probably knew the control they had couldn't last long. She'd been making six or seven figures a year since she was fifteen.

As he made himself a cup of coffee in the little alcove the sisters kept supplied for guests, he added another thing he knew about Victoria. She was kind. The test tonight had proved it. She'd had to give up hiding, her safety, to help him. There weren't many people who would do that. Not in Gabe's world.

He thought of Yancy and wished he could tell his son that Tori was worth saving. Worth protecting. But maybe Yancy already knew that.

"What you doing up so late, Professor?" a low voice said from a few feet away.

Gabe turned, forcing down any reaction. He hadn't even seen the huge deputy sitting in the dark beside the bay window. He must be losing his edge.

"Evening, Deputy. I must have been lost in thought."

Fifth Weathers stood and grabbed a juice from the tiny half fridge beneath the cups. "Can't sleep for thinking," Fifth said. "I have the same problem tonight."

Gabe pulled his disguise about him like an invisible cloak. "I took a tumble when I ventured out on my walk tonight. I think it may have upset me more than I originally thought."

"The ladies mentioned it when I came in. They were very worried about you. Said you hurt your leg and head." Fifth studied him. "Don't see much evidence now. Fast recovery, Professor?"

"It was just a scratch on the head. I traded the bandage for a Band-Aid." He lifted his hair so the deputy could see the proof. "I was frightened by a stick I thought was a snake. My leg is still hurting, but a hot shower helped."

Fifth leaned forward. "I'd think it would take a lot more than a snake to frighten a man like you."

Gabe caught a glint in the deputy's eye and he knew he was walking on thin ice—the lawman was clearly suspicious of him. After all, he was a stranger in town. Fifth was young, but he was no fool. "I find as I grow older I'm afraid of many things. Falling is one of them."

"I know what you mean. When I got out of the academy I never gave much thought to getting hurt in the line of duty. I played football through college and had eleven guys trying to kill me every weekend. But when I came here and saw how bullets took down a legend of a sheriff, I couldn't sleep. Can you imagine what it must have been like being shot?"

"No," Gabe lied. "I can't."

They talked for a few more minutes about the storm, and then Gabe headed up to bed. An uneasy feeling had settled over his shoulders. Logic and experience told him it was time to disappear. Let someone else finish the job. He had more money than he could ever spend in bank accounts spread across four states. Not even a quarter of a million was worth hanging around for and being made by a cop. It would not only blow his cover, it would be the end of the job. In this line of work, a man had to be no more than a shadow.

Only, this time he couldn't leave. No matter the danger. This time he wasn't planning to take someone in. His mission now was to make sure she stayed exactly where she wanted to be. He owed this one favor to a son he'd never known.

Gabe needed to be near to protect her. And to do that he had to make sure the deputy wouldn't interfere. He figured that Fifth Weathers wouldn't be an easy man to bury, so he'd better come up with another plan.

Chapter TWENTY-NINE

At dawn, Yancy woke and stared at Tori sleeping next to him. Her midnight hair had come loose from her braid and flowed over her pillow. She was so beautiful. So perfect. It made no sense that she could be here in his little back room of the office. He was just a handyman, a carpenter maybe. Not the kind of guy who slept with a woman so pretty.

She'd cuddled against him last night. She trusted him. In this crazy mixed-up world he was her hero. Yancy had never been anyone's hero. He'd never had any expectations to live up to. Men like him didn't even meet women like her. But she'd come to him last night and for some reason she'd stayed.

He climbed out of bed. He wanted everything to be ready when she woke. Taking her clothes from the dryer, he draped them over the one chair in his room. He put on coffee in the meeting room, even though he knew no one would be in for another hour or two. Then he pulled on his coat and slipped out the side door of the office lobby.

He wanted to get to the café when it opened, so he could buy breakfast and have it waiting when she woke. They'd laugh about the way she'd looked last night and talk about the professor she'd met in the storm. He might even offer to take her over to the bed-and-breakfast so they could check on the old guy. Yancy hadn't really been that polite to him when he'd dropped by, offering to buy the house, but Tori had said he was a sweet man, so Yancy figured he could make another effort to be friendly. After they talked to the professor, he'd see if she'd be willing to come back to the lobby and meet all the retired teachers. He'd like that, and he knew a few of them would make her laugh.

Yancy planned as he waited to order, hoping

she'd let him take her home later. If she said no, he promised himself he wouldn't push it. She was afraid of something, and if keeping where she stayed private made her feel better, then he wouldn't mind not knowing.

Of course, if she felt safe enough to sleep with him, she must trust him.

Last night, with her cuddled in his arms, he knew, for the first time since he'd met her, she felt safe and the feeling made all worries rest for the night.

The new waitress at the café didn't ask why he was ordering two breakfasts or why he wanted extra jelly, one of every kind they had. She just placed his order, took his money and told him to have a great day.

In fact, he planned to have maybe one of the best days ever. When Tori woke, they'd eat, and then he'd take the day off and they'd do something fun. They could go to the canyon if it wasn't too muddy or drive into Lubbock and see the huge windmill museum. He didn't really care what it was as long as they were together for a while.

Yancy was still thinking about what they might do as he walked back in the lobby of the long office that had once been the check-in counter for a cluster of bungalows that made up a small motel.

All was quiet.

He slipped into his back quarters to set up breakfast.

The first thing he saw was his bed, all made up. Tori's clothes were gone from the chair. Her yellow rain boots had vanished, as well.

For the first time since he'd moved into the space, the room seemed empty, hollow, dead. She was gone and he had no idea which way to look.

Yancy dropped the two breakfast boxes in the trash. A sorrow built in him. He felt her loss deeper than any loss in his life. He was a man who'd learned not to want much, not to dream too large, but he wanted her. Maybe not forever, but at least for a whole day.

One whole day of being with Tori would be enough, he told himself. He wouldn't ask for more. And, for the first time, he didn't want to settle for less.

For a few minutes he felt like he didn't even breathe. He had no idea how to find her. He'd just have to wait and hope that she returned. With the list of chores that needed tending around the place, he stormed out back to his toolshed. Maybe he could work hard and long enough to forget about the ache in his heart.

A lifetime of disappointments seemed to settle in his gut. One day. One day with her was all he'd asked for. All the birthdays and Christmases never celebrated didn't matter. All the lies that things would get better, that something would go his way, that he'd win just once, didn't matter.

Yancy put all his wishes in one day that would

never happen. He didn't blame her; he blamed the whole world, from the father he'd never met to the cook at the café taking so long.

The hours dragged by endlessly. It wasn't the lack of sleep or the heavy lifting he did cleaning out the rose garden or dragging huge bags of mulch from the shed to the flowerbeds. It was the loss of Rabbit, of Tori. She was never his Rabbit. She was never his, period.

He didn't eat all day and barely noticed when several of the residents asked him if he was feeling bad. Yancy told himself he would simply push through the day, survive, like he used to do in prison when no sun shone in his world. Like he did during his childhood when his mother would say things would get better, but they never did.

It was almost sunset when he walked over to his house, telling himself maybe it would cheer him up to see the work they'd done.

He hoped she'd come tonight, but she hadn't taken the time to say goodbye this morning. If she didn't come, at least he'd feel closer to her at the house where they'd worked together.

When he opened the workshop door and flipped on the light, he saw a board propped against his toolbox.

Anything out of place stood out in his shop. Yancy liked everything in order. But when he stared at the piece of scrap wood, he didn't care if the entire barn burned down, tools and all.

Written in a painter's bold script were four words. *Missed you. Love, Rabbit.*

Yancy lowered his head against the workbench and let out a breath. He didn't have all the answers, but she'd said enough to make him believe in hope.

She hadn't vanished. She'd be back.

The door creaked.

Before Yancy could move, a male voice said, "You all right, son?"

Yancy turned and smiled at the professor. "Yeah, I'm fine. How can I help you?" If it hadn't been for the professor, Tori might not have gone into town and wouldn't have passed his place at all last night.

Yancy wished he could thank the professor for his part in what had happened. For the best night of his life. "I'm glad to see you're still here, Dr. Santorno. We haven't had time to get acquainted."

Santorno seemed to be surprised at the greeting. He ventured in another foot. "I didn't mean to bother you, but I wanted to thank your friend for helping me out last night. The little dear may have saved me."

"I'll tell her if I see her," Yancy said.

"You know where she lives?" Santorno asked. "I'd like to do something special for her. Maybe take her flowers. Women like that, I've heard."

Yancy shook his head. Even if he had known

where Tori disappeared to, he wouldn't have told the professor or anyone else.

The professor sighed. "Too bad. I brought her some of the Franklin sisters' muffins. If you see her, would you give them to her?"

"Sure." The guy was just being nice. Maybe Tori was right and he was just a sweet man, but something about him told Yancy it might be best to keep him more in the stranger category than friend.

Santorno put down the basket of muffins, but then hesitated.

Yancy waited. The guy obviously had more to say. Yancy hoped it wasn't a pitch to make another offer for his house.

"I was wondering, Yancy, if you'd be willing to talk to me about this house you own, the gypsy house. I've heard from a few people that it has a colorful past."

"I guess I could, but the Franklin sisters know more about the history than I do." Yancy saw the professor's shoulders drop. "But if you're willing to ask while I'm working, I'd be happy to tell you what I know."

Yancy was surprised at how pleased the man looked. He even adjusted his dark glasses as if he were about to cry. Maybe this research he was doing was real important to him. If so, Yancy could spare some time.

"Wonderful. I'll go get my notepad."

The professor was at the door before Yancy thought to add, "But if Tori comes, you have to leave after you thank her. We've got work to do tonight."

Santorno nodded several times. "I understand. I'll be thankful for any time you can spare."

Yancy smiled down at the message on the board. On impulse, he took a hammer and nail and hung it above the door. Now every time he walked out of the shop he'd see Tori's note.

Missed you. Love, Rabbit.

He'd look up and know that someone loved him.

"I wish I'd said it first," he whispered, "because I've felt it from that first night." He reached up and tapped the bottom of the board. "I'll be waiting, Rabbit."

Chapter THIRTY

Scarlet Mars rising

Parker walked along the lane where the oak tree spread its long shadows. She couldn't help wondering why she was taking a chance with a cowboy at this stage in her life. If she were healthy, if she had years to live, it would be one thing, but Laceys never lived past forty and she was now less than three years away.

She'd told Tori about the doctor in Dallas. Tori

suggested she might be overreacting. Maybe it wasn't as bad as Parker thought. After all, she hadn't given him time to say much. But Parker knew the signs. She wouldn't waste her time on false hope like her parents had.

Parker breathed in the pure air, loving the silence around her. In this place she could hear herself think. She wouldn't worry about what waited for her in Dallas. For once, she'd run toward life. Toward Clint, no matter how short the time was that they had. She'd make a memory she could hold on to.

If it didn't turn out for the better, it was just a fling she might regret, but it wouldn't matter in the overall canvas of her life. If the time they spent together meant something, then that would be nice for her to remember.

But what if she left him hurting?

The memory of Clint Montgomery ten years ago flashed in her mind. He'd been young, barely in his thirties, and still had a wildness about him that said he'd never settled for anything.

Only that day, he'd been a broken man when he'd sold her the little slice of land next to his place. She remembered he didn't even seem to see her in the room. His eyes were as dead as coal. He looked like a man bucked off his only dream.

Would those brown eyes go dead again if she led him into love and disappeared as quickly as she had appeared? The thought of hurting him tore at her heart. No one could kiss like he did and not feel deeply. She'd tasted wild passion in the man, and if she left, he might suffer loss again.

Parker told herself she was overthinking the whole thing. All he'd offered was a one-night stand. *Love* probably wasn't a word Clint knew how to use. She'd made a habit of never using it. Love wasn't something she'd had time for. Or sex, for that matter. Of course, she liked sex. It just wasn't worth the emotional tumble she had to take when the skydive into love was over.

Some people were wired to love someone till-death-do-us-part, but not her. Not Clint. She wasn't sure he even had enough heart left in him to break.

Looking up, she saw him at the end of her lane waiting and remembered him saying that he was waiting for her to run to him. Well, she wouldn't run; she'd never run after a man. When she got in his truck, she'd set the rules this time. She'd let him know just what she wanted out of this affair. An affair. Short. Passionate. And over when she went back to Dallas.

If there was going to be an affair. The thought of being nude in front of a man who didn't seem to listen to a word she said wasn't all that appealing. All she wanted was a memory. If that was all he wanted, then maybe they'd talk. If not, she'd get out of the pickup and forget all about the cowboy.

When she walked up, his head was down, his

elbow out the open window and a book propped on his steering wheel.

"It's too dark to read," she said.

He didn't answer. He simply closed the book, climbed out of the truck, held the door open and said, "Get in, Parker."

She huffed, starting a new mental list of things that needed to be discussed. No one ordered her to do anything. He needed to start listening to her now and then. Maybe talking to her more. No, wait. Maybe she'd like him better if he just kept quiet.

Climbing into the cab, she tried to think of where to begin. The man had so many things wrong with him that he'd need a team of specialists to figure him out.

He folded in beside her and closed the door, then leaned toward her and kissed her on the mouth. From her reaction it might as well have been a slap, but he didn't seem to notice.

When he pulled back smiling, he said, "I missed you, pretty lady."

"I don't even know who you are." She frowned. How could she think of being attracted to a man who had no idea how to read her?

"I plan to end that problem right now." He circled the pickup around and headed toward his place. A few minutes later they passed his little brown house and drove toward an old wooden windmill. From there they turned left and went over a rise in the ground so gentle she'd never even noticed it. The brown house disappeared behind the rolling landscape.

She saw fences and watering troughs and an old tractor that looked like it had got stuck in the mud thirty years ago and no one had bothered to dig it out.

Parker was beginning to feel as lost as Hansel and Gretel. She wouldn't have been surprised to pass the gingerbread house with a witch at the door, waving them in.

Finally, just as full dark settled over the valley, they pulled up to a barn painted the same blue as his pickup.

"You brought me to see a barn?" she whispered to herself more than him. At this point, she didn't even want to talk to him. Any man who thought she liked looking at farm animals was so far off the mark she considered him hopeless.

He jumped out of the pickup and held the door for her. "I brought you to see where I live, Parker."

She climbed out. "But you live in that mud-colored house at the turnoff by the main gate. Right?" It was stucco, so close enough to mud, and whoever decorated it twenty years ago must have got all the furniture wholesale because dull brown had gone out of style.

"No, you *thought* I lived there. If I hadn't had to take my horse back to the corral that night, I might not have seen the door open and known you were in the old place. I only stop by there a few times a week to collect my mail and do the ranch office work."

He tugged her toward the barn. "Come on. You need to see where I live."

She might have dug in her heels in protest, but now she was interested. She'd thought the little dull house was bad. How much worse could his life get? He lived with the pigs and cows?

He pulled a wide, sliding barn door open. "This is where I store stuff. You know, like a garage? Folks do still have them in Dallas, right?"

Now he was talking down to her, and she felt like decking him.

In the dim light she noticed a couple of pickups parked. One was an old piece of junk with the paint all scratched off. The other looked like it was from the forties and in mint condition. Several other cars were lined up, each looking like it was being repainted or restored. Workbenches lined the space between each vehicle, forming individual stalls. Toward the back was a Mustang in good condition and a Jeep that looked new.

"You restore cars for a living?" She thought of asking if maybe this was one of those chop shops where people steal cars and take them apart to sell, but not even a thief would drag a car all the way out here to take it apart.

"No. It's just a hobby. I live upstairs, and I come

239

down here when I can't sleep." He took her hand and led her up a long line of stairs made with unfinished wood. The open trapdoor rested against the wall.

When he reached the top, he flipped a light and the loft came into full view. One huge room with an area for living space, bedroom and kitchen. The walls, which held what looked like framed ranching magazines, were polished oak, and the floor had been stained darker, giving the space a welcoming warmth. All the furniture was fine quality and circled around a fireplace in the middle of the room. A huge desk faced one window to the east that stood ten feet high and almost twice as wide.

In a way, the space—cozy and welcoming— reminded her of a loft apartment in the warehouse district in New York. The kind a rich artist would kill to have.

"You want to know me, Parker. This is me. I'm not a rancher or a farmer, though I play around with both."

"You're a writer," she whispered as she moved along the wall, seeing his name on every cover of the framed magazines.

"Not exactly. Mostly it's research I write about. My own research as well as others, some schools like A&M and Tech and companies that work in the ranching industry. They're usually inventing or improving products and want me to have a look. The business of raising cattle isn't as simple as it used to be."

"But what about the mud house?"

"It was on the land when I bought this place. My wife and I lived in it right after we got married and planned to redo your house as our residence. But she got sick, and she couldn't handle the stairs at your place. I had just an office here then, not much of a quarters."

He moved to the big window and stared out into a starless night. "So we settled in the stucco house. We knew she didn't have long. I haven't slept a night in it since she died. She wanted us to farm. She never thought I'd make any money writing articles."

"But you do?"

"Thanks to the internet, I do. I started out with a blog, then an online journal, then the *Montgomery Report*, a daily news blast for farmers and ranchers. Turned out it pays well."

Parker calmed. She could handle a writer. A cowboy, she wasn't sure of, but a writer couldn't be that difficult.

"So, what do you think, lady?" He pushed his hat back and stared at her. "You still afraid of me?"

"I wasn't afraid of you," she lied, knowing she had to get the conversation away from her as fast as possible. "I'm sorry about your wife."

He nodded once and looked away.

Parker guessed the pain of her loss still haunted him even after ten years.

"Ask whatever you want, lady. If you're set on talking, then we'll talk."

She knew she had to step on safe ground. He was making an effort and she wouldn't torture him. "Don't folks think it's a little strange that you live and work in one big room, in a barn, in the middle of nowhere?"

"No one's ever been here. If I have to meet with someone on the ranch, I do it at the stucco house. It's closer to the road."

"No one?"

"No one," he repeated.

"Then why did you bring me here?"

"So we could talk and get to know each other." He watched as she crossed the room, touching the soft leather of the couch and the warm wool of a blanket folded over the back. "You know enough yet, Parker? I'm about talked out."

She moved to the other side of the window. "I guess. You're an interesting man, Clint Montgomery, and it doesn't take much to see we have little in common. It's like we live on two different planets. You in this silent, beautiful world of nature and me in busy, noisy Dallas. I appreciate your bringing me here, showing me your place, but I don't understand much about what you do."

Looking up, she realized he probably wasn't listening again. He was paying far too much attention to the dark roll of his land beyond the window.

"You haven't even offered me a glass of wine." Parker had no idea why she said that except that a glass of wine would really be nice right now.

"All I have is beer," he muttered, still not looking at her.

Parker wasted a dirty look on the back of his head. "Of course. One more way we don't—"

Clint swung around so fast she jumped.

"Stay here," he ordered. "And stay away from the window. Once I'm down, lower the trapdoor and throw the bolt. Don't open it until you hear my voice."

"You're leaving? You can't do that. I don't even know the way home." She followed him toward the stairs. "If you're going after wine, it's not necessary. I really don't drink that much."

He reached inside a cabinet by the steps. "Someone's on my land. I'll be back as soon as I can. Remember, drop the trap and bolt it."

Parker stared at the rifle he pulled out of what looked like a coat closet. "What if you don't come back?"

He was taking the stairs two at a time when he yelled back, "Take the Jeep. Keys are in it. Head north. You'll find your way to the main road."

"North?" She heard the barn door close. "North? Which way is north?"

Chapter THIRTY-ONE

Clint dialed the sheriff's office as he ran to his truck. By the time he started the engine, Deputy Weathers had picked up.

"Fifth," Clint snapped. "They're back on my land."

"I'm on my way."

Clint dropped the phone in the cup holder and gunned the engine. He'd seen tracks of someone on his land twice before, but none of the hands working for him had seen any strangers. No one had any business stepping one foot on his property without his permission.

He'd mentioned it to the deputy when he'd eaten breakfast with him the other day. Fifth went through all the possible reasons and Clint hadn't liked any of them. Someone might be stealing cattle. They might be messing with a few of his tests on new feeders. They might even be hunting, which Clint never allowed on his land. Too many drunken hunters couldn't tell the difference between cattle and deer. If they were on his land they'd already broken the law. Every gate leading onto his land had signs posted.

One other possibility occurred to him. He knew that Parker was protecting a girl at her place. Maybe some ex-husband or abusive boyfriend was looking for the houseguest. If so, the two women wouldn't have a chance. They had no car and probably no gun.

Parker had had art supplies shipped to him in those first few days. Maybe whoever was looking for the woman had come across Clint's address when he was trying to locate Parker and her friend.

Deputy Weathers met him at the main road.

"I called in backup." Weathers pulled close to the pickup. "In ten minutes we'll have someone watching the back road going into your place."

Clint nodded. "Climb in, Deputy, and I'll show you where I saw someone moving across the land. He was on foot. Looked like a soldier, armed and on full alert. I'd bet my boots it's not some guy hunting deer at night."

Weathers parked and joined Clint in the cab. "What's your best guess?"

"Maybe someone who's been hired to destroy an experiment going on in the pasture. It's just a new piece of equipment, but there might be someone who doesn't want it on the market." Clint had heard of rival companies corrupting research, but he'd never seen any proof of it.

"I'm thinking the stranger isn't alone. They're probably cattle thieves. They could pick up a few calves and haul them off in the back of a one-ton truck on a night like this."

Clint shook his head. "The man I saw was

carrying a rifle. He wouldn't need that to rustle beef."

They drove awhile, crossing over pastures, without seeing any sign of hunters or rustlers.

"We're wasting time," Clint finally admitted. "Whoever he was, he's gone now. If he came on foot, he could follow the creek bed and be off my land without making a sound." Clint didn't add that the creek ran behind Parker's place, as well. He didn't want to get her involved if he didn't have to, but the need to protect her was strong.

"I'll come back in the morning and we'll start again," the deputy agreed. "Who knows—it might be some guy training for jungle survival or a nut running across open land with a weapon, trying to get in shape."

Clint grinned. "You think we got nuts like that running around here?"

Weathers swore. "I know we do. I'm related to some of them." The deputy used his cell to report in to his backup stationed at the south gate.

Clint relaxed. Weathers was right—there was nothing more they could do tonight.

"Speaking of nuts, I once saw a man with a pie plate taped to his head," Weathers commented as Clint drove toward the deputy's car. "He said that it kept Martians from reading his mind."

"What did you do?" Clint asked.

"Nothing. I figured if the Martians were dumb enough to choose *his* brain to explore, I wanted to stay out of the fight. As far as I know, it's not illegal to wear a pie plate or talk to aliens."

"You're a logical man, Fifth."

"I used to think so, but lately I don't know."

Clint laughed. "Madison O'Grady driving you crazy?"

Fifth turned toward Clint. "Does everyone in the county know I'm seeing her?"

"Sure. Rumor is they're taking bets at the volunteer fire department on how many inches long your first baby will be at birth."

The deputy climbed out of Clint's truck. "Tell them not to bother. She doesn't even like me, thinks I'm an idiot, and claims she wouldn't go out with me even if I drove to Wichita Falls and asked her."

Clint laughed. "Keep trying, Deputy. Sounds like you're making progress."

Weathers was shaking his head as he climbed into his cruiser.

Clint turned the truck around and drove back home. Parker was waiting. Part of him wanted to be with her so badly that he thought of yelling for whoever was out there to keep roaming. He didn't plan on wasting any more time looking.

When he got back to his barn, all seemed quiet, and his Jeep was still parked in the first spot. She hadn't given up and gone home. He guessed that was a positive sign.

When he tried to lift the trapdoor, it was bolted.

"Parker, let me in." She couldn't have missed the noise of him driving up or opening the sliding barn door.

"Who is it?" she yelled back.

"It's me—Clint. Don't you recognize my voice?"

"No," she answered. "I really haven't heard it all that much."

"Parker, throw the bolt so I can lift this door."

After a long pause, he heard the bolt slip. He shoved and was in his room before she changed her mind.

Parker must have jumped back because she looked startled. Then she tried to act calm, as if nothing ever got to her. As though nothing he could do or say would ever matter to her.

He fought the urge to grab her and kiss her. Damn, she was the most kissable woman he'd ever met. He even wanted to kiss her when she was complaining about him not listening to her.

"Did you find your intruder?" She folded her arms over breasts he'd already touched lightly and was looking forward to exploring a great deal more.

"No." He moved to the sink and washed his hands, just for something to do. The sight of a stranger on his land had made adrenaline dance in his blood. He needed to calm down before he touched her.

She sat on a stool and watched him. So much for

talking. He had no idea what to say to her. She probably wouldn't be interested in watching a movie or reading. And right now, she looked like she wasn't interested in touching him either.

He was about to ask if she was ready to go home, when she said, "I read some of your articles. I found them interesting. You're a good writer."

"Really?"

"Yes. You're obviously well respected in your field. One magazine was honored to have you weigh in on their new research. In one of the bio lead-ins, I saw that you have master's degrees in both business and ranch management. I didn't even know there was a degree in that."

He got it. He wasn't as dumb as she'd thought he was but she still didn't look interested. He was learning her finally. Parker wouldn't allow any of her emotions to show even if she was feeling something. She had to be in control.

Only he'd seen fire in her eyes when he'd touched her. A hunger when she looked at him, a need she was trying to hold back. Her battle wasn't with him; it was with herself. Even now, when he'd opened up to her, shown her his place, she was doing her best to push him away. She seemed to want to stay as frozen as one of those people in the paintings at her gallery he'd visited once.

Clint had seen her clearly that night he'd

stepped into her world. The paper had announced the gallery party like it was a big event, so he figured he was invited. People were everywhere, but he'd watched only her. She moved like a queen among the artists and patrons. Her perfect white suit. Her high heels tapping across the cold marble floors. A woman in total control of her environment. A woman made of ice. He'd seen how beautiful she was that night. He'd also seen how totally alone she seemed, even in the crowd.

He'd come to offer to buy back the little sliver of land he'd sold her, but when he saw her, he'd changed his mind. He had a feeling that if she ever shattered, she'd need the little house in the middle of nowhere to run to.

Clint had left her pricey Dallas gallery without ever speaking to her. A month later, he'd offered to lease her plot in exchange for upkeep on the house. If, or when, she shattered, when she ran, he wanted to make sure she had a place to escape to.

That night Clint had seen her, really seen her. Her little farmhouse had become a project for him. She'd become a part of his silent life.

Even tonight, Parker Lacey had no idea how completely he saw her as she sat staring out the window into darkness. She seemed like she was waiting, but she wasn't sure for what.

She couldn't know that she was about to learn to breathe.

He flipped the light off and moved in front of

her. The moon shone through the window, outlining them. "We've talked enough," he whispered, as he raised his knuckles to brush her cheek. "I'll take you home when you say it's time, but right now, I think we should communicate in another way."

She'd opened her mouth to question him, but he covered her lips with his. The kiss was soft, careful, hesitant, and she reacted as he hoped she would.

Her arms circled his neck and he pulled her off the stool and against him. Her whole body seemed to melt over him.

The kiss deepened, and her grip grew tighter. She was starving, and so was Clint. The time for talk or games or indecision was over. His lady of ice was melting.

He could feel her heart pounding against his chest as he let her know just how much he wanted her. Without breaking the kiss, he moved his hands over her and felt hunger growing inside her. He could sense that she needed to be held and touched and loved so passionately that she forgot that there were differences in their worlds.

When he finally pulled away, he took her hand and led her to the long couch. Without a word, he pulled her down with him. "I want to take my time touching you. I want to taste every part of you. That's as far as I'm going tonight, Parker." He moved his hand down her throat all the way to between her breasts. Then he pressed firmly with his palm so he could feel the rise and fall of both her breasts against his hand.

Her breathing quickened.

"You all right with this?"

She closed her eyes and leaned back. He was offering what she hadn't known to ask for.

He leaned closer, brushing her ear with his words. "Are you all right with this, Parker? You have to answer."

"Yes," she said, then didn't breathe at all as his hand caressed her breast.

"Yes," she whispered again.

There was no more need for words. He did exactly what he said he'd do. He took his time, undressing her slowly, learning every line of her slender body. She leaned into the soft leather of the sofa, raising her arms above her head, letting him prove he knew how to please a woman. Then he stood and removed his shirt and boots.

He covered her gently, letting her body take his weight. He kissed her so deeply she cried softly with pleasure as his bare chest moved over hers.

When she tugged at his belt, he laughed. "No, not yet. Not until you know exactly how I feel about you."

When she cried out his name, he kissed her tenderly, shifted and let her cuddle into him as her breathing slowed. Then he began again, building passion one touch at a time.

The second time she lost control, letting a desire

it seemed she'd never known take her, and tears ran down her cheeks.

He held her tightly, feeling so close to her that their breathing matched. Then, as he had before, he touched her lightly, letting her settle. Her skin cooled and she relaxed against him, only this time, she didn't stop holding on to him.

When she was completely relaxed, he began building a fire inside her once more. His kisses grew deeper, his touch bold. She pushed him away sleepily, but he didn't stop. All she had to say was one word and he would have taken her home, but after a moment she responded, silently telling him she wanted more.

The third time, he whispered, "Run to me, Parker. Come to me without hesitation."

And she did, holding nothing back. He felt her passion build as though she were starving for more, demanding, needing him. She made love to him fully and he was lost.

When they finally drifted down to earth, she lay in his arms, soft and relaxed. He kept touching her, loving the dampness of her skin and the way she moved into his touch.

Without a word, he lifted her up and took her to his bed. He planned to make love to her again before dawn but now he needed to hold her.

As she drifted to sleep, his hands kept stroking her. "Spend the night with me, pretty lady," he whispered. "Spend the rest of your life."

Chapter THIRTY-TWO

Harmony

Tori felt a peace she'd never known in the days that followed her night with Yancy in his little multicolored room behind the office. She painted in a whirlwind of colors, smiling, remembering as she worked.

Parker seemed happier, too. She slept until noon the day after they'd both stayed out all night, then worked making frames. There was a peace in the little farmhouse.

Neither talked about what had happened to them that night. Tori thought maybe, like her, Parker wanted to hold her experience close for a while. Sharing it might take the shine off a perfect night.

The third morning, when Tori came down to make a sandwich, she noticed a Jeep parked out front. "Where did that come from?"

"Clint loaned it to me. He told me to keep it while I'm here."

"Who?" Tori asked as if she didn't know who had left a smile on Parker's face that didn't seem to fade.

"The cowboy next door." She winked. "My cowboy, I guess."

"Oh." Tori grinned. "The grumpy one you don't want to have anything to do with. The one who waits at twilight every evening at the end of your lane."

"Yes, I believe that's the one. He's coming over tonight for dinner."

"Really?" Tori fought down a giggle.

"He's known about you since you came." Parker shrugged. "I trust him, Tori, but if you don't want to see him I'd understand. It's your call."

Tori shook her head. "I think it's time. When we hatched up this plan of me getting away, I don't think we considered the long-term strategy. I can't stay here forever. At some point I'll have to face my parents and deal with them."

Parker nodded. "I know a few lawyers in Dallas who can help you with the legal issues. You're not crippled or mentally ill, Tori. You never were. They just tried to make you seem that way."

"I guess they thought I was weak enough to be manipulated, but you're right—it's time I grew up. I need to make it plain that getting drunk at a party when I was still a kid doesn't equal a suicide attempt—it was just poor judgment. Being shy doesn't mean I'm weak."

"You're not weak," Parker said firmly.

Tori nodded. "It's time I took charge of my life."

Parker smiled. "We should celebrate."

Tori straightened. "How about I invite Yancy over tonight, too? I'd like you to meet him. He's not only kept me from being lonely here, he's helped me believe in myself again."

"I think it's time I met this fine man." Parker's logical mind was putting everything in order. "You've been missing so long the news has probably died down. We're safe here, as long as no one except Yancy and Clint know about us and neither knows who you are. This place is so far out of the loop, the world could probably end and no one in Crossroads would notice."

Tori felt a bit guilty that there was one more person who knew about her, but she didn't tell Parker about the professor she'd saved. After all, he was harmless.

An hour later they climbed into the Jeep, took the back roads and went shopping at a country store thirty miles away. The selection wasn't wide, so they settled on simple foods. Broccoli and mushroom pork chops, made with canned mushrooms. Spaghetti and meatballs using a ready-made sauce. Bread created by popping open a can of refrigerated biscuits and desserts made with ingredients that came together in a box. Since neither Tori nor Parker cooked, they mostly picked the menu by pictures. When they got home, both realized they had enough meals for a week.

"Let's cook them all, then eat leftovers tomorrow." Tori couldn't wait to get started. Everything looked so easy.

Parker agreed. "And tomorrow and tomorrow and tomorrow."

They laughed through the afternoon as they made a mess of the kitchen. A few things they made looked nothing like the picture on the box, so they tossed them like a bad science experiment.

At six, Tori borrowed the Jeep and drove over to get Yancy.

He was right where she knew he'd be, working in the shop. She tried to sneak in, but he looked up when the door creaked.

"Evening, Rabbit. You're early. I was just setting up."

"Have you eaten?" She moved closer, needing to touch him.

"I brought a sandwich. We could share it if you like. The professor, who said you saved his life, brought over muffins as a thank-you." Yancy seemed nervous. "How's that for supper?"

"No good," she answered. "How about coming back to my hideout for dinner?"

"Are you sure?"

She pressed her hand over his resting on the table. "I'm sure. It's time I told you all about me. I'm not an outlaw, Yancy. I just ran away from a life I didn't want."

"You're not married, are you?"

She knew he'd been trying to make sense of her secrets. "No. I've never slept with anyone but you."

Tori thought she saw him blush beneath his tanned face. "But, Yancy, there is more to do in bed than sleeping."

"So I've heard."

She smiled, knowing that somehow even at twenty-four and thirty-two, they needed to pass through this part slowly. Moving gently from friendship to flirting to loving. She'd almost rushed into passion a few times and hated how it didn't feel right. She guessed he'd had his heart broken, too. They were both a little shy, a little broken. Maybe they could mend together. If sleeping curled up beside him could feel so good, Tori couldn't wait to see what happened next.

"I'll come to dinner, but I don't need to know any more about you." He took a breath. "I know enough to love you, Tori."

Moving into his arms, she whispered, "The truth may frighten you away."

"I doubt it." He kissed her forehead. "I think I loved you the minute you tumbled out of my loft, and I can't think of anything you can tell me that might scare me off."

They just held one another for a while. Then she helped him put up his tools. It was dark by the time they made it back to the house. She'd told him how she'd run away. The bus rides, the boys' clothes, the backpack, and walking from the bus station to find Parker's place.

Yancy didn't say much. She knew she'd shocked

him with the invitation and now with her chatting, but his hand never let go of hers. Whatever secrets remained between them could wait. They now had each other and that was enough for the moment.

Once they were at the house, she introduced him to Parker. Yancy was polite, but quiet. He sat on the kitchen stool and listened to them talk.

Tori told him about how she and Parker had met in an airport. "I was crying because I didn't want to go back home."

"That must be hard," Yancy commented.

"It was." Tori could tell he didn't understand. "I told Parker I wanted to run away, and she not only agreed to help me, she said she'd join me in the hideout."

"What about your parents?" he asked. "Are they worried?"

"I don't know," she answered honestly. "But I don't think so. Parker and I have been talking about sending them a note just to let them know I'm fine and they can stop looking for me."

Yancy turned to Parker. "Anyone looking for you?"

Parker shook her head. "No. I have no family and I'm sure my employees think they're on vacation while I'm away."

Tori saw that Yancy was a bit confused. The story didn't seem to have all its parts. "We'll talk about it later," she whispered.

He nodded.

"I'm glad you came tonight." She leaned close when Parker went outside to welcome Clint. "I miss you when you're not close."

"It seems strange to share you. I thought you were my rabbit." He kissed her, but when he pulled away, there was a sadness in his eyes. "I wish we were back in the shop, just me and you. I have a feeling that time of just us is going to come to an end."

"No, it won't, Yancy."

Their friendship ran deep, but their relationship was still newborn. Tori saw Yancy's big heart but she wasn't sure others would. Parker was nice to him, but the very proper art director didn't seem to relate to Yancy.

When Parker introduced her cowboy, Clint, Tori saw that he was good-looking, but his intense gaze made her feel like one of the fish in a waiting room aquarium. She couldn't relate to him any more than Parker could to Yancy.

Parker didn't talk to her cowboy much either; she didn't even look at him. To Tori's surprise, Parker seemed nicer to Yancy than she was to Clint Montgomery. She almost felt sorry for the neighbor.

"Thanks for the doughnuts, Clint," Tori managed. "And the cookies and socks were great. I know they were for Parker, but I enjoyed them, too."

The cowboy looked at Parker as he answered,

"You're welcome. I'm sorry I almost ran over you that one night right after you arrived."

"I'm guessing not many people walk that road."

"It's a private road. Only goes to my place and here."

Well, this is interesting, she thought. She couldn't wait to see what they'd talk about next.

"Those your paintings?" He surprised her with the question.

Tori glanced to the far wall. "Yes." She held her breath. Since she was a teen, everyone who had seen her work thought they got to decide whether it was any good.

"They're beautiful," he said simply. "You could make a living at it."

"You think so?" She fought down a laugh.

"I do."

They both turned back to the kitchen when Parker laughed. Yancy was busy tossing something burning out the back door.

"We are not having appetizers tonight, ladies and gentlemen," Parker announced. "They seem to have vanished."

Yancy played along by hiding the pan behind his back.

Tori grinned and glanced back at the cowboy.

When Clint stared at Parker, he had the look of the big bad wolf who'd just noticed a fourth little pig running around without a house. He didn't see anyone else in the room.

This was going to be one terrible dinner party. She should have kept Yancy to herself, and the cowboy should have kept his communications coming in boxed deliveries. Even Parker, who was always organized and in control, was beginning to unravel.

When they sat down at the little table, Yancy bumped one of the legs and spilled part of the sauce. Parker rushed to clean it up and collided with Clint, sloshing even more sauce. Clint frowned and said he'd prefer not to wear his dinner. No one laughed. No one knew if he was joking or not.

When Parker moved to the kitchen and Clint went to the bathroom to clean up, Tori leaned over and whispered to Yancy, "I wish we were back at the workshop sharing a sandwich."

He smiled. "Me, too. I've seen Montgomery around. He's not as friendly as folks say."

Tori's eyebrows shot up. "They say he's friendly?"

Yancy winked. "No, they say he's rattlesnake-mean, but I'm not sure he makes it that high tonight. If they're a couple, they must have had one hell of a fight right before they walked in."

"I don't think so. Parker's crazy about him."

Yancy nodded as if he understood. "I knew a guy who kept a huge tarantula in his bedroom."

Tori giggled. "Don't tell me he loved it."

"He did, till it bit him one night. After the guy

found out he was going to live from the bite, he had the pet made into a paperweight."

"That's a terrible story." She leaned into him, seeing his lie in his mismatched eyes and loving that he was trying to make her laugh.

Clint had just walked back into the room when gunshots ripped through the silent night.

Both men reacted immediately. Turning off lights, closing shutters.

"What was that?" Parker asked as she peeked around the door.

Clint pulled her back inside and out of the line of fire. "Those were shots. It sounded like they came from my land or from the road. Either way, they're close enough for a stray shot to come this way." He closed the door. "Any of you got any reason to have someone shooting at you?"

"Not lately," Yancy answered as he pulled Tori beneath the stairs.

Tori shook her head. "I don't think I've ever heard shots fired except in the movies."

Clint pulled out his phone, hit Speed Dial and clicked it to Speaker.

One ring before someone answered, "Sheriff's office. What is your emergency?"

Clint's even voice relayed the facts. "Deputy Weathers, someone's on my land again and this time they're firing shots."

"Anyone hurt?"

"No."

The voice came again. "Location."

Clint seemed calm, but his arm was around Parker's waist. "I'm at the little house farther down my road. The two-story hiding behind a hundred-year-old oak."

"I'm on my way," the voice on the phone said. "I'll call the sheriff from my car. He'll want to be informed." The phone went dead.

The room was silent for a moment. Then Parker asked, "Don't people say hello or goodbye anymore?"

Tori didn't miss the gentle way Clint took her hand. Maybe he wasn't the stone-cold wall he seemed. "Probably illegal hunting, Parker, but it's not safe to go outside. Inexperienced hunters see a pair of eyes looking their way and they fire."

No one spoke. It seemed only a few minutes before Tori heard the lonely sound of a siren. She wanted to slip up the stairs and vanish. There was no way the shots had anything to do with her, of course, but if she stayed downstairs, this deputy and the sheriff would know she was in town. Knowing her parents, they'd probably posted her picture in every station from here to Canada.

Yancy must have read her thoughts. "Why don't you disappear, Rabbit," he whispered. "We can talk to the police. Whatever this is, it doesn't involve you."

Tori looked over at Parker and Clint.

Parker nodded.

As she heard the sound of car doors opening, Tori slipped up the stairs and sat in the darkness of the landing, watching, listening.

"You okay with keeping silent about Tori?" Parker asked Clint.

"I won't say a word unless the deputy asks," Clint answered. "This has nothing to do with her. If she wants to remain unknown out here, it's no business of mine." He turned away from Parker and opened the front door.

Tori watched a big man dressed in the tan uniform of the sheriff's department enter. He had to be over six-six, and to her surprise, he had a woman with him who was almost as tall. She was wearing creamy beige pants tucked into chocolate-brown knee-high boots and a leather jacket. They were a striking couple; they matched.

Clint stepped forward. "Evening, Fifth," he said, sounding none too friendly, as usual. "Did you bring a date to a 911 call?"

The deputy didn't seem to take offense. "I'm off duty, technically, but we were working on a case at the sheriff's office when you called. Madison O'Grady, meet Clint Montgomery. We're on his land." He turned from Clint to Yancy. "I'd also like you to meet my friend Yancy Grey."

Yancy just smiled and gave a quick wave as if he didn't want to get too close.

Tori fought down a laugh. She would have

265

reacted the same way. Strangers were never welcomed at first sight.

Madison, a beautiful, auburn-haired woman in her midtwenties, wasn't the least bit shy. She stepped forward and held out her hand to first Yancy, then Clint. "Among other things, I'm a helicopter pilot, Mr. Montgomery. If the sheriff or Fifth thinks it will help, I'll be happy to stay over tonight. We could be in the air at dawn, flying over your place."

Clint shook her hand but didn't smile. "I'd appreciate the help. I'm sure whoever is on my ranch will be long gone, but thanks to the recent rain, we might be able to track tire marks. At the least in the morning I'll know where they're coming in."

Fifth smiled, as if pleased that she'd offered to help. "Montgomery's spread is big, but nothing like the Kirkland Ranch. With any luck we'll find something fast, and you can make it back to work before the morning is half-over."

The sheriff pulled up and Clint went outside with the deputy. Yancy climbed back on his stool, showing little interest in becoming part of the posse. Parker moved around the kitchen, nervous as always and seeming to want to keep busy. Madison took the other stool and stared at Yancy.

"How long you been friends with Fifth?" Madison asked.

"I don't know. Ever since he's been in town,

I guess." Yancy looked nervous. "Is this an interrogation? Do I need to ask for a lawyer?"

Madison laughed. "Funny. I probably deserved that. Truth is, we were on a date, but he just didn't know it."

"Oh." Yancy didn't look any more comfortable. "I've been on a few of those myself. If you don't mind a little advice, I'd encourage you to let him know. Speaking for the whole male race, we're as likely to guess wrong as right."

Tori smiled down at him, loving that he wasn't flirting or even understanding the tall woman, yet he was doing what Yancy did. He was being friendly because he probably thought it was the right thing to do.

Tori saw Parker insert herself into the conversation, probably to make things less awkward. Thirty minutes later, when Clint returned, she and Madison were laughing like old friends.

"Nothing," Clint announced. "We didn't find a single clue. Whoever is on my land just seems to disappear when I go after them."

No one looked surprised.

"The deputy's waiting," Clint added as Parker shook Madison's hand. "I'll see you at dawn. Fifth told me where you park your helicopter."

Madison nodded at him and waved at Parker and Yancy as she walked out.

Tori breathed out in relief. Slowly, she let her tense body relax. They were gone. No one had asked about her, and she'd managed to remain invisible.

All three downstairs stood there, silently, until the cruisers pulled away. Then Clint spoke first. "You can come down, Tori. No one asked about you."

She slipped back into the light, walked down the stairs and hugged Parker, then Yancy, then Clint. "Thanks," she whispered to Parker's cowboy.

He gave her a twitch of a smile. "Anytime. Glad to help. No sense getting you involved in my problem."

Then they all moved to the table. The meal an hour ago had looked, if not good, at least edible. Now not so much.

"Anyone up for hamburgers?" Clint offered.

After some discussion over who would go and who would stay, they decided to all go in Clint's pickup. Yancy and Tori claimed they didn't mind squeezing into the small, windowless backseat in the cab. When they drove through the hamburger place, Yancy tossed a blanket over Tori that she complained smelled like a horse, and yet didn't remove the blanket until they were driving away from the take-out window. Everyone in the pickup heard her laughing softly.

They were all comrades now, coconspirators. The conversation flowed easily.

Chapter THIRTY-THREE

Low clouds moved over the land, making the night as black as the bottom of a well. Gabe Santorno dropped from the oak tree that stood at the bend in the road leading up to a little farmhouse. He was getting too old to be climbing trees. Hell, maybe he should think about retiring. Only where did old warriors go when they could no longer trust their skills?

Maybe Victoria Vilanie should be his last assignment. Only this time he wouldn't be bringing the prize home. He wouldn't be collecting the bounty. This time he would let it go.

When she'd picked Yancy up at dusk, he'd been watching, waiting in the trees at the edge of Yancy's few acres of land. Gabe guessed where they were heading and took a chance tracking them on foot. He couldn't keep up with the Jeep she was suddenly driving, but there were few farms or ranches in the direction she was going. Her place had to be close if she usually walked the distance to visit Yancy.

Sure enough, by the time he made it to the little farmhouse, the Jeep and a blue pickup were parked outside. He'd almost missed the house because of the old tree, but the oak offered him a great hiding place to watch. From the branches, he could see a mile in any direction.

Gabe waited until full dark, then slipped like a shadow into the tree. In the daylight, someone might have seen him, but at night, he looked like one of the thick branches.

The windows of the farmhouse were open, and he could see the two couples moving around. From their body language he knew they were definitely two couples, but the four of them were not friends.

He waited, spending most of his time watching Yancy. Gabe couldn't help but think about all the years he'd missed being in his son's life. What had he looked like when he learned to walk? When he'd been a kid? When he'd been barely grown and had to go to prison. Gabe hadn't been there to catch him as a toddler when he tumbled or help him through his teens or fight for him when he went to prison.

He'd never been there, yet he could tell, somehow, that Yancy had managed to grow into a good man. The kind of man a woman like Tori might love.

Maybe Jewel Ann had had something to do with that.

He'd asked a few people about her but no one knew more than that she'd stayed with the Stanley widow until after the baby was born.

Gabe wished he could ask Yancy. Maybe he

knew. But the question would be far too personal. Besides, Gabe's profession was finding people. When this was over, if Jewel Ann was still alive, he'd find her.

Then, when he knew about Jewel Ann, maybe he'd tell Yancy who he was.

Gabe was proud of his boy, and it was a kind of pride he'd never known. Even if he hadn't been there for Yancy's childhood, Yancy was a part of him. Maybe the only good part left.

When the shots came, Gabe spotted their point of origin easily and was out of the tree and crawling over dry buffalo grass before the blast stopped, echoing in the night air. The shots weren't aimed at the house or at him. Gabe knew what they were, though.

Whoever was firing was trying to draw the people out. If it had just been a normal night, maybe the people would have stepped on the porch to see what was going on, thinking that maybe a car was backfiring or someone was shooting off fireworks.

But country folks know the sound of gunfire. Yancy and the cowboy inside the farmhouse made sure they all stayed inside.

In truth, Gabe had seen the ploy work a few times. People are naturally curious. They usually look out to see what's going on. If the two couples in the house had stepped on the porch, the shooter would have known there were two women in the place. And if he was tracking Victoria Vilanie, he might not get a good view to ID her, but he'd have enough to know the house was worth watching.

Information that Gabe remembered Charlie Watts providing echoed in his thoughts. Victoria's dad had said he didn't care if she was dead or alive. He wanted her back. For a quarter million, some of the bounty hunters might decide that *dead* would be the easier way. They'd make sure no one connected the bullet that killed her to them. Then, a few days later, they'd show up as if just arriving in town and identify the body.

Gabe was almost to the neighbor's fence when he saw an outline of a man running low to the ground. The runner reached the main road and turned toward town, his form blending with the brush and mesquite trees growing wild. The shadow knew what he was doing. He'd be invisible before any car lights could catch him. Like Gabe, he was in shape, able to run two miles.

Car lights turned on the road from town. Gabe pulled back and disappeared in the grass. By the time the sheriff's cruiser passed, lights silently blinking, the shadow traveling in front of him was gone.

He moved deep into the night heading toward Crossroads. Tori and Yancy were safe tonight but Gabe's fears had come true. Another hunter had found Victoria Vilanie's trail and he wouldn't stop until he snatched her up—or worse, killed her.

As Gabe slipped into the back of the Franklin sisters' house, he knew what he had to do.

Find the shadowy hunter and stop him.

Yancy was going to get the chance to be happy that Gabe never got.

Chapter THIRTY-FOUR

Fifth Weathers leaned back in his office chair and stared at Madison. Between roaming around Clint Montgomery's place and checking on things at the office, they'd been hanging out with the sheriff for an hour. Sheriff Brigman had finally called it a night and gone home. Fifth got what he'd been waiting for—a minute alone with Madison.

"Well, did you notice?" Fifth whispered, even though they'd both heard the front door close.

She nodded. "But I don't think Sheriff Brigman did. He never went in the house. I thought of mentioning it to him, but I couldn't see that the news would have anything to do with the shots being fired half a mile away."

"Right. But I couldn't get the obvious out of my mind. Three people at the farmhouse. The table set for four."

"And when you left me there, I couldn't miss

how every few minutes at least one of them glanced at the stairs as if they expected someone might come down. All three were helping hide something or someone."

"They were terrible at pretending," Fifth said.

"Maybe that's because they're honest people. They must have seen themselves as protecting someone. But from who? Surely not us."

Fifth grinned. "My first thought was that the shooter had gotten inside and was holding a gun on them, but Parker wouldn't have set him a place at the table. Besides, if they'd been in danger, Montgomery would have told me when we went outside. Whoever was there was being hidden, protected."

Madison nodded as if she knew Fifth was testing her. "The professor, maybe. They could have all known him. You said he wasn't in his room when you left the Franklin Bed-and-Breakfast."

"Yeah, but he could have gone to eat or visit with friends. I swear, the guy has been here a few weeks and he already knows more people in town than I do." Fifth rubbed his forehead. "It doesn't make sense. Why would three people, two of them I consider my friends, lie about there being someone else in the house? Why would they protect the professor from me? I sleep ten feet away from the man every night."

"I don't know. I'm still trying to figure out who Dr. Gabe Santorno is. I can't tell if he's a good guy or a bad guy. I just know he's not who he says he is. I checked this morning. There is no Dr. Santorno at the University of Texas. If he's lying about that, he's lying about why he's here."

"I say we bring him in and question him," Fifth said.

"You do a lot of interrogation?" she asked.

"No. Most of the locals start confessing in the cruiser on the way to the office."

Madison laughed. "You read Santorno's bio from his army years. I'm guessing he wouldn't tell us anything he didn't want us to know even if we tortured him. And remember, as far as we know, the man has done nothing wrong. Maybe UT canceled his class and he doesn't know it yet, or maybe he's just hoping to get the job next year. People stretch the truth all the time to make themselves sound better. If we give him a few days, maybe he'll slip up and we'll see who the man behind the professor mask is."

"Well, we can't starve him out. He's eaten enough at the Franklin sisters' place to last until fall."

Madison stood, crossed her arms and began to pace back and forth, deep in thought. "If those three weren't hiding the professor, then who? If they are honest people, like you say, they wouldn't be harboring a criminal." She turned and retraced her steps. "And doesn't it seem strange that those three would be together. Maybe Parker and the rancher. They live next to each other. But Yancy? Why was he out there?"

"They were about to eat dinner. Maybe he was hungry?"

She ignored him and kept pacing.

The third time she whirled to retrace her steps, she bumped into Fifth.

He reached out and steadied her, but he didn't turn her loose.

"What are you doing?" She tugged on his arms, but he didn't let go.

"Stop thinking and relax, Madison."

When she shoved, he let go and slid his hands inside his jacket to keep them to himself.

To his surprise, she didn't move away.

He figured now might be the only shot he got all night. Madison wasn't the cuddle-up-and-talk type. "I love working with you. I love the way you look at every angle, but how about we take a break?"

"Fifth, this is serious."

She was so close he could smell her hair, and every time she breathed, he prayed her chest would brush his chest. Her brain might be running full speed, but his had turned down another track.

"So is this." He leaned his head against her throat. "I love the smell of you. I love the feel of you against me, Madison. I love pretty much every inch of you. Do you have any idea how hard it is to wait until you make the first move?"

She pushed him away. "I'm not going back to the bed-and-breakfast with you, Fifth, so we have to be all business. Hiding out in your room kind of feels like we're at my parents' house. Besides, I told my cousin Connie I'd stay with her if I had to sleep in town tonight."

"What about the Kirklands' big house? They don't even live in it. Quinn's your relative, too. She'd let you stay there."

"Quinn doesn't even know I'm in town. Besides, if I told her I was working with you on a case, she'd tell Staten and he'd tell the sheriff that I was staying over. If you came along with me, everyone would notice your cruiser parked out in front of Kirkland's headquarters all night. Half the town knew we ate lunch together. If you stay with me at the ranch no telling what will happen."

"I get the point." He stepped away. "It's not like we're star-crossed lovers. Everyone around wants us to get together, but I'd like to have some time to date before we have to pick out rings."

"Me, too. Besides, we don't really have a case with Santorno. Just a person of interest. I doubt my department will let me take off much more time."

"How about, when this is over, I come to Wichita Falls and we have a real date. I'll find a hotel room that looks nothing like your parents' house."

"No," she said.

"No?" Fifth looked crushed. He'd thought she was as interested in him as he was in her.

She grinned. "I have an apartment. Central heat and air, private balcony, plenty of parking, king-size bed."

He tugged her close. "I get off at five on Friday. I can be there by seven. You pick the restaurant."

She kissed him on the cheek. "How about takeout?"

"Perfect."

Chapter THIRTY-FIVE

Fulvous-orange warmth

Parker talked the outlaws she seemed to be running with, Tori, Clint and Yancy, into eating their burgers over at Yancy's house. She wanted to see what Tori had been doing. Sometimes talent transferred from one art form to another, and sometimes it didn't. Clint went along with going anywhere except back to the farmhouse, and Yancy seemed to love the idea of showing off his place.

They ate standing around a beautiful hand-carved bar. Parker could see the love Yancy had for the house in every corner of the place. After they stayed long enough to roast marshmallows for dessert, she and Clint dropped Yancy off at the retirement home.

To Parker's surprise, Tori climbed out, too.

Parker had to bite her lip to keep from commenting, but Tori was an adult. If she wanted to spend more time with Yancy, that was up to her. They'd all had a tense night with first the shots and then having to hide Tori from the deputy.

When Parker watched Yancy take her hand as he and Tori ran for the side door of the office, she grinned. Maybe Tori just needed to be held tonight. Parker couldn't help but notice the way he'd looked at Tori all evening. Like she was treasured. Like the little artist was the most important person in his world. As they disappeared into the building, Parker couldn't help but smile. Maybe it was time for Tori to have a little peace in her life.

Clint left the truck in Park. He reached over and took Parker's hand. "She's safer here," he said, as if he knew what Parker was about to say.

He'd done a good job of blaming the shots on men out hunting on his land, but now she knew he had the same fear she did. Maybe whoever was out there was looking for Tori. It made no sense, but she had a feeling they both knew that somehow the shots and Tori's hiding out at her place were related.

"Tell me about her," Clint said. Then, before she could start, he added, "Whatever you say won't affect one thing. I'll still keep her secret if that's the way you want it. I'm guessing she's not on the run from the law or you wouldn't be putting her up at your place. And somehow I doubt she's a serial killer."

He pulled her hand toward him. "I just need to know the truth, Parker. If it comes to a fight, and after tonight I think it might, I want to know what I'm fighting for because I plan to be standing next to you when trouble comes."

"All right. I'll tell you as you drive home."

Without a word, he put the truck in gear and turned toward her place.

Parker relaxed. As Clint drove home slowly, she told him Tori's story and he listened, asking questions now and then. By the time they were back at her house, he had a plan. "All Tori has to do is call in. The police. Her parents. The press. Once she does the reward is gone, and so will be anyone looking for her. If she's no longer missing, no one will be looking for her. She doesn't have to tell her parents or even the police where she is. Just that she's safe and living where she wants to be."

Parker shook her head. "If she talks, someone will find out. What if her parents show up? What if your ranch is overrun with reporters? The press loves stories about writers and artists who they think go nuts. They'll talk about it on air, claiming she must be on drugs or imbalanced. Just calling in seems the right thing to do, but it's not that simple."

"I could post a sign saying trespassers on the property are shot on sight. But it sounds like her parents might try to prove she's not in her right mind. After talking to her, even I can tell she's sane, but it sounds like her stepdad might already be spinning his own story. That could be bad for her."

They walked into her house talking easily now. He helped her with her coat and hung it on a peg by the back door. She turned on the stove and heated water for tea that she doubted he'd drink.

After they tossed the untouched dinner and cleaned up, they sat on the couch and ate one of the desserts. They kept talking—really talking—and in the end both agreed that Tori's presence should be kept quiet. Somehow they'd find a way to settle this, but both thought it would be best if she would remain the invisible artist holed up in Parker's hideout.

Neither talked about what had happened at Clint's place a few nights before. For Parker that kind of tender loving couldn't be put into words. She'd never known a man could make her feel so totally alive even though she'd known from the first that it was just a one-night stand. He'd never mentioned more and she refused to draw him in with promises of a life together when she knew there might not be one.

He made no effort to touch her while they sat on opposite ends of the couch, but Parker remembered every detail of their night, every touch, every kiss, every time he'd made love to her as if he'd been starving for her for years. It wasn't just sex. It was loving. The kind of full-out, complete loving that she'd never known. Despite what he'd said about wanting a fling, she had a feeling it would be all or nothing with Clint if she let what they'd started continue.

Only she couldn't. She had a date with a doctor in Dallas as soon as Tori's life was settled. A date with death perhaps, even though the doctor hadn't said the word *cancer.*

Looking at her cowboy, Parker wished for more. If he said he'd stand with her and fight to help Tori, she knew he would. That was all she'd ask for.

Her body ached for his nearness, but she couldn't go to him. Somehow it would be surrendering to need, and Parker wasn't built like that. She would not get any more emotionally involved. It wouldn't be fair to him. It wasn't her nature. She didn't have the time. It was better for them both if she ended this with one perfect night shared together.

"Did you ever think about painting?" He broke the silence between them.

She looked up, glad he was studying Tori's work on the wall. She wasn't sure she could meet those chestnut eyes. "I've thought of painting a few times, but it was always a someday thing and I've run out of somedays." She looked at the fire, not him, when she'd realized what she'd said. All her life she'd known she would die young. She'd feared it until finally she'd simply accepted the fact.

Laceys never grow old.

She had no regrets . . . except maybe the time she missed spending with him.

"Oh, you know." Parker had to say something before he started asking questions. "If you don't use a talent, you lose it. I guess I lost it. For a few years I sent art supplies and a letter asking the housekeeper to store it in the attic. I thought I'd slip away from Dallas and come here to paint." She looked around her little house with its high windows and rooms painted to match the colors of this land.

"Thank you for watching over this place for me, Clint."

"You're welcome. Flip and I had a great time arguing about the colors to paint the walls. I wanted it ready in case you ever did come." He stood and moved to the window. "You know, I saw you once at your gallery."

"I don't remember seeing you."

"There were a ton of people in the place. You looked like a princess in a tower that night. I figured if you ever decided to come down to earth, you might come here."

"You were right."

He didn't ask more about her painting. He just stared into the night.

She wanted to know more about Yancy, but Clint was of little help. Clint wasn't a man who talked about others. He barely talked at all. So she filled the silence, telling him about her gallery and how she'd started her own business when she inherited a little money.

A little after ten, he stood and pulled her up into his arms. With a gentle kiss, he whispered, "I'm staying here tonight. I'll sleep on the couch, but I don't want to leave you here alone." He grinned. "I'd say there is a good chance that Tori won't be home until tomorrow."

"I agree. Thanks for the offer to stay. I don't think I want to be alone in the house." She had no idea how to tell him how much their night together had meant. She had a feeling she'd long for his warm body lying next to hers for the rest of her life. But they'd said there would be no strings, no forever. She knew it would hurt him when she left, but she couldn't tell him why. Better that he remember her passion than think of her as sick. If he'd lost his wife, he'd already lost one love to illness. She'd not ask him to do it again.

Her leg hadn't bothered her lately. But Dr. Brown was still waiting for her to come back so he could make her more comfortable. Funny how not wearing high heels and never carrying a bag eased her back pain, but the knee weakness was still there.

"Well." Parker straightened, pulling her emotions under control. "I'll say good-night. Thank you for all you did tonight."

"You're welcome." He waited.

"Well, good-night."

"You've already said that, Parker."

She forced herself to move toward the steps. "There is coffee in . . ."

"I'll figure it out." He didn't move. He just watched her.

She almost said good-night again, but there was nothing else to say. He might be just downstairs but she swore he seemed a million miles away.

When she started up the stairs, she glanced back.

He was making a bed out of a blanket and one of the decorative pillows she'd bought online.

"You'll turn off the lights?" she said.

"I will," he answered, without looking up.

She waited, hoping he'd say something, anything, that wouldn't put an end to their night.

But he didn't.

She climbed the stairs into the darkness, feeling hollow inside. It had been too much to dream of repeating their night in his loft. Those kinds of things happened only once, if ever. They barely had enough in common to spend one evening talking. There was no future between them—just one perfect night she'd remember. Tomorrow they'd probably have little to say and the day after that he'd go back to being a stranger.

As she walked into her bedroom, she turned on only a desk lamp. She wanted the room to be as dark as her mood had become. She'd survived all her life trying not to feel, and she told herself she didn't plan on changing now.

Dressing in her colorful pajamas, she remembered how Clint had made fun of them. As she moved through her routine, brushing her teeth, putting lotion on her hands and face, she felt like he was so close, yet he seemed like a million miles away.

When she turned out the desk lamp, she noticed only a pale blue glow of the moon through the big, curtainless windows.

Parker had always loved the beautiful way evening shadowed the world in cool, watery blue. When she'd been a kid she'd thought of it as fairy light. She moved to the top of the stairs so she could see the color gently washing over her house, Tori's paintings and Clint sleeping on the couch below.

She'd have to go only halfway down to the landing. Clint wouldn't even know she was there, but she had to see the colors of the night sky. She wanted to see her cowboy sleeping.

Parker was almost to the landing when she saw Clint standing there, his back to her. She could see his white socks and his dark jeans that looked black now. His back was bare to his waist, and his hands were spread wide on the landing railing. His head hung low as his hands clenched on the smooth wood of the banister.

She lowered one last step to join him on the landing. "What are you doing, Clint?"

He took his time turning around. "I'm coming up, if you'll welcome me."

Letting go of the railing, he turned and faced her. "Parker, I think I understand what you're afraid of. I don't want to take your somedays. I don't want to change anything about you or your life. I just want another night with you. This night."

She smiled and watched him. He was asking for so little . . . and yet so much. More than she'd ever given of herself. Less than she'd need.

She wanted him more than she'd ever wanted anyone or anything in her life. She'd give all her somedays if she could say yes, but she couldn't hurt him. He mattered too much to her.

But one more night. One more time in his arms. Then she'd walk away. They were old enough to know nothing lasts and they were young enough to understand a need too deep to ignore.

For once she couldn't talk. She just stared at him.

Finally, he snapped, "Why are you here, Parker? Did you forget something or just come down to torture me?"

Her heart shattered as she looked at him, knowing her need mirrored his.

"Yes. I forgot something," she finally whispered and reached for his hand. "You."

Without another word, they climbed the stairs. He made it to her doorway before he pulled her against him and kissed her hard. He was starved for the feel of her, hungry for her touch. His fingers slid over the silk of her pajamas and slipped beneath to her skin.

"I can't get enough of you, lady," he whispered.

She felt her body warm to his touch and relaxed in his arms.

"One more night," she whispered, knowing that one more would never be enough.

Chapter THIRTY-SIX

Safety's illusion

Tori slept, curled against Yancy. They'd talked late into the night, telling each other all the secrets in their lives. She'd cried when she'd talked about her real father and he'd held her tight like, if he could, he'd take all the pain for her.

"My mother says I saw him die, but I don't remember that. All I remember was standing in his workshop doorway and seeing him on the floor. Dark crimson blood slowly circled round him. I didn't scream or anything. I just watched the blood.

"Then my mother dragged me away and screamed. She told everyone later that the sight of him had shattered me, but I think it was more that it shattered her. I just felt numb. Like, with the blood, all the color went out of my life. I wore black. I painted with blacks and grays. It wasn't that I was in mourning. There was just no color in the world."

Yancy didn't say a word. He just held her as she cried.

"Finally, I realized my daddy didn't die. He lives on in his work. When I designed your banister using his idea, it made me smile."

Yancy kissed her cheek. "He'd be very proud of you. You're like him in your art, but you're not like him in life. You're stronger, Tori."

She shook her head. "I don't know."

"I know," he added. "You ran. You got away."

Tori smiled. "I did, didn't I?"

"You can do anything you want. I believe in you and so does Parker."

Hesitantly, they spoke in *what-ifs*.

What if they promised, no matter what happened next in their lives, that they'd always meet one weekend a year somewhere exciting? Yancy said he'd pick the state fair in Dallas. Tori picked Paris near a bridge she loved.

What if they could live anywhere in the world?

Tori wanted to travel. Yancy said he'd stay right here.

What if they got married and had kids? He wanted girls. She said definitely only boys.

What if they moved to the country? He wanted to raise cows. She swore chickens would be easier.

They laughed and played at arguing and held one another, but at first light, Tori slipped from his bed. She knew he'd said he would take her back to Parker's place, but she loved to walk. In the half-light when shadows still swayed, all the world seemed newborn. She loved the sunlight crossing across the land as if, just for a moment, it tiptoed into dawn before bolting forward into full day.

Walking had always helped her think and dream, and with Yancy, there were so many things to dream about. The idea of having days, years to paint without stress seemed a special kind of heaven. Having one person to love her, truly love her, made the world a rich place.

She silently slipped out the side door of his place. First light. For a few minutes she thought she could see almost all the colors on earth.

So she'd leave Yancy sleeping and hurry home before he even had time to miss her. She'd slip up to her attic studio and paint until she heard Parker banging around below making breakfast. They'd talk about all that had happened the night before. Then it was time Tori made some decisions, and no one would be more help than Parker.

Tori left the sleeping edge of town and ran toward the farmhouse she now thought of as home, her head already full of plans.

For a half mile, she took the empty road, listening for a car so she could vanish before it neared. By the time the sun began to peek over the horizon, she was on a path between a stand of cottonwoods and almost in sight of the private road leading to Clint's place and Parker's house. A few more minutes and she'd see the roof of the house. The attic windows would sparkle in the sunrise, welcoming her. Her work was there waiting for her.

Everything seemed so beautiful. Early spring. Cool and crisp.

She hesitated when she had to cross through the one place where the tree branches doubled across one another. It was the only part of her walk that made her uneasy. The wild branches tried to snag her and the wind always seemed a bit colder as it whipped around the buffalo grass that reached almost to her waist.

Tori tucked her head down, pushing her chin into Yancy's coat as if she were a turtle. She knew the path by heart, but still kept her eyes on the ground for fear she'd trip over a branch that had fallen.

Halfway through the stand of trees she thought she heard something moving behind her. It seemed more than a squirrel skirting around her, and she worried that it was a wild pig. Those ugly animals could weigh several hundred pounds and had tusks sharp enough to rip flesh.

Tori moved faster, wanting to be out of the trees.

Glancing back, she tripped over a root and almost tumbled on the uneven ground. She slowed, took a deep breath and tried to calm herself and think logically. Wild pigs made noise, lots of noise. She'd never seen one on Parker's place, much less this close to town. What she'd heard could have been caused by the wind or a rabbit or even a shy deer darting out of sight. She forced herself to calm.

More movement rustled the dry grass. A twig snapped behind her, but she didn't turn around.

Tori kept moving. Not too fast or she might fall. Not too slow.

Then, steady as a saw, she heard breathing.

Suddenly, her world went black.

No color.

No light.

Something rough and heavy was thrown over her face and yanked down over her shoulders. A rope tightened at her waist, trapping her arms inside what felt like a sack. She tried to push it away, lift it off, but the prisoning bag tightened as another strap circled her shoulders, trapping her completely. She screamed, but her cries seemed only to echo in her own ears. No one could have heard her now.

Tori fought to stay conscious as big, beefy hands jerked her up. What felt like his shoulder rammed into her middle, knocking the air from her lungs, and a low male voice swore.

He threw her over his shoulder as if she were no more than an empty bag as he began to run. When she kicked and struggled, he hit her hard on the bottom. "Give me any trouble and you'll regret it."

She kicked harder, getting in a few blows on his leg.

Suddenly, he swung her down and held her tight on each side until she got her footing. "I told you not to give me any trouble." He released his bruising grip on one arm. "Maybe we should get something clear before we go any farther."

A moment later she felt what had to be his free hand slam into the side of her head. When she cried out, another blow hit her just below her chin, sending her head snapping back.

"I'm not putting up with any crap from you." His voice echoed around her now. "You come easy now, girl, or I swear you'll regret it."

Tori barely felt the third hit; she'd lost her fight. She tumbled into a well without sound, feeling or thought. She gave no resistance as his hands grabbed her again and tossed her over his shoulder.

The last picture in her mind, of Yancy sleeping in his multicolored room, melted away like old crayons left on a summer sidewalk.

Chapter THIRTY-SEVEN

Fifth Weathers felt like something was wrong before he even made it down to breakfast at the bed-and-breakfast. He hadn't heard one sound from the professor's room last night after he'd come in. The guy was a pacer, a light sleeper who often went down for a snack in the middle of the night or clicked his lights on or dropped papers or dressed in the middle of the night and took a walk.

Last night Fifth hadn't heard anything. Not even the shower running at six, as it usually did. This mystery man, with holes in his past, reminded Fifth of one of those portraits in a horror gallery, the one that looked sweet until you stepped closer and a skeleton appeared behind the harmless face.

When he passed the professor's door, Fifth thought of tapping on it. He'd already tried the knob on his way to the shower. It was locked. By the time Fifth sat down to the empty table at breakfast, he'd decided Professor Gabe Santorno was either laid out dead on his bed or he hadn't spent the night in his room.

Where would a harmless bookworm like him go? Fifth couldn't even imagine the guy picking up someone in a bar and going home with them. He might have been a ranger years ago, but he was a professor type now even if he didn't have a class to teach.

"Morning, Fifth." Daisy was as cheery as ever. "How's the morning treating you?"

"I'm fine," he lied. In truth, he was counting the hours until Friday night. "How are you?"

"Can't complain." She set down his usual three eggs, toast and half-dozen sausages. "Philip from the bakery was late delivering our rolls this morning. Seems some farmer who dropped in for coffee at dawn swore he saw a man running near the north road carrying a body. Philip felt the need to stop and tell everyone on his delivery route the frightening news. It'll probably be noon before he makes it to the school." Daisy straightened as if doing her duty. "I told Philip the person he needed to tell was you or the sheriff. He said he would as soon as the office opened."

"He could call 911."

She shook her head. "He wouldn't do that even if he was on fire, having a heart attack and taking gunfire. Philip used to date Pearly. He swore he'd never talk to her again, and since she's the only 911 operator, we just all have to pray he doesn't have to face an emergency."

"What about the farmer? He could call."

Daisy shook her head. "No. He told Philip. That seemed to be enough. He'd be burning daylight if he hung around until eight."

Fifth would have been worried, but Daisy had

295

a new story every few days. Last week she'd claimed an egg-sucking dog was breaking into houses, gobbling up eggs by the dozen, and last month she'd heard some nut was poisoning the water supply just because he couldn't get his cable to work.

He'd head into the office and find out what was going on as soon as he shoveled down a few bites.

When he swallowed, he asked, "Is the professor up and gone this morning?" Fifth kept his voice from sounding too interested in the answer.

"Haven't seen him." She shrugged. "Come to think of it, I didn't hear him unlock the front door last night. I always hear that lock clanking like it's a gate on the Tower of London. One of these days I'm going to replace it, even if Rose does think the old thing makes the door look quaint."

"Dr. Santorno?" Fifth asked, gently guiding her back to their conversation.

"Oh, yes, the professor. I do hope the poor man is all right. After that terrible fall he had in the rain the other night, my sister and I have been worried about him."

"What fall?" Fifth had forgotten about the fall. It hadn't sounded like a big deal when he'd heard about it earlier and the professor hadn't looked any the worse for wear the next morning. But now he needed Daisy to run through the facts again.

"Oh, it was the night it rained so hard last week. He said he stepped sideways to miss what he thought was a snake and ended up in that deep ditch over by Yancy Grey's old house. If some kid hadn't come along, no telling what would have happened. He might have lain there and died. Our professor. Makes me shudder to even think about how it could have ended."

Fifth frowned. How could anything happen in his town without him knowing every detail, and when in hell had Gabe Santorno become "our" professor? He wasn't some stray dog the sisters had adopted from the pound. Fifth might be the sisters' deputy, but Santorno hadn't been around long enough to belong here.

"Who was the kid who helped?" Fifth, for once, had lost his appetite for breakfast.

"I didn't get a good look. When I saw the professor all muddy and bleeding, I didn't think about the kid. The professor said she was a petite woman, but he didn't get her name." Daisy smiled. "I'm afraid I wouldn't make a very good witness. I thought she was a boy. Dressed like one as I remember, but had on yellow rain boots. I remember seeing them as I closed the door. She was almost to the street by then, but those boots were shining in the streetlight."

Fifth asked a few more questions, but all he got were repeat answers. Daisy had a habit of saying things twice, and if you didn't get away fast, she'd run through it all again just as a refresher course. "Miss Daisy, would you call the sheriff and tell him everything? I'm working on another case but he'll want to start checking into this one."

She stood at attention. "I will, Deputy."

"Thanks. Your help is deeply needed." He'd made her day. If there was any truth to the story a farmer related to Philip, who related it to Daisy, who related it to him, the sheriff should know about it as soon as possible.

As he walked to his car, he dialed Madison. "Morning," he said when she answered.

"I'm already at the chopper. Where are you and that cowboy? We're supposed to do a flyover to see if we can find any tracks of shooters on his land."

"What are you wearing?" Fifth grinned.

"Shut up," she answered.

He laughed. "I love it when you yell at me. Once I figured out it was your own brand of foreplay, I see it in a whole different light." He didn't have to see her face to know she was blushing beneath those beautiful red curls. She might think herself tough, with a smart mouth, but she clearly wasn't used to someone who was so attracted to her he'd wade through all the bull. Man, when Madison O'Grady wrapped herself around him, he felt nothing but loved—or maybe used. She was a demanding woman. He'd better start working out so he could keep up.

"Fifth." She woke him out of a great fantasy. "Why'd you call? I don't have time for this kind of thing."

"You had time for it last night before we left the office and again when we had to stop on the way to your cousin's place. I love the way you catch your breath every time . . ."

"We are not having this conversation, Fifth." He could hear the slight giggle in her voice. "I'm standing out here waiting for you and Clint Montgomery to show up so we can fly."

"I'm driving toward you right now. We'll talk about that catch in your breath later. I've got to be all business right now." He knew they had to talk before they were with Clint. "One question, darlin'. When we were at Parker Lacey's farmhouse next to Montgomery land, what did you see by the back door?"

"Is this a test?"

"Yes."

"A hook by a bolted back door with a flyswatter hanging on it. Blue handle, I think." Madison was silent for a moment. "A rug so old it looked ragged. A pair of rain boots."

"What color?"

"Yellow."

"Bingo."

"I give up. What do I win?"

Fifth turned onto the north road, passing Yancy's place. "I thought that was what I saw, but

I knew you had time for a better look. I think the boots belonged to our invisible guest in the house, and I also think there's one man in town who knows who she is besides the three mute, honest people at the farmhouse."

"Really. Who?"

Fifth wished he could see Madison's face as he said, "Gabe Santorno. The professor we both know is far more than he claims to be."

"Holy cow," Madison whispered. "There just seems to be more and more pieces of this puzzle that don't fit together. We've got an invisible guest in a farmhouse being shot at and a stranger who's lied about his past."

"Don't forget he was an army ranger, an arms specialist, and has had no documented means of employment for the past ten years."

He filled her in on everything Daisy had told him at breakfast.

"The boots belong to the same person. Our invisible guest. The fourth place setting," he ended.

"And all we know about the invisible lady is that she has three good friends hiding her and she's petite." Fifth made a mental note to stop by the farmhouse as soon as he finished with the flight. "If I find the professor, I plan to ask him a few questions. Apparently, the guy didn't come home last night."

"I see your cruiser," Madison interrupted. "The cowboy's blue pickup is right behind you."

"Right. We'll talk about this later, babe."

"Don't call me 'babe,' " she snapped.

"You got it, babe." Fifth laughed as he ended the call. There was something about a mad redhead that turned him on.

When Fifth pulled up he was all business. The three of them talked for a few minutes, then climbed into the chopper. Montgomery told them where the entrances on his land were and they flew over them all, crossing back and forth.

Sure enough, when they flew low, they saw fresh tracks in one field, but not on Clint's land. The tracks were on the land he'd sold Parker Lacey, and from the looks of it, whoever had driven across her land had broken the lock on the gate to get in or out.

Fifth leaned up between the two front seats. "Do you know of any reason someone would want to cause trouble for Parker? She seems like a nice lady."

"None at all." Clint sounded angry. "I farm that field every spring. The lock was solid and there was nothing in the pasture to steal."

"Maybe they were after her?" Fifth almost added *or whoever she's hiding,* but he didn't want to put Clint on the spot. Not just yet.

Clint shook his head. "She owns a nice art gallery in the trendy part of Dallas." The cowboy seemed to think about it and added, "She's been a good neighbor."

Twenty minutes later, they landed near where the pickup and cruiser were parked.

Fifth said he'd go into town and collect the sheriff, and then the three of them could walk to where the tracks turned around. Maybe they'd get lucky and find a clue.

Madison shook hands with Clint and said she had to get to work, but she'd be happy to help if she could.

Montgomery looked at the small helicopter that had saved them so much time. "Does the government just issue you one of these like some folks get a company car?"

Madison laughed. "No. At work I fly a V-22 Osprey. This little chopper is all mine."

Clint nodded. "Right, the Osprey. Half airplane, half helicopter, totally badass."

"You know it?"

"No, I read about it in the paper when I was in New York. Since then I've seen a few flying around here. Test flights out of Amarillo, I'm guessing." Clint tipped his hat. "You must be one hell of a pilot, Madison."

"I'm working on it."

Fifth could tell Montgomery had made a friend. He didn't know whether to be proud of his almost-girlfriend or jealous. Clint was older, but not that much older.

"We'd best be moving," Fifth interrupted. "I'll meet you at your place, Mr. Montgomery." Fifth suddenly wanted to keep it formal between them all.

"Right." Clint nodded a goodbye and headed for his pickup.

Fifth waited for Montgomery to drive away then walked Madison back to the chopper. "He probably Googled *helicopters* last night just so he could impress you."

She laughed. "I don't think he had time."

"Why?"

"The guy hasn't been home. Didn't you notice that he was still wearing the same clothes he had on last night? Spaghetti stains and all."

Again, Fifth was impressed by how observant Madison was. "So, if he slept somewhere, I'm guessing it was the farmhouse."

"From the looks of him, he didn't sleep much, if at all."

"Right," Fifth said, as if he'd noticed that, too. "Question is, which one did he sleep with? The owner he said was a good neighbor or the invisible guest with questionable taste in footwear."

"I'm guessing Parker, because I saw nothing, not even friendly flirting, between her and Yancy Grey. I'm not even sure they were friends, even though Yancy must have been invited to dinner. So if Yancy was in her house, he wasn't there to see Parker."

"Right," he said again as if he was with the

program. "Only I didn't see much between Montgomery and Parker. They didn't look like they fit together. She's a polished lady and he's a shit-kicking cowboy."

"When he came back in the house last night, he only looked at her. For a few seconds everyone else in the room didn't make it into his line of vision," Madison countered.

"So, let me get this straight. We're looking for an invisible person who three, maybe four people—if you count the professor—are trying to protect. All we know about her, besides her shoe choices are terrible, is that she's petite and matches up with Yancy Grey."

"Right."

Fifth shook his head. "I've been in town two years and have yet to see a woman match with Yancy. The guy's a loner. Talks to old people all day. Works every night on an old house that will probably take him years to build."

"Work on it, Weathers." She laughed as she kissed him on the cheek and climbed into her chopper. "You may find he has time for something else."

"I will. See you Friday about seven." Fifth pushed his luck. "And wear a dress."

"Not a chance, Weathers. I don't plan on wearing anything."

Fifth stood perfectly still and watched her fly away. He was in way over his head, he realized.

After Friday night's date with Madison, he had a feeling he'd never be the same.

Hell, if she thought Montgomery looked bad after a night rolling around in bed, she'd probably think he'd died. Madison had already left a few bruises on him that Fifth wished he could show off.

Chapter THIRTY-EIGHT

Alone

Tori awoke in total darkness. There didn't seem to be enough air to fill her lungs. She pushed at the thick bag that covered her. The bottom was tied too tightly around her waist to even get a few fingers out. She felt like she was in a straitjacket with a hood. The tie around her shoulders had slipped loose, making the heavy material no longer press against her head and chest.

Slowly she worked one hand up to her face and felt blood on her cheek, and also dripping from her lip. Her left eye was so swollen she didn't think she could have opened it enough to see light, even if there had been any light inside the bag.

Rolling first one way, then another, she couldn't do more than a half turn before hitting what felt like a wall covered in something. The space was too small for her to straighten her legs out completely.

For a moment, she panicked, thinking she was in a coffin. All was black, without any color. It crossed her mind that maybe this was what death felt like.

But she knew she was hurting far too much to be

dead, and something sharp below her left hip poked into her side.

No, she wasn't dead. At least not yet. But whoever tossed her here had taken no care. Her attacker had wanted to hurt her at least enough to take any fight out of her. He'd wanted to frighten her.

Slowly she tried to calm her breathing and think. What did she know for certain? Someone had followed her at dawn or been waiting for her in the trees. If he knew she'd cross there, then he probably knew where she was staying and maybe even that she'd spent the night with Yancy.

When he'd caught up with her in the trees, he'd obviously planned to kidnap her. He had the bag and ropes with him. She had no idea what time it was now; she could have been out an hour or a day. It could still be morning or after mid-night.

Whoever had attacked her was a man. Big, thick, with a fist that felt like a sledgehammer. He'd been impatient and angry, taking out his frustration on her. He'd frightened her so completely she hadn't put up much of a fight. He took her easily—almost too easily for it to be his first time kidnapping someone. When she'd fought, he'd used more force than was necessary. She guessed that crying or pleading wouldn't work on a man like that.

Tori moved her feet. Her boots had disappeared.

The flooring beneath her felt like cheap carpet. The air smelled of motor oil.

She was in the trunk of a car. He hadn't bothered to tie her legs or her hands beneath the bag he'd wrapped around her. He hadn't gagged her.

Tori concentrated. He must have thought she wouldn't be able to get out, and that wherever he'd parked the car would be too far away for anyone to hear her screams. She thumped three times on the side wall of the trunk. Then three more and three more. *SOS,* she kept saying as she pounded. But no one outside answered the code for help.

No one came. She was alone.

Closing her eyes, she tried to think of a color, any color, to make herself calm. But none came. Her world was suddenly only black.

Chapter THIRTY-NINE

Gabe waited for the sisters to leave the house for their early morning hair appointments, then slipped into the bed-and-breakfast. He took a shower, changed his clothes, ate most of the muffins they left next to the coffeepot, and all the while he was silently cussing himself.

He'd watched Tori and the others eat dinner in Yancy's house last night. He'd stood in the shadows and smiled as they'd laughed and talked.

For a moment, he'd bought into the possibility that they were safe. Yancy had friends and someone to love. Things Gabe had never allowed himself to have.

When the man in the blue pickup had dropped Yancy and Tori off at the retirement center, Gabe knew the two were settling in.

He'd been in the building a few times, visiting with the retired teachers, so he knew that Yancy lived in the little room behind the office while he fixed up his old house. Gabe had even added the office number to his phone when he'd promised the teachers he'd come back again. In truth, they were a wealth of information, about the history of the town and the people.

The office/sunroom area wasn't fancy, but no one would bother the young couple tonight without Yancy hearing the door.

Gabe had waited until the light went out in Yancy's room before he moved on. He'd even seen his son's room once, when he'd walked to the back of the office, looking for a restroom. Yancy kept neat quarters. Not big, but to a kid who'd just got out of prison when he came to Crossroads, the room must have seemed grand.

Now, with the lights out, Gabe knew the couple was in for the night. His guardian duty was over, but not his work. He planned to walk the few miles to Parker Lacey's farmhouse and check things out now that he knew Tori wasn't there.

Since he feared someone was watching Tori, it would be wise to make sure the windows were locked. It might not keep out the professionals, but it would slow down the amateurs. With her parents offering so much money for her return, there was no telling how many people were looking for her, and her encounter with the highway patrolman put her in the general area.

But when he got to the house, Clint Montgomery's pickup was parked out front beside a Jeep. Apparently, Yancy and Tori weren't the only two having a sleepover. Checking the paperwork in both glove compartments, Gabe found that each vehicle belonged to Montgomery.

Gabe had spent the next three hours roaming through Clint Montgomery's property: first, the front house, which obviously no one lived in. Then he checked out the other buildings on the man's land. He'd found something very interesting in the last barn. A writer's loft apartment.

He sifted through the unlocked loft, learning everything he wanted to know about the cowboy. He even found a desk computer that wasn't protected by a password. Gabe saw that as an open invitation. Montgomery's finances were solid. He subscribed to what looked like every farming or ranching magazine online. The only game running was solitaire, and the past ten web searches dealt with cow diseases or crop rotation. The only thing that seemed out of place was a subscription to an art magazine from Dallas. The rancher didn't seem like the type to follow the art scene, but Parker Lacey might have something to do with his interest. Gabe also found a full cabinet of rifles in Clint's loft, none of which had been fired lately.

Tired, Gabe had returned to Yancy's apartment a few hours before sunrise. He'd curled behind flower bushes that were just starting to bloom and slept for a while. Funny how much he knew about this town. At first he'd been looking for clues that would help him locate Tori; then his search widened to include any friends or relatives he'd left behind when he'd run all those years ago. Only the relatives were dead and any close friends had moved on. Now he searched for a stranger, someone who didn't belong but was an expert at fitting into a community.

With only a few places close where an outsider could rent a room, Gabe had thought it would be easy, but the man who hunted, the man like himself, hadn't left his scent anywhere. Chances were good that he'd broken into an abandoned house or one where the owners were away. The guy could learn enough about the people who lived there to pass himself off as a relative dropping by to check on the place. The people might be on vacation or in a second home somewhere or even in the hospital.

The con wasn't as easy in small towns as in cities, but it might work.

Or maybe the hunter had pulled a travel trailer or had driven a truck he could sleep in. Because of the canyon, there were several places he could have parked, even down in Ransom Canyon. A man alone, in a camper or even camping gear, wouldn't be noticed in town.

It wasn't until he heard the click of the side door to Yancy's place that Gabe realized he'd fallen asleep. As always, he was instantly awake and alert.

Tori slipped like a fairy through the first hint of dawn. For a few minutes Gabe just watched her. She was happy, dancing almost. Whatever had happened in Yancy's little room off the office had been good. Once she stopped just to twirl in the crisp morning air, and Gabe grinned, thinking about how happy she seemed.

If she was happy, he'd bet Yancy was, too.

He'd been so busy watching her he hadn't noticed a shadow following Tori until it was too late to call out and warn her.

She was on the road now, running as if in a hurry to get to the little attic room he'd watched her working in sometimes all night.

The shadow of a man ran behind her in the ditch. He kept his head low, rising up only slightly when he knew his entire body was camouflaged in crossing wisps of morning fog. The runner was tall, broad-shouldered and dressed totally in black.

When they crossed the open field to the stand

of trees planted along the ridge as a windbreak, Gabe had to double back. Tori might not turn around, but the stalker would.

He'd take one look back just before he entered the trees and followed her. The man trailing Tori would need to know that no one saw him. No one could later link him with the girl who was about to disappear.

If Gabe could have reached the man, he would have taken him out without a second thought. He'd killed before in combat. Silently, quickly. But they were moving too fast for Gabe to reach them in time, and Tori might have looked back if he made any noise.

He wanted her to keep running. That might be her only chance. If Tori could get far enough ahead? If Gabe could overtake the stalker?

Too many *ifs*.

Gabe had to circle round to stay hidden from the rapidly growing light. He crossed fifty yards to the right then slowed, moving soundlessly between the trees. Hoping to cut the man off before the stalker could reach Tori.

For a few moments he lost sight of Tori. Then the man disappeared into the trees as if melting.

Gabe ran now, not taking the precautions he should have. Knowing that this location was perfect for a kidnapping. No one close enough to hear her cries. No one watching.

A sound, like a struggle, echoed through the

trees, and Gabe listened, trying to pinpoint their exact location. Trying to see through last year's vines and dead leaves still hanging on low branches.

Another sound, as if someone were hitting something. The scuffle of feet.

Then nothing.

Gabe suddenly didn't care if he made noise. Something was wrong. The man was hurting Tori. He plowed through the branches, breaking them as he ran. One caught his open palm, cutting deep enough to scatter blood. He barely noticed.

When he reached where he thought the sounds had come from, there was nothing but silence.

He heard the click of an engine being turned on and moved toward the familiar clamor. Just as he broke through the trees on the other side of the windbreak, he saw a small gray car pull onto the country road near the gate of Montgomery's ranch.

As he memorized every detail of the car and the man driving, something caught the corner of his eye.

A yellow boot at the edge of the trees.

Tori was gone. The sun warmed his face, but nothing could warm his heart. He would not sleep until he found her and the man who had taken her. If she'd been killed, the hunter in the small gray car wouldn't have time to draw a breath when Gabe found him.

An hour later he'd showered, bandaged his hand and put on his disguise, along with all the weapons he might need. Gabe would also need all his skills to lie his way into Yancy's and Parker's trust.

First stop, the hardware store, where he filled the back of his car with tulips of all colors. Second stop, Yancy's office at the retirement community.

Gabe adjusted his glasses and walked into the sunroom. He took his time moving between the retired teachers, stopping to visit briefly, even accepting a cup of coffee.

Finally, he made it to Yancy, who was standing behind what had once been the counter at the motel office.

"Morning, Yancy," Gabe said, noticing that his son looked tired but happy this morning. He wouldn't appear so calm if he'd known what had happened at dawn.

"Morning, Professor. You in to take more notes this morning?"

Gabe shook his head. "No, I'm here for your help."

Yancy looked up from paperwork he was studying. "I'd be glad to help any way I can. It's a slow morning."

Gabe made sure no one was within hearing distance. His caution seemed to pique Yancy's interest. "I'd like to give the little angel who saved me the other night a surprise. We probably both know how much she loves spring, so I just bought out the first shipment of tulips at the hardware store. I'd like you to take them to her."

Yancy didn't move. "I'm not sure who you're talking about."

Gabe was ready. He began. "You know exactly who I'm talking about and I understand why you hesitate. I would in your shoes, as well. In fact, I admire you for it."

Yancy wasn't buying anything Gabe was trying to sell. He beefed up the lie. "Tori and I are good friends, Yancy. She trusts me the way she trusts you."

"What do you know?" Yancy asked as he seemed to be widening his stance and about to make a stand.

Gabe didn't react to the younger man's hard manner. "I know she loves you, for one thing. She told me. She also told me she was going to tell you her real name." Gabe lowered his voice. "Victoria Vilanie, a fine painter." He figured if Yancy was sleeping with Tori they'd probably gotten around to proper names. "I also know she's in danger. More than you know."

Yancy relaxed some. "How do I know you're not part of the danger?"

"You don't, I guess. That's why I'm asking you to take the flowers to her. She trusts me. She told me she's staying on a friend's farm, but I didn't ask where it was at the time."

"Well, I'm not telling you, Professor."

Gabe grinned. "I wouldn't expect you to. I'd just like you to deliver the flowers for me. You can tell her I'll meet her at our usual place for ice cream this afternoon if she takes a break from her painting."

Yancy let out the breath he'd been holding. "You do know her. If she told you she paints, you must be a friend. I'll take the flowers, but it'll be a while before I can take a break."

"Oh, that's fine." Gabe clapped his hands as if he were delighted. "I'm meeting with a farmer for coffee this morning across the street." He handed Yancy his keys. "I'll be back in an hour or so for my car."

When Yancy stared at his keys, Gabe added, "You did right, son. When you've got a treasure, don't take any chances, even with a harmless old fellow like me. Thanks for delivering them. I about broke my back loading them." Gabe leaned forward a little as if in pain. "You tell her the flowers are just a small thank-you."

Yancy studied him. "How'd you hurt your hand, Professor?"

"Changing a flat. Just a scratch." Gabe gave a quick wave and hurried across the street to the café. He didn't want to give Yancy enough time to back out of the favor or ask any more questions. He was betting on Yancy wanting to see her more than him simply doing a guy he barely knew a favor.

Twenty minutes later when Yancy turned off the main road heading toward Parker's farmhouse, Gabe was standing in the trees watching.

He had no idea what Parker and Yancy would do when they figured out Tori was missing, but whatever it was would keep them busy while he looked for the small gray car. If he hadn't had Yancy deliver the flowers, it might have been hours before they found Tori missing.

The kidnapper might be holed up somewhere close, making sure no one had noticed her gone. Maybe waiting until night. If he'd been out all night stalking Tori, he might need sleep before he drove hundreds of miles.

While the kidnapper killed time, he'd probably wrap up all the loose ends so that he couldn't be tracked.

Gabe usually went as far as to remove any records on the hotel computer and to swap the license plates on his car with those from a similar car. The kidnapper would do the same. Hunters never wanted to be hunted. To keep their job, they needed to be no more than a shadow. A person people might remember seeing some-where, but they could give no details.

As soon as this bounty hunter knew there were no roadblocks or clues to who he really was left behind, just as a precaution he might drop hints to anyone he'd talked to that he was heading in the opposite direction. Then, in the cover of night, he'd head out with Tori locked away in the trunk.

As Yancy disappeared around the bend where the oak tree stood, Gabe put on his fedora. He began walking northeast, away from town, away from Montgomery's place. He'd seen the small gray car head that way. It had been parked in mud when the hunter had hidden it in the trees preparing for the grab. With luck, there would be tracks where he turned off the road. It couldn't be far. If the kidnapper had been watching Tori, he knew she went through the trees on her way home. He must have been tracing her on foot and would have left tracks.

The shots near the farmhouse last night told Gabe something important about the man who took Tori. He was getting impatient, something a hunter should never be. He may have had some kind of special training, but he was reckless, sloppy.

Despite all the noise Gabe had made at dawn, the hunter hadn't noticed him, which told Gabe that the hunter was tired or ill or simply pissed off that it had taken him so long to find his mark.

Gabe was out of sight by the time Yancy probably knocked on Parker's door. Let them run around panicking. He had no doubt they'd call the law. That's what honest people did. But he would find Tori faster without Fifth looking over his shoulder.

Chapter FORTY

Yancy thought his brain would explode when he found out Tori wasn't at the farmhouse. He'd been setting all the tulips on the porch while Parker went upstairs to get her. Parker hit the door a few minutes later in a panic. "She's not in the attic. Her room hasn't been slept in. She's not here!"

Parker's words were like shots to Yancy's heart. "She left my place two hours ago, at least."

Parker paced back and forth while Yancy just tried to breathe. "Clint left early, maybe half an hour after dawn. He was meeting the deputy who'd stopped by last night. They were going to fly over his land, checking gates for signs of the trespasser who had been firing shots off last night."

"Where is he now?" Yancy asked.

"I don't know. Home, I guess. He called to say they didn't find anything but a broken lock and a few tracks. He would have said something if he'd seen Tori walking."

Yancy tried to think. "I heard the side door open about first light. I thought of running after her, but she'd slipped out without waking me before. She likes the walk between my place and here when the world's changing." He fought the urge to join Parker in her pacing. "I didn't want to order her to stay. I was afraid of holding too tight. Afraid she'd bolt if I did."

"Is there anywhere she would have gone besides your place or here?"

"The old house we're working on, maybe. She likes to walk the land, but I think she limits it to your farm." Yancy shook his head. "She wouldn't be anywhere else in daylight. She'd be worried about someone noticing her."

"I've never heard her mention any place she goes but to see you." Parker grabbed her coat. "Let's check your house first. Then we'll retrace her path from your place to here."

Yancy nodded. It didn't seem like much of a plan, but it was better than doing nothing.

Thirty minutes later, they'd checked both his house and the barn. Nothing. They'd walked the path back and forth.

Clint pulled up, having noticed them in the windbreak of trees. Without asking too many questions, he joined them in the search.

Yancy did little but listen to his heart pound and Parker thinking aloud as she kept coming up with ideas of where else Tori would be. None of them seemed logical. Tori was too shy, too afraid. Too happy here to run.

When they found her yellow boot in the tall grass by the trees, all theories stopped. They looked at each other and knew the truth. Their greatest fear had come true: someone had taken Tori.

Clint spoke first. "We're calling in the sheriff. He's already overdue to be out here. Who knows —the tracks he's coming to look at and the broken lock on the gate may have nothing to do with the shots last night and everything to do with Tori. If I'd only been in the air thirty minutes earlier."

Yancy chimed in. "If I'd insisted on taking her home, she wouldn't have been walking. She . . ."

Parker broke in. "And if I hadn't been born, I wouldn't have bought this place and Tori would not have been here to be kidnapped."

Circling her shoulders with his arm, Clint added, "You win. It's all your fault." He pulled her close and hugged her.

Parker hesitated, then accepted the cowboy's hug.

Yancy knew Parker must feel as though her effort to help Tori was a terrible failure.

He felt sorry for Parker. All Tori had wanted was peace and the lady had tried to offer that. But Tori's parents had put a reward for information out there. They'd blown the whole thing up, probably to get Tori's name in the news. It wouldn't have been so bad if the police thought she was missing, but with money offered, a quarter million, it had put her life in danger.

"When we call the sheriff, ask them to keep it

quiet," Parker said. "We don't want reporters here."

"Wrong," Yancy whispered, his eyes closed as if in pain. "Bring them all in. It's time they know the truth."

"I agree," Clint said. "If we broadcast it everywhere maybe someone somewhere will help us find her."

Clint punched in Fifth Weathers's cell number. Fifth must have picked up the phone on the first ring because Clint started talking. "Get here fast. We've got a kidnapping on our hands." A moment later, he handed the phone to Parker. "The deputy is driving. Sheriff's firing questions. You talk faster than I do."

Parker gave details as all three walked back to the road. They were waiting a few minutes later when the cruiser pulled up.

Time seemed to be moving in slow motion as they drove back to the farmhouse to make calls and plans. Sheriff Brigman knew what to do. How to call in help. Where to get experts checking the corner pasture, which was now referred to as the crime scene.

Yancy sat on the steps of the porch, letting all the panic whirl around him. He wanted to help, but couldn't see how. With all their talk, no one seemed to know what to do.

Only Yancy knew what he should have done. He should have held on tighter. For once in his life he shouldn't have let go so easily. He thought about all the people he'd known in his life. He'd let go; he'd walked away; he'd never cared enough to stay and fight.

But he cared enough now. He should have told Tori to wait so he could have driven her home or walked with her. He could have protected her until she was back at the farmhouse. Then he could have walked back to town. No one was looking for *him*. No one would kidnap *him*.

He kicked one of the tulip pots off the porch just for the hell of it. Suddenly, something hit him like a slap. The professor had lied. He'd said he met Tori for ice cream sometimes in the afternoon. That couldn't be true. For one thing, Tori never came near town until dark, and even then, it was only to his house; and two, she'd said she hated ice cream. She'd claimed it froze her brain when she ate it fast and froze her tongue when she ate it slow.

He knocked another pot over as he stood and ran into the house. Fifth not only listened to every word, he took notes. The others gathered around as Yancy explained how Gabe Santorno had met Tori. About how he'd dropped by, wanting to know where she lived, so he could take gifts. About how he asked all kind of questions.

"Anyone else know about the professor?" the sheriff asked.

Fifth raised his hand like a kid in school. "I've

been watching him. As far as I know, the man's done nothing wrong around here, but he's not what he seems. I do have one fact that might help. To my knowledge the professor did not sleep at the bed-and-breakfast last night."

"So," Yancy noted as if he were part of the investigating team, "he could have been out in the dawn light, waiting for Tori."

"But why?" Clint asked. "If he wanted to kidnap her, he could have done it that night in the rain."

No one had the answer.

Fifth added one more fact. "If Gabe's out there and he has Tori, he's armed. He's ex–army ranger, so if he's our kidnapper, he won't be easy to capture."

The sheriff stood. "Call in backup. Order roadblocks on all four major highways. Notify every law-enforcement agency. We've got a full-scale kidnapping on our hands and our only hope is finding them before they have time to get out of the county."

Yancy backed away from the others. Nothing made sense. If the professor was the kidnapper, that meant he already had Tori when he'd shown up at the retirement center with all the flowers in his car. Why would he want them delivered to someone who he knew wasn't at the farm?

Unless he wanted everyone who cared about Tori in one place. Or, more important, out of his way.

Yancy swore his brain was about to explode. He couldn't tell the others his theory. Hell, it didn't make any sense even to him. If he told them and they reconsidered the professor as a suspect, and he was guilty, Yancy might have cost them valuable time.

It occurred to him that everyone in the room had a job to do but him.

If the professor was trying to distract them or get them all in one place, maybe the best thing for Yancy to do was be somewhere else.

If the professor had nothing to do with the kidnapping, maybe he could help. Tori had liked him. Maybe the best thing Yancy could do right now was find the professor.

Chapter FORTY-ONE

Fifth flew into action like a quarterback in the last two minutes of the Super Bowl. Within an hour he had everything about Gabe Santorno mass-emailed to every law-enforcement office in the state. He'd printed maps and passed them out to a dozen teams from other sheriff's offices. The highway patrol had set up roadblocks. Alerts were being posted.

Since Yancy still had Gabe's car, the suspect would have had to steal a vehicle to get out of the county. That would take time, especially if he was weighted down with a woman. With luck, he was still in the county.

Fifth could hear Parker in the other room, talking to her office and the press. By noon every station for a hundred miles around would have the details about Victoria Vilanie. She'd come to Texas to paint, but her parents panicked and offered a reward to have her back. Someone kidnapped her for the money. No, she wasn't on drugs. No, she wasn't suicidal. In fact, she'd been living quietly, being the most creative ever.

Parker knew how to spin the story to make everyone care and hopefully make everyone want to help.

By noon Pearly stopped answering calls on the sheriff's phone. Fifth thought of yelling at her because if the sheriff's line didn't pick up, all calls were passed to his phone, but when she brought him coffee, he reconsidered.

"Thanks," he said, surprised. In two years she'd never even offered to hand him a pack of sugar when she delivered the sheriff's coffee.

"Calm down, Deputy. It may be a long day. I've been around long enough to know that nothing happens for a long stretch then everything seems to happen at once." She still didn't sound too friendly. "If you explode it'll make a terrible mess."

"I should be in the field searching, not stuck here."

"Right." She stood at attention. "Me, too."

Fifth almost choked on his coffee. The thought of Miss Pearly running around with a weapon in her hand was a nightmare.

She patted him on the back, as if that would help. "Don't worry. Any leads will come in here first. When the call we're waiting for comes in, I'll man the phones and you go get that son of a bitch who kidnapped our little artist."

Fifth raised an eyebrow. *Now* Tori belonged to the town? When had that happened? Hell, he'd been here two years and no one had ever referred to him as "our little deputy."

"Keep the coffee coming," he said to Pearly. "I'll help you man the home front until we get a lead. Then I'll be on the road."

She raised one hand. Every long nail was painted a different color. "I'm on guard."

Fifth went back to work, feeling like the lone settler in the middle of a raging prairie fire with no one near but a squirrel.

A few minutes later when the press crews showed up, he was surprised at just how well the squirrel could handle herself.

Between Pearly and Parker, who appeared to have been born with a press-handling gene, the camera crews were all given packets and pictures of Tori in her plaid shirt and jeans. She was smiling from the porch of Parker's house.

"It's just a shot I took with my cell phone, but if we blast it out, there is a good chance someone, somewhere will remember that they've seen her."

Fifth had never met Tori, but if she had friends like Yancy and Parker, she must be something.

"The team found blood in the field!" Pearly yelled. "The sheriff wants you there, Deputy Weathers."

Fifth shot out of the office so fast he almost knocked a group of reporters down. He heard them yelling and complaining, but Pearly shouted over them all, "If you don't want to get plowed over, get out of our deputy's way!"

Chapter FORTY-TWO

Madness

Tori had been in the trunk of the car for what felt like hours. Her face hurt. Blood still dripped from her lip. She was lying on something that was cutting painfully into her hip. She was thirsty and frightened and alone.

Finally, she heard someone unlocking the trunk.

Tori didn't move. She had no way of knowing if she'd been rescued or the man with the beefy fist was back. She hadn't seen his face, but she knew it would be one of a monster.

"You still alive in there, girl?" he yelled as he poked her hard in the chest with a couple of his thick fingers.

She jerked but didn't make a sound.

"Good. We're about to head out and I want to make a few things clear. I'm getting paid the same amount no matter what shape you're in. You cooperate and don't make a sound and I'll stop somewhere before dawn and let you have a drink, maybe go pee in the bushes. You cause me any trouble, you'll be sorry." He laughed. "I guess you already learned that lesson."

This time, as if just for a reminder, he hit her in the stomach so hard she feared he might have broken her bottom rib. "I'm not putting up with any crap, you understand?"

He patted her middle, where his fist had landed. "That oughta take some of the starch out of you. I find if I have a nice talk first it saves time later. And don't even think about running or I'll break one of your legs."

She kicked at him, but only ended up hurting her foot on the side wall of the trunk.

The kidnapper laughed. "After you bump along on these back roads for a few hours you won't be so playful." He slapped at her head, batting it back and forth inside the bag until she stopped struggling. "I like hitting you when you're all covered up. This way I don't have to see the blood.

"Now go to sleep, Victoria," he said as he grabbed her ankle. "We've got a long ride and I don't want to hear a word out of you." He twisted her leg as if it were a twig. "I could snap these bones without half trying, girl. You cause me any more trouble and you'll be limping the rest of your life." He swore. "That is, if you don't bleed to death. Rumor is your folks don't much care if you come back alive or dead."

"Yancy," she whispered. "Yancy."

"No one's coming to get you, girl." The man shook her leg, as if making sure she had no more fight in her. Each jerk made her land on the sharp object below her hip. "You're going back where you belong. I ain't going to kill you unless you die easy."

"Go to hell!" she shouted, a moment before his fist slammed into the side of her head, ending all thought.

Chapter FORTY-THREE

Hours passed before Gabe finally found the right road. Half-dried mud clods were scattered on it, the way they did when a muddy vehicle clambered over an old cattle guard. Mud from a freshly plowed field where Tori had been kidnapped. The car had to have turned off here, but why? The road looked so rarely traveled he could see the tracks in the dust of a dozen days.

The sun was long past noon, and so bright with spring it turned the land almost copper. Gabe had heard a few sirens and knew the lawmen were doing their jobs. Everyone with a badge would be out hunting for Tori. Making enough noise, causing enough excitement to keep the snakes in their holes for a while.

Gabe was concerned with only one snake. He'd seen him for only a few seconds, but he knew the make of the man. The patrols might be looking, but they'd never notice this old dirt trail that turned off a deserted road near the canyon. There must have been hundreds of trails like this along the canyon rim. Gabe knew, because he'd traveled several since dawn.

A few miles northeast of Yancy's place, tucked away on rugged ground, was an abandoned farm that nature seemed to have reclaimed. Little more than a lean-to of a barn was still standing, but the house looked like it had burned years ago and no one bothered to rebuild.

The bounty hunter had found the perfect place. If he went out the back of the barn on foot, he didn't have to go near a road. He could drop into the canyon, cross through a lake community and be in town within minutes.

Gabe moved like a man trained to be invisible. All mannerisms of the bumbling professor who walked as if older than his years were gone now. He moved like a trained hunter, aware of everything around him.

He knew he was in the right location and he

needed to be on full alert. One moment's slip might cost Tori's life. He saw a few primitive trip wires that would warn the kidnapper that someone was approaching. They were designed as warning devices, not as protection. Gabe stepped over them, leaving them untouched.

As he suspected, the barn hid the small gray car. The bounty hunter could have driven into town days before without anyone living close enough to see him coming or going. The man would have been able to hike into Crossroads unnoticed when he followed Tori.

Inside the barn, the kidnapper had set up a tent, and it looked like he had everything he needed to camp out. Only, thanks to the barn, he had a roof over his head, as well.

The only disadvantage to building this kind of hideout was that it took a while to pack up and leave. Gabe spotted his prey walking the edge of the canyon, picking up traps he'd set.

All Gabe had to do was watch for his opportunity, slip in and find Tori. Once he had her and he knew she was okay, he'd figure out the rest of the plan.

When Gabe flattened against the outside wall of the barn, he could hear a radio. The guy was listening in on the police frequency, but he was too far out to get a clear signal or maybe his equipment was old.

Gabe moved to where he could see inside the

barn and still have his eyes on the hunter by the canyon.

One inside wall held maps of the area. From the looks of it, the hunter was planning to travel only back farm-to-market roads to get away. It was a gamble. He was far less likely to be stopped, but if he *was* spotted on a back road, he'd be far more likely to be searched.

Gabe hated it, but he knew he had to wait. It would be suicide to charge the place now. He'd wait for his chance. If it didn't come, and the man climbed into the driver's seat, he'd have one, maybe two shots before the car got past him. But if he shot the driver then, he'd be putting Tori in great danger, because she'd be rolling around right next to the gas tank. If he missed and the car got by, Gabe would lose Tori. Correction: Yancy would lose Tori.

Gabe wasn't about to let that happen.

The big guy finally came back. He unscrewed the plates from the car and stuffed them in his jacket. Gabe smiled. The hunter was taking the time to go after local plates. A good move on his part and a great opportunity for Gabe. The kidnapper wouldn't risk stepping foot on the working farm next door or being caught jogging into town. The only option was to head east and climb down into the valley where a small lake was located.

This time of day, there wouldn't be many people at home in the lake houses. Maybe he'd get lucky and find a license plate right away, but even if he was fast it would still take him thirty minutes. By that time, Gabe could have Tori out of there and moved to safety.

Gabe kept low as the hunter did exactly what he thought the man would do. He went out the back of the barn, where no one would see him from the road or from the only farm around. Gabe could barely see him moving across the field, keeping low, blending into the landscape. As soon as he was out of sight, Gabe slipped into the barn.

The car's trunk was locked. It took him two, maybe three minutes to find something to pop the lock.

When he opened the trunk, Tori didn't move and Gabe feared he was looking at a body wrapped up, ready to bury. For one long heartbeat he feared he was too late. She was already dead. Then she twitched slightly, and Gabe sighed with relief.

He worked the knots on the bag tied at her middle. They'd been jerked so tightly they wouldn't give. Gabe pulled his knife from the strap around his left calf and cut the ropes. Then he lifted the heavy material away from her body and ran his knife up, slicing the thick bag open.

The sight before him turned his stomach. Tori's beautiful long hair was wet and matted with blood. Her face was bruised so badly he almost didn't recognize her.

"Tori, honey." Gabe kept his voice low. "Can

you hear me? Can you wake up?" He moved his hand lightly over a wound on the side of her head. It wasn't deep, but she'd need stitches.

She jerked. "No," she mumbled. "Stay away. Don't hit me again."

"Tori, it's the professor. Remember me? I'm here to help you the way you helped me when I fell in the ditch."

"No. Don't touch me. No!" She started to cry.

Gabe reached for his phone. He needed help. If he forced Tori, he might hurt her more. Right now she didn't want to go anywhere with him and he had only minutes to get them both away from this place.

He dialed the number he'd recorded for Yancy from the retirement center's office.

Some old guy answered on the third ring. "Cap here."

"Cap." Gabe tried to keep his voice calm. "This is Professor Santorno. Is Yancy around?"

"Nope, haven't seen him."

"If you can get ahold of him have him call me. I've got something he's lost. He'll want to know I have it."

"I'll try, Dr. Santorno, but we don't usually try to keep up with him. He's probably out searching for that missing girl."

"It's important," Gabe interrupted.

"I'm on it. I'll call around until I find him," Cap answered and hung up.

Gabe turned back to the girl his son loved. "Tori," he tried again. "Tori. It's me—the professor. We have to get out of here before the guy who kidnapped you comes back."

One of her eyes was swollen shut and the other was tightly closed. Whatever she'd suffered through must have been bad and she didn't want to see anything more. He gently moved his hand down her side and felt blood soaking her jeans near her left hip and at the small of her back.

Gabe pulled a small camping shovel out from under her and fought down an oath that would have frightened her. If it took him a day or a year, he'd come back and find this bounty hunter and make him pay.

"Tori. Open your eyes."

"No. The world is black. All black." She curled into a ball. "Don't touch me. Don't hurt me."

Gabe cupped her face as gently as he could. "Tori, look at me! Please, look at me."

This time he must have got through. She opened one eye and he saw the terror in her gaze. She'd been so terrified that she now stood on the edge of sanity.

"Look at me, Tori. What do you see? It's just me—the professor. You know I'm here to help you. I'm going to get you out of here." He was burning precious time, but he couldn't just grab her and run.

She tried to pull away, but he held her bloody

face gently, though securely. "Look at me. See me."

She finally opened her eyes.

"I see," she cried. "I see one blue eye and one brown."

He felt her calm in his hands. She was coming back. "That's right, honey. One blue eye and one brown, just like Yancy's eyes." He pulled a bandanna from his pocket and wiped the blood from her nose and mouth. "You've got to help me get you out of here. Yancy's worried about you."

"You're here to help me?"

"Yes. Just like you helped me, remember?" He slipped his arm beneath her legs and slowly lifted her out of the trunk, noticing that the small shovel she was lying on had cut deeper across her back than he'd realized.

His phone sounded with a low beep. Gabe clicked it on with one hand.

"Yancy here. Where are you, Professor? I'm in town but I can be heading your way." He didn't sound too friendly, but he would come.

Gabe gave directions, then added, "I found her. I've got Tori. She's safe, but we've got to get out of here fast. Park a hundred yards from the barn and stay with the car. I'll bring her to you."

He clicked on the speaker so that Tori could hear Yancy.

"I'm on my way," Yancy shouted. "Tell her I love her."

Gabe smiled. "I think she already knows that, son."

Tori took the phone and cradled it to her as she relaxed in Gabe's arms. He lifted her out, closed the trunk and carried her into the afternoon sunshine.

"I'll get you to him as fast as I can," he whispered. "Do you think any bones are broken?"

"No," she answered. "But I hurt all over. I couldn't see the man who hurt me. He wouldn't stop hitting me."

Gabe kissed her head. "You're safe now, Tori. He won't hurt you again. As soon as I know you're safe, I plan to come back and have a talk with the guy."

Tori rested her head on his shoulder as he carried her out of the barn. They had to make it off this farm and to the dirt road that was only slightly more traveled. If Yancy could follow his hurried directions, he should be there to meet them when Gabe stepped out into the open.

Chapter FORTY-FOUR

Yancy almost plowed into Deputy Weathers when he swung out of his parking spot across the street from the county offices.

Fifth jumped out of the way and yelled, "How blind do you have to be not to see me standing here?"

Yancy slammed on the brakes. "Get in."

Before Fifth's butt settled in the seat, Yancy had hit fifty.

"You do know you're speeding with an officer of the law . . ."

"Shut up and listen." Yancy didn't take his eyes off the road. "The professor just called me. He's got Tori. She's safe."

"He kidnapped her?"

"No, he didn't. He apparently went after the man who did. Why would he call to say she's safe if he was the one who kidnapped her? He's saving her, but he needs our help. He said that wherever they are they need to get out fast. I think they're still in danger." Yancy knew he was rambling, but he couldn't seem to stop. Somehow the old professor who fell down in the rain had managed to track down Tori.

"What do we do?" Fifth asked. "Call for backup?"

"You can try but my guess is they'll never get there in time. We're flying out to pick up Tori and the professor first. We can't wait." Yancy took a sudden turn on an old road so fast, the dirt flew out from the car. "Be ready for anything, Fifth. I have no idea what we're heading into."

"I was born ready." Fifth didn't look the least bit nervous.

Yancy passed what looked like a trail shooting off the old road, then threw the car into Reverse and went backward just as fast.

He made it a few hundred yards down the trail and stopped.

"Why are we stopping? I see the barn up ahead." Fifth was pushing on the dash with both hands as if he could keep the car moving forward.

"The professor said to stop where we'll have room to turn around. A hundred yards out. He said he'd come to us."

Yancy pushed the car into Park and climbed out. Fifth followed.

The air was still, silent. Yancy scanned the horizon, looking for anything or anyone moving. Then he saw them. The professor was running with Tori in his arms as if she weighed no more than a stuffed animal. His steps were quick, like an athlete's. The glasses and his funny hat were gone. Yancy saw the soldier Fifth had told them all he'd been. He saw the true man the professor was today for the first time.

"There he is!" Fifth shouted the obvious.

Yancy broke into a run, forgetting that Gabe had told him to stay with the car. The land hadn't been used in years and there were dead trees and mounds of cacti making the place seem like an obstacle course. He was almost to them when he tripped over a hidden wire, sending off a sudden pop and a cloud of white smoke. He didn't slow. He could see Tori now. She was hurt; blood seemed to be everywhere: on her clothes, covering her face, in her hair. Yancy just ran toward her. Nothing else mattered now.

"Take her!" the professor yelled as he almost pitched Tori into Yancy's arms. "Run to the car and stay down. Get out of here, Yancy. I'll make sure you have a few minutes' head start."

Yancy held her tightly against his heart and felt her arms wrap around his neck just as securely. In his peripheral vision, he was aware of the professor unstrapping a weapon from his leg. The man might not be the bad guy in this as they'd thought, but he was far more than what he seemed.

Gabe was helping Yancy and right now that was all that mattered. They had to get Tori to safety.

When Yancy made it to the car, Fifth was holding the door open. "How is she? Where's the kidnapper? What is the professor doing?"

Yancy didn't bother to answer. He laid Tori in the backseat and grabbed a first aid kit from the trunk.

Tori took it from him. "I can do it," she said with a determined tone.

Just as Yancy climbed back in the driver's seat, he heard shots.

Fifth started answering his own questions. "Holy cow—the professor has a gun. He's dragging up branches as if making a stand."

"That's not him firing," Yancy answered. "It's the kidnapper. The professor is trying to hold him off while we get away."

"Hell." Fifth pulled his weapon. "I'm not going

anywhere. I plan to be in the fight. I can't leave the professor out there alone. It's my duty to arrest the kidnapper and back up the professor."

"I got a feeling he can take care of himself," Yancy said as he turned back to Tori.

Fifth was too busy to listen. He called for an ambulance as he ran toward the professor.

Yancy turned to check on Tori, and everything seemed to happen at once.

The professor yelled for Fifth to stay back.

Someone fired from the barn.

Both Fifth and the professor returned fire. The noise rumbled across the land like rolling thunder. More rounds came from the barn. Yancy watched the professor tumble backward on the ground.

Fifth, even though he was about as big a target as they come, stood there like a giant poster of what a deputy sheriff looked like. He fired again and again as he walked toward the professor on the ground. He didn't even look nervous; he was just doing what he'd been trained to do.

The last round echoed. Then there was silence. Yancy almost didn't breathe as he watched Fifth kneel beside the professor.

No fire came from the barn, but the deputy kept his gun at the ready.

Then Yancy heard the faraway sound of sirens. It was over. Tori was safe, and the man who'd saved her was on the ground.

Chapter FORTY-FIVE

Slate-gray sunset

Parker heard the ambulances fly past the county offices but she couldn't stop the meeting she was having with several lawyers. When they found Tori, she wanted to have lawyers briefed and ready to fight for the girl's rights. There was no way her parents would get their hands on her again and try to make her out to be a mentally unstable girl who needed constant supervision.

She wouldn't allow herself to think that Tori wouldn't be found safe and sound. If she planned. If she organized. If she controlled all she could, then everything would turn out just fine. Clint was out looking with everyone else. As soon as anyone found Tori, he'd call in. Then Parker would be ready to help.

Thanks to her contacts, she knew the people to talk to in Dallas. Tori would never have to leave the state of Texas unless she wanted to. Her money might be tied up in court for years, but the money she made from now on would be hers. The little artist could live anywhere in the world she wanted to, even right here in Crossroads, Texas.

Pearly opened the door to the jury room, where Parker had been talking with lawyers.

"Miss Lacey. I thought you might want to take this call."

"Who is it?" Parker tried her best not to act upset about being interrupted.

"It's a call from Yancy Grey's phone." Pearly smiled. "It's Victoria Vilanie. She wants to speak to you."

A cheer went up in the room and Parker ran to the phone. "Tori! Are you all right?"

"I'm fine. I'm with Yancy. I just got banged up a little. The ambulance is pulling up now to take me to the hospital in Lubbock. Will you come?"

"Yes." Parker walked out of the room. "I'll meet you there."

"I'll have Yancy text you all the information, but he's going to have his hands full when we get to the hospital."

Tori sounded so sad, so exhausted. "It was terrible, Parker. A man kidnapped me so he could take me back. He hurt me."

Parker closed her eyes, trying not to cry. "It's over now."

"No, it's not. The professor saved me. He found me." Tori's voice broke and the phone was silent for a moment. "Parker, he's been shot. Fifth went with him in the first ambulance. The deputy said he might not make it."

Parker fought to keep standing. She felt light-headed. She thought of the night at LAX when she'd found Tori crying. She'd had to help, but

345

she'd never dreamed that that one decision would change so many lives . . . or maybe end one.

Then, from nowhere, a strong arm went around her, holding her up, pulling her into his warmth.

"I have to get to Tori," she whispered to Clint.

"I know. I just heard. I figured you'd need a ride."

He didn't ask a single question. He just rushed her out and they were in his pickup before she had time to fall apart. All the way to the hospital she talked, telling him this was all her fault. She should have planned better. She should have guessed trouble would come. How could she have lost control? She'd built her world around always being in control.

Four hours later they were sitting in the waiting room while the doctor stitched up the cuts on Tori's hip and back. The artist had two cracked ribs, more bruises than she could count and an eye that probably wouldn't see light for a few days. Butterfly stitches ran the side of her face, but she couldn't stop smiling.

She was alive.

Gabe Santorno, on the other hand, was fighting for his life down the hall. The bullet had gone through his chest, missing his heart, but doing serious damage.

When Yancy stepped in the waiting room, Parker stood and hugged him as if she'd known him forever. "How is she handling all this?"

"She's fine. Talked to me the entire time they were stitching her up. I don't know how it happened, but being kidnapped almost seems to have made her stronger. She says no one, not even me, is ever going to push her around again." Yancy shrugged. "I'd never push her around anyway, but she felt the need to tell me so just in case."

"So, what happens next?" Parker grinned. Tori certainly was a different woman from that night at LAX.

"The doctors want to keep her a few days to run tests. Then she says she's going back to Dallas with you."

"I told her I'd help her." Parker saw how sad he suddenly looked. "But, Yancy, when this legal mess is straightened out, you do know she's coming back to you."

Parker saw it in his eyes. He didn't know. He didn't believe. "She loves you, Yancy."

"She'll forget about me no matter what she says now." He tried to smile. "Besides, she's so full of painkillers she's talking out of her head. She told me when she looked up in the professor's eyes she saw my eyes. That pulled her out of her dark place, she said."

"I'll go sit with her awhile. How about you go check on the professor?"

"Sure. I owe the man big-time."

Parker watched Yancy walk down the hallway

toward the surgery waiting room. It didn't seem fair that the man who had risked everything to save Tori might die alone.

Clint handed her a jacket. "You'll need this if you're staying over with Tori. Tell the nurse you'll need a blanket, too. The chair's not bad to sleep in and it's no problem to get an extra tray delivered for meals."

Parker didn't ask him how he knew about hospitals. She had a pretty good idea what the answer would be. They'd talk about it when he was ready, but knowing Clint, that time might be never. "Thanks. I'm staying with her until we leave for Dallas. I'm going to be with her until this is over."

He nodded, as if understanding what she wasn't saying. His hug said all the words neither of them seemed able to say.

It was over. She'd miss him every day of her life that she had left, but she couldn't stay. She had to help Tori.

And when that was over, she'd go back to Dr. Brown and the hospital. There were some things in life that she couldn't run away from, not for long.

She'd rather be alone on her last days than see Clint have to endure watching her die. The thought of her cowboy's chestnut eyes turning dead with sadness would break her heart. He'd get over a breakup now. Maybe even remember their few nights together with a smile now and then.

Dear God, she loved this man. He was stubborn and didn't belong in her world any more than she belonged in his. But no one had ever loved her so gently, so tenderly, so completely. For a long while, they just held each other.

She wanted this one last hug to be enough to last her through what was to come. She prayed the memory of her would give him comfort and not pain.

When she pulled away, she didn't look up at him. She simply turned and walked away, knowing she was leaving her heart behind.

Chapter FORTY-SIX

Yancy felt like a zombie haunting the halls of the hospital as he moved between Tori's bedside and the waiting room outside intensive care. He liked to visit her early, relieving Parker so she could go home and shower. Then he'd come back in the afternoons for a while and listen to them talk about all their plans. Parker wanted to do a special gallery show of the work Tori had painted at the farmhouse.

Tori said it would take time to get the paintings in shape. She'd need an apartment and a loft to work.

Parker seemed to be constantly making lists and talking on the phone. Yancy just held Tori's hand. He realized he couldn't dream as big as her. He thought of when he'd got out of prison and all he'd wanted was a warm coat.

Tori's dreams were grand.

Every night he'd drop in and watch her sleeping. Slowly, the bruises were fading; she was growing stronger. He loved her and he knew she loved him. That was enough for now.

On the fourth morning, the hospital released Tori and also moved the professor to a regular room.

While Parker packed up Tori's room, Yancy sat on her bed and held her close, trying to think of how to say goodbye. "You sure you don't need a coat? I could loan you one," he whispered.

"I'm fine. Parker says it might hit eighty today. Besides, I'll be in the car." Tori kissed his cheek. "Don't worry about me. You watch over Gabe. He'll need you by his side. No one should be in the hospital alone."

"I know. I'm kind of getting attached to the guy, now that he saved your life. The Franklin sisters are sending sweets every day, even though he's not awake long enough to eat many. I'm trying to eat them before they go bad."

Tori looked down. "No one has told me what happened to the man who kidnapped me. I need to know."

"Fifth shot him, then fought like crazy to keep him alive. He ended up sharing the ambulance

350

with the professor. Fifth rode up front with the driver."

"Did he live?"

"Six hours," Yancy said. "Fifth cried but he said he'd done what he had to do."

Tori nodded. "That man hurt me and didn't seem to care, but I didn't wish him dead."

"If Fifth hadn't fired, we might have all been killed."

She held Yancy's hand in both of hers. "I have to go to Dallas. Promise me you'll take care of Gabe."

"I promise," Yancy said as the nurse told Tori it was time to go.

"Don't walk me out, Yancy, or I don't think I can leave."

He kissed her and whispered, "I love you."

"I'll be back, Yancy, I promise."

He nodded, but he didn't believe her. He watched from her window as she was loaded into a car, his heart breaking. Then he walked back to the professor's room.

The guy had been talking out of his head for days. Yancy just played along. He couldn't see arguing with a guy who had one foot in the grave. But for once, the professor was resting, so Yancy sat down in the chair next to him and closed his eyes. He wanted to dream awhile that he was back in his workshop, with Tori by his side.

It was almost dark when the sound of Gabe's voice woke Yancy up.

"I'm sorry, son. I never got you a birthday present. I should have bought you one every year. And tons of Christmas presents. A ball, a bike, I don't know. I never knew."

Yancy patted his arm. "That's all right, Professor. It would be just more stuff to carry around."

"I would have loved you."

"Thanks, Professor, but I'm not really into that kind of thing."

Gabe shook his head. "No. A father should love his son."

"Oh, that kind of love. Well, Professor, if you were my dad, I'd be honored to have you, but my dad's dead."

Gabe opened his eyes. "No, he's not. I'm right here. If I'd known about you, son, I would have found you."

Yancy saw the truth in the professor's eyes. "You've got gypsy eyes," he whispered. "Just like me."

"I've got gypsy blood, too. Just like your mother did. I loved her, you know. I always liked to say her name fast so 'Jewel Ann' sounded like one word."

Yancy couldn't breathe.

"How'd she die, son?"

Yancy fought back tears. He'd never once looked for her. "I don't know that she did. I ran away when I was fourteen. She was too stoned to notice, I'm sure."

Gabe nodded slightly. "Well, that settles it. I'm going to live. I've got to go find her."

Yancy frowned, wondering if living or dying was ever much of a choice. "You do that, Professor," he whispered. "You do that, Pop."

The professor drifted off then, leaving Yancy to think. At midnight, when he woke, Yancy had his questions ready.

Galen Yancy Stanley's eyes were clear as he answered every one of his son's questions. He told the truth, the complete truth, for the first time since he'd climbed in the truck heading for Denver the night he'd been beaten. It was dawn before the professor finally leaned back and closed his eyes.

Yancy smiled. "You know, Pop, you didn't have to get me any Christmas or birthday presents. You piled them all in one when you saved Tori. I don't hate you for leaving me. I'm just glad you came back."

An hour later, Yancy called Tori and told her his news.

Tori didn't sound surprised. She simply said, "I already knew it. I saw it in his eyes."

Chapter FORTY-SEVEN

Summer orange

Clint Montgomery stormed the doors of the Dallas hospital. He'd waited six weeks for Parker to call and she must have lost his number. He'd called her assistant at the gallery so many times they'd be exchanging Christmas cards come December.

Finally, he bullied Yancy enough to give him Tori's number. Then the minute he got the artist, Tori started crying and saying that Parker had checked herself into the hospital and wouldn't tell her what was wrong.

Clint was in his truck before the line went dead. He was finished waiting around for Parker to figure out that they belonged together. He didn't care if she was in the hospital or on the moon. He was going to her and talking until she realized they were meant to be together. If she wouldn't come back to the ranch, he'd pack the horse trailer up and move to Dallas. He planned to tell her how he felt about her in words that left no doubt. After all, what did he have to lose? She already wasn't taking his calls.

"Sir! Sir!" A chubby little nurse trotted along

beside Clint. "You can't come in here with those things on."

He faced her. If she thought she was going to keep him from seeing Parker, she had another think coming.

"You have to take them off."

The nurse jumped back when he growled, "I'm here to see Parker Lacey. I was told she's in 403."

"Right." The nurse straightened to her height of five foot nothing and pointed down at his boots.

"I have to take off my boots. Hell, this place is worse than the airports."

"No, sir. You have to take off the spurs."

"Oh," he said, feeling like a fool. "Of course, miss."

Clint figured he might as well get used to the feeling of being an idiot; it was probably going to happen again any minute. Unless Parker was sedated she'd probably start yelling at him at first sight. Parker had told him from the first that what they had wouldn't be a forever kind of thing. Only he hadn't listened, because it wasn't what he wanted to hear. It still wasn't. He wanted her. Whatever was wrong with her, they'd deal with it. He wanted to be with her the rest of her life, whether it was counted in weeks or years.

He glared at the nurse. "What's wrong with Parker Lacey?"

"I can't . . ." the nurse began. "Unless you're her immediate family?"

"I'm all the family she's got." Clint lifted his left hand that bore the wedding ring he'd never taken off.

"She was scheduled for a knee replacement, but the doctor canceled it. He said he had to deal with a more urgent matter first."

"Hell." Clint handed his spurs to the nurse. "I've heard of folks coming into a hospital with one problem and catching another."

"I don't know about that, sir. Maybe you'd better ask your wife."

"I plan to do that. Hang on to my spurs. I'll pick them up on my way out."

"Okay, cowboy. Room 403 is the second room off the elevator."

"Thanks." He ran.

Three minutes later when he walked into Parker's room, she was crying.

He didn't need to ask. He knew the diagnosis must be bad. All the fight went out of him as he walked to the side of the bed and pulled her into his arms.

For a while he simply rocked her while she cried. All the things he'd thought he had to say could wait.

When she finally settled in his arms, he said, "I don't care what it is, Parker. I'm here and I'm not leaving. We'll fight this together."

To his surprise, she smiled. "All right. We'll fight, but it might be hard. It could bankrupt us, wear us out, drive us nuts. We're not young, Clint. I'm thirty-seven and you're forty-three."

She was still smiling, and he considered the possibility that her illness could be mental. "Whatever this is, we'll fight it together."

She must have been on heavy drugs. Parker just kept smiling.

"All right. I'll take you up on your offer to help, but it'll be a twenty-four-hour fight for years and years. I'm pregnant."

Clint Montgomery did something then he'd never done in his life.

He fainted.

When he came to, he held her and they talked for hours. He told her how much she mattered to him. The sight of her the day she bought his slice of land had pulled him out of a hell he'd been in for months. The night he watched her at the gallery and decided to make sure her little farmhouse was ready for her when she needed to run. The night he'd made love to her so completely.

They talked of the next six months. Her doctor had said she had a problem with her back and knee. She would have to wait for surgery while she took it easy during the pregnancy. "He almost cussed me out for running away from the hospital before I left for Crossroads and not having surgery before I got pregnant."

They talked about where they'd live and where they'd raise their child.

Finally, Parker told him her greatest fear. "Laceys don't live long. I worry about bringing a child into the world."

"Marry me, Parker," Clint whispered.

"Didn't you hear me? Laceys don't live long."

He kissed her gently. "I heard you. Laceys don't live long, but Montgomerys do."

Chapter FORTY-EIGHT

Home

Yancy stepped out of the cool, fall night and into his workshop. As always, he tapped the board above the door. *Missed you. Love, Rabbit.*

"I love you, too," he whispered, wishing she could hear him.

Everyone in the world seemed to have paired off but him.

Clint and Parker had married in July, and no one had seen them since. Word was they were on his ranch. She'd turned over the day-to-day running of her gallery to her assistant, Minnie. Word was that Minnie had turned out to be more of a general than Parker.

Even Fifth bought a ring, and had shown it to everyone in the county offices, but he said he wasn't proposing to Madison O'Grady until they got to New York City. He'd laughed and said there was only one place for him to get down on one knee and pop the question.

When Yancy asked where, the deputy had said, "Fifth and Madison, of course."

Rumor was, the whole O'Grady family was adding money to a pot to buy them tickets. Last Yancy had heard, Pearly and the Franklin sisters were planning the shower.

Yancy was alone, but he wouldn't complain. He had a dad who called him once a week. Gabe had turned out to be a cool guy, and once he'd got out of the hospital, he'd taken up his real name again and started traveling. Gabe hadn't said he was looking for Jewel Ann, but Yancy had gypsy blood. He could feel things and he knew that was exactly what Gabe was doing.

Every few weeks Yancy got a present from some place he'd never visited and the note with it always said the same thing: *I'll be home for Christmas, son.*

So, Yancy worked every night, hoping to have the old gypsy house complete before his dad came home. It'd be different this year. He'd have a tree, maybe put some lights on the house. Invite friends over.

Yancy grinned. His heart might ache for Tori, but he was a rich man.

Just then, something shifted in the loft above

and he looked up. Tori, dressed in jeans and her paint-spotted plaid shirt, appeared above him. "You need some help?" she said, smiling.

"I do." He couldn't stop staring at her. She was so beautiful.

Then, without hesitation, Rabbit jumped.

And Yancy caught her in midflight.

Center Point Large Print
600 Brooks Road / PO Box 1
Thorndike, ME 04986-0001 USA

(207) 568-3717

US & Canada:
1 800 929-9108
www.centerpointlargeprint.com